Cover art designed by
Solutions
Author photo by Carso

MW01147975

ISBN-13: 978-1548233259
ISBN-10: 1548233250

Note: This is a work of fiction. While the names of some
public figures, locations, and actual world events are real, the
characters in these pages and their exploits are entirely
fictitious. Any resemblance to actual persons, living or dead,
is entirely coincidental.

Pulling a novel together in a way that looks good, reads well, entertains readers, and still hovers near the surface of plausibility is a real challenge, and can't be done without the help of a multitude of people. I'm fortunate to have a comprehensive network of talented friends and family who are always eager to lend an ear, offer their suggestions, and loan out their skills and expertise on a multitude of subjects. I'd like to extend a heartfelt thank you to the following folks in particular:

Traci Granzow—my sweet, always-supportive wife. Without her patience and sacrifice, this book never would have been written. Mel Granzow—my adorable daughter, who always seems to know when dad needs a hug. Kev Granzow—my brother, business partner, and cover artist, who continues to astonish me with his talent. Curt and Betsy Granzow—my folks, who are always quick to offer a new creative angle to help move a story forward or a supportive word. The three Stephens/Stevens: Stephen England, Stephen Carroll, and Steven Hildreth Jr.—These guys are as funny as they are brilliant. They make ideal beta readers and make up just the kind of peanut gallery a guy needs to stay humble and entertained. Matt Snyder, Chad Michael Cox, and Tracey Kelley—the trio that makes up my long-time writers group. These three are all outstanding authors with very different styles, and they've helped me gain perspective on my work and push through some difficult writing roadblocks. Chris Hernandez and Ross Elder—Sometimes the information a writer needs can't (and shouldn't) be found on the internet. When it comes to explosives and security systems, these guys know their stuff, and were a big help in adding a dose of reality to this novel.

Those were the great days of excavating...anything to which a fancy was taken, from a scarab to an obelisk, was just appropriated, and if there was a difference with a brother excavator, one laid for him with a gun.—*Howard Carter, English archaeologist*

PROLOGUE

Ancient Minoan palace site of Phaistos, Crete
July 1908

He'd never been handsome. With thin lips perhaps a little too close to his nose, and dark, inexpressive eyes perhaps a little too far apart, Luigi Pernier had never, even in his youth, been considered a man with an attractive visage. His wife had often praised his earnest nature. His professors, his intelligence. His employers, his work ethic. But no one had ever mistaken him for comely.

Today, that had changed. It was subtle, a glow about him the others in his party had confused with his excitement about the day's finds. Rejuvenated by finally discovering something worthwhile in this barren soil, they thought. Encouraged by the unearthing of relics that would finally validate the expedition and establish his reputation as a skilled archaeologist. But there was something more. Something ineffable.

Before he'd entered the palace temple that morning, his hands had been calloused and rough from months spent digging, worn ragged on pick and spade handles. Now, just a few short hours after he'd discovered the mysterious clay disc—the Disc of Phaistos, he would call it—crawled to it on hands and knees in the darkness, he saw only bronze skin, more supple than a spring calf's, as lovely as the Minoan figures preserved in painted friezes on the temple walls.

Luigi stepped out of his tent, his dark hair teased by the cool breeze. A fertile tapestry lay before him, unfurling to the distant waves of the Mediterranean, punctuated by gently swaying olive trees and low evergreen shrubs. He checked his hands once more in the bright moonlight. The change wasn't imaginary. The disc had healed them, made them beautiful.

But the others had seen its power. Luigi had seen the way they looked at him when he spoke of bringing the disc home to Florence. The way they eyed it like dogs before a piece of raw steak—chained, but scraping at the dirt. Hungry for it. They would try to steal it. No doubt they already waited nearby, watching for the lantern light in his tent to be extinguished, listening at the door for the sound of heavy breathing as he dreamt.

Sweeping aside canvas tent flaps and ducking back inside, he slid the disc from a velvet bag hidden beneath his pillow and ran a finger over the corkscrew of symbols covering both faces. Moths fluttered around the lantern suspended from the tent's apex, their silhouettes dancing along the fabric of the walls like frantic shadow puppets.

It was his. He'd found it. Everything discovered on this expedition, lost for millennia, was found only because of his leadership. He may not have freed all the relics from the earth himself, but they were his all the same. Not the museum's, not the investors', his.

A torrent of surprised shouts interrupted his contemplation. Stuffing the disc back under his pillow, his hand sought the leather holster hanging from his chair. His fingers wrapped around the walnut grips of his Bodeo revolver. Thumbing back the gun's hammer, which unfolded the trigger, he stepped outside. They'd be in for a fight if they thought they could take the disc from him by force.

The rancid smell of burning plaster filled the air. His rage vanished, overcome by confusion. Had there been a fire? A man on horseback, a blur of movement in the dim light, charged through the camp. With each gallop, heavy canvas bags slapped the mount's withers.

"My things!" Luigi ran to intercept the escaping horseman. "He's stealing my things!" He waved his arms in an attempt to frighten the horse and throw the rider. Desperate, he moved directly into the rider's path. The beast snorted, hooves thundering over the hard soil, undeterred. Before Luigi could leap clear, the mount's wide chest slammed his shoulder. The back of his skull impacted the dirt. Rolling himself over, world spinning, sight hazy, Luigi leveled his revolver at the escaping bandit's back and fired. Orange sparks leapt from the muzzle, a cloud of sulfuric smoke lingering. The thief rode on and disappeared into the darkness.

Forcing himself to his feet and batting away the hands of his colleagues, his skull throbbing, Luigi rushed toward the temple. Had he gotten everything? The camp came alive as laborers and archaeologists ran from their tents toward the blaze, collecting buckets of water to combat the flames. Smoke poured from the ruins so black, it could be seen vividly even in the darkness. Ignoring the heat, shirt sleeve pulled across his mouth and nose to guard against the smoke, Luigi hastened inside the temple, eyes stinging as he searched frantically for the artifacts.

Only shards of broken pottery and crumbled bits of broken terracotta remained. Everything else had vanished, bounding across the Greek countryside in the possession of a thief— probably an uneducated laborer—who would surely sell them for a handful of drachmas or barter them for a few bottles of wine.

Philistine.

Retreating to safety, Luigi pulled hungrily at the clear air before slamming his fist against the temple's stone wall. A trickle of fresh blood shimmered in the firelight as it coursed between his otherwise unblemished knuckles.

ONE

Washington, D.C.
Present day

C autiously testing her footing, Susara Eaves dared another step forward. Dabbing her brow with the cuff of her shirtsleeve, she inched along the narrow ledge surrounding the museum's central vault. A 6,500-year-old Sumerian gold jar sat on display in the room's center, glittering inside a glass vitrine case rigged to set off the museum's alarms should the relic inside be shifted.

She'd accounted for and disarmed all the sensors in the vault but the one inside the case and the one scanning the floor. The only way to reach the jar without setting off the latter was to stick to the vault's perimeter, leaping atop displays and racks, clinging to the few areas wide or sturdy enough to allow a handhold.

Her legs shook from exhaustion. After an agonizing half hour spent carefully advancing toward the gold jar, she'd reached the final step. Only one long leap stood between her and the glass case. If she made the leap and landed atop the case, and if the impact didn't trigger the case's sensor, she could begin cutting into the case using the battery-powered oscillating multi-tool in her pocket. She'd equipped it with a diamond blade intended for cutting tile and stone. It would make quick work of the case's thick ballistic glass. After creating a window large enough to slip a hand inside, she could disarm the case's sensor before extracting the prize. But the jump was nothing short of impossible. Sure, a basketball player or Olympic long-jumper might find such a task laughable, but she was neither.

Still, she prepared to try it, imagining in her mind's eye the trajectory of her body, gauging the distance as she rocked on her heels.

Measured breaths.

Focus on the case.

She leapt.

The alarm shrieked as she collided with the side of the case and toppled to the floor.

"*Fok die kak*," she cursed. She'd left South Africa over a decade ago, but her Afrikaner lineage bubbled to the surface with her frustration.

She stood and trudged toward the room's corner, where she disarmed the system and brought up the lights. Illuminated, it became clear the room wasn't a vault at all, but a full-scale model staged in a corner of a large warehouse. It perfectly simulated the underground storage chamber beneath the National Museum of Iraq, which had been robbed in the fall of the previous year. Susara knew who'd done it. Still, she couldn't figure out *how* the thief had managed to reach and extract the Sumerian jar from its display without setting off the alarms. She'd spent days constructing this reproduction of the vault—every display and dimension replicated to the inch using construction lumber and resin models—and nearly a week trying to imitate the theft in every way she could imagine. Her latest attempt was the best explanation she'd come up with so far, but the thief would have to be as athletic as he was clever to pull it off successfully. Dragging her palm across a whiteboard mounted to the wall, she erased her latest notes.

Her phone buzzed in her pocket.

"Eaves," she answered, puffing from her face the errant hairs pulled loose from her ponytail during the jump.

"Agent Eaves, you told me to call you if I heard anything about Lane Bradley," a nervous voice said. One of her informants in Europe. He didn't call often, but his intel was seldom flawed.

Her heart beat more quickly.

"You've located him?" she said.

"Stuttgart, Germany. You'd better move fast."

TWO
Stuttgart, Germany

L
ane Bradley didn't care how imaginary Reichsritter
Conrad Poldi's fantasies were. The man's money was
very real.

Poldi was an eccentric, though not the Howard Hughes,
sorting-one's-peas-by-size variety people found inspiring or
amusing. Known throughout the antiquities world for his
rabid belief in conspiracy theories and his penchant for the
occult, the German collector spent his fortune—made on the
sale of his sewage treatment business—filling his small
medieval-style castle with artifacts from all corners of the
globe. He claimed relics from ancient civilizations bolstered his
power and increased his life energy.

"Mr. Bradley, I presume?" The spindly collector bowed
exaggeratedly and swept his silk cape to a side. His bare head,

pale and sprinkled with liver spots, reminded Lane of a speckled egg. "I'm delighted you could make it this evening despite the inclement weather. These spring rains...so inconvenient."

"The rain doesn't bother me, Reichsritter Poldi. It's a pleasure to finally meet you," Lane said, approaching the slender figure at the end of the stone-lined hall. The German descended from his marble throne. Poldi's self-appointed title of Reichsritter was medieval in origin—one bestowed upon imperial knights of the Holy Roman Empire. Though obsolete and ostentatious, Poldi insisted his guests use the title whenever they mentioned his name.

Lane's connections had stressed that part: Don't forget the title.

Burly security contractors wearing black T-shirts and Kevlar vests paced restlessly like shadowy sentries in the darkened hallway behind the eclectic collector. Lane forced a smile and extended his hand.

Poldi shook it daintily as he looked him over. "With your reputation as an adventurer, Mr. Bradley, I really thought you'd be taller. Your voice, too; I'd imagined you with a much deeper timbre."

"You should hear my falsetto."

"Why, you can't be more than 175 centimeters tall," the German marveled, straightening as if to more accurately compare Lane's height to his own.

"I make up for it in density."

"Indeed. Muscular fellow, aren't you? Must be all that climbing into buildings in the night," Poldi tittered.

"I believe I have something you want." Lane tried to steer the conversation back on track. He could tell already their trade wasn't going to be a swift one. Despite what he'd said before about the rain—that it didn't bother him—he'd felt an uneasiness, a growing sense of foreboding the moment he stepped out of the taxi and into the castle keep. That feeling seemed to slip beneath the collar of his shirt, clinging on, damp and chilling as an autumn brume. He wanted out of here.

But he wanted those museum passcodes more.

"Likewise, Mr. Bradley. Perhaps you'd care to sit for a moment, first. You must be exhausted from your journey. Besides, I'd like to get to know you. You strike me as a valuable connection to have in the stolen antiquities industry."

Lane winced. "Stealing is an ugly word. I prefer to look at it like...relocating. I'm just moving artifacts from places where they're likely to be destroyed to collectors such as yourself who will ensure they're cared for. Museums are great for school field trips, but when it comes to keeping artifacts safe, no one will protect them more fiercely than someone who's spent a fortune to acquire them."

"I'd like to think I'm proof of that." Poldi nodded toward his security team. "Please, Mr. Bradley, take a seat." He gestured toward a large trestle table nearby, a pentagram carved deep in its top. Rain dribbled down the hall's towering stained-glass windows. Overhead, a trapped sparrow fluttered among the thick oak beams of the arched ceiling. The light was faint; the dozens of large candles spread throughout the cavernous space still weren't enough to illuminate the room more than dimly. "Our mutual friends have spoken very highly of you and your career. An autodidactically trained archaeologist who specializes in war zone artifact extraction—that's a mouthful." Poldi shivered and made a loud pop with his jaw.

"Yeah, doesn't fit well on my business cards." Lane followed the sound of the sparrow with his eyes. "I look at preserving history from a different perspective than most of my peers. You look at the best-preserved pieces throughout history, and most have come from private collections like yours. Collections where the piece's rarity and monetary value is recognized and appreciated." He ran a hand through his short hair—a brown so dark it appeared almost black—still wet from the rain.

"You have a magnificently square jaw," Poldi said abruptly, staring hard at Lane's features. Head cocked to a side, his tongue bulged the pallid skin of his cheek.

"Um, thanks. Gift from my father."

"He must have been a handsome man."

"I'm sure he'd be flattered. How about we get down to business?" Lane shifted his weight on the hard slab bench.

"Of course. You have the mask of Shoshenq the Third, as promised?"

Unsheathing the tarnished gold mask from a bag at his side, Lane placed it gently on the table. The rain suddenly picked up in its ferocity, battering the castle's stone walls like waves crashing against a ship's hull. The mask stared back at him emptily, wearing a haunting smile. The golden face ended just above the ear, sheared clean across the forehead. A grinning lobotomy patient.

"The Arab Spring uprisings were tumultuous. They'll assume this was destroyed along with the hundreds of other pieces that burned up in the Museum of Egyptian Antiquities." Lane spoke with a thinly veiled melancholy. People called him a thief, but he was the last refuge for these irreplaceable pieces of history. He could never save them all.

Donning white inspection gloves and accepting a jeweler's loupe from one of his men, Poldi began scrutinizing the piece. The man's tongue snaked between his lips. Hungry. "I have to ask, Mr. Bradley, why wouldn't you accept money for such a precious piece as this? The security codes to the Heraklion Museum hardly seem like adequate compensation. They proved so easy to attain. Little more than a phone call and a wire transfer for a few thousand euros." Poldi held the mask inches from his face, dwelling on every detail with the loupe tight to one eye.

"I'd like to see that we do business together in the future. Consider this an effort on my part to ensure your satisfaction." Lane slipped a hand into his pocket, fingers caressing the worn leather binding of a small journal.

Poldi gently placed the loupe on the table. "But the codes…surely, the risk of stealing antiquities from the Heraklion Museum outweighs their worth." His finger wandered unconsciously toward the breast pocket of his vest, tapping the fabric lightly as if to point to where he'd placed the codes. "Especially with so many priceless relics ripe for the picking in the turbulent Middle East and Levant."

"I'd rather not discuss it."

"Oh, come now, it's simply to sate my curiosity. What's a little honesty between a thief and his buyer?"

Lane considered the situation for a moment, eyes scanning the rafters overhead, before he capitulated. "You could say there's one particular artifact in that museum I have a soft spot for."

"A Minoan snake goddess would look lovely on your desk."

Lane shook his head.

"Or perhaps you long to drink deep the wine from a bull-headed rhyton to strengthen your spirit force? Why, I have three of them here. Surely that couldn't be reason enough to risk being caught."

"Let's not do this. I came here to trade. Let's trade."

"Ah, I know." The collector wagged a willowy finger at Lane, ignoring his request to get down to the business at hand. "The Phaistos Disc. One of history's most enigmatic discoveries. Such a little thing—the size of a CD-ROM—yet so full of mystery. Yes, I can see where that would be of exceptional interest to you. I've thought about it often myself. It could be the secret to life itself, or a child's board game. No one can decipher it. It's fascinating."

A series of loud blasts outside the castle broke the rhythmic patter of the rain. Both men jumped. Gunfire crackled. Poldi's security team shouldered submachine guns and sprinted toward the noise, their radios echoing the bellows from their comrades.

Poldi held the death mask tight to his chest as he leapt from the table. "What have you done?"

"I haven't done anything!" Lane protested, scrambling from his seat. "Give me the codes. Quickly." The two men collided and struggled for possession of the mask.

"No, you're trying to swindle me. Those are your men outside," Poldi groaned.

"I don't have men. I work alone."

"Then you were followed." Ripping the mask from Lane's hands, Poldi skittered into the shadows.

Pressing himself tight to a wall, Lane glanced down at the wrinkled paper in his palm he'd lifted from Poldi's pocket during the scuffle. The Heraklion Museum's access codes.

He had no idea who was assaulting the castle or why, but he did know he was trapped in here with no clear way out—a rare misstep that had him cursing under his breath, frozen in place.

Poldi's mercenaries began overturning heavy furniture, barricading themselves in, guns trained on the hall's entrance.

There was an eerie pause in the gunfire. Then, outside the hall, the clatter of booted steps as men—sounded like a dozen or more—approached. Muted commands. The door splintered and flew open. A steel canister rattled and bounced across the floor. Lane pressed his hands to his ears, pinched his eyes closed, and yelled. The flash-bang grenade exploded, filling the cavernous space with white light and deafening noise. Uniformed Bundeskriminalamt, German federal crime police, pushed through the door.

Having taken no more than a few steps inside, the first of the officers in the fatal funnel dropped on hands and knees as a mercenary's bullet struck his plate carrier. He clutched at the wound and gasped for breath, his handgun clattering to the floor. The other officers, chased back by the onslaught, retreated to the safety of the hallway, leaving their comrade to his fate at the hands of Poldi's mercenaries. Sprinting into the line of fire, rounds snapping by, Lane grabbed the fallen policeman around the waist and dragged him into an alcove. No more had they reached safety before a full-blown firefight erupted between the two parties.

The officer tore away the mask covering his face. His features were…effeminate. Lane swallowed hard, the color draining from his face. He was a *she*.

Her chestnut hair, pulled loose from beneath her ballistic helmet, fell before long-lashed, jade-colored eyes glinting with intelligence. A goddess in body armor.

Leaning against the officer in the tight space as the firefight raged on around them, Lane shouted, "You OK?"

Pulling air through her teeth, she fought back the pain from the bullet's impact. Without a word, she gripped Lane's wrist in one hand, the back of his neck with the other, and smashed his face against the wall. Wrenching his arms behind his back, she kicked behind his knees and drove him to the floor. "Move and I'll end you," she said.

THREE

Bundeskriminalamt headquarters
Wiesbaden, Germany

Two things ate at Susara more than anything else: being told she couldn't do something, and having someone prove it. When she'd first arrived at the New Era Recovery Office six years before, she'd been laughed at—ridiculed by her peers—for saying she would be the one to bring Lane Bradley down. He had a reputation as the elusive target no one could lay a finger on. Seasoned investigators and recovery agents had retired before they'd slipped so much as a single useful page inside his case file. Like some kind of evanescent phantom, Bradley would slip across international borders, empty a museum, and vanish before the first government official arrived on scene. When the agency set a trap for him, he always seemed to know. They'd end up arresting one of his competitors whom he'd mislead to think the trap was an easy score.

Perhaps it was her youthful zeal—her diploma still warm from the printer—that made Susara so certain when she said she could capture him, but she'd meant it all the same. And they'd laughed.

For that, Lane Bradley had become her pet project. The ultimate professional challenge.

It turned out they had good reason to be skeptical.

Years had passed since she stormed out of that conference room, and until today, she had almost nothing to show for her unrelenting pursuit: shoe prints; security and traffic camera composites that, when combined in the lab, came out looking like a Frankensteinian grab bag of clumsily mashed-together body parts; and one partial fingerprint. None of it was adequate for a court case.

But none of that mattered now. Finally, she'd caught him red-handed. She'd been the one to bring him in, too, just like she'd said. It should have been one of the hallmark accolades of her career. But something nagged at her, one simple fact that kept her from enjoying her victory: He'd risked his life to save hers back at Poldi's estate. That was something even the *Bundeskriminalamt* officers she'd led there couldn't lay claim to. Such behavior didn't fit the image the agency had painted of him as a cold, calculating, opportunistic mercenary.

Susara massaged the raised bruise on her sternum. The 9mm bullet had struck her vest like a supersonic fist. There was no ignoring the fact that she'd been just seconds from collecting dozens more such injuries. Or worse. Others might have taken such a near miss to be a warning. A call to change to a safer career, or to rethink one's life choices. But Susara

17

was exactly where she wanted—and needed—to be. It would take a stronger deterrent than a bullet to stop her.

Stepping into a dark room adjoining the interrogation area, she began observing Bradley through a one-way mirror. He was handsome. Younger than the camera composites had suggested. Most of the criminals she trailed possessed the swarthy appearance of war criminals, not beachfront bartenders. A bit unkempt, perhaps—his Henley shirt well worn, his jeans holey around the knees—but he exuded the carefree attitude of someone who couldn't be perturbed by anything. Even his short, Ivy-League haircut seemed carelessly messed. He evoked the kind of effortless cool cigarette companies strived so hard to capture in their advertising. With his stocky build, bronze skin, and chiseled jaw, the addition of a set of aviator sunglasses and he'd have been a shoe-in for any Hollywood war movie.

"Here you are." One of the *Bundeskriminalamt* officers nudged her arm with the file she'd requested. Though bulging with documents, most of them were blank or filled with unrelated filler text. No organization in the world had much on Bradley, and what little they did have was circumstantial evidence and outdated intel. But he didn't know that.

She set about squaring the edges of the file. The pages had been hurriedly printed and tossed inside the folder, and she didn't need that small detail distracting her while she questioned her suspect.

The *Bundeskriminalamt* officer stared at her a moment longer than was prudent. She glared at him. Clearing his throat, he nodded and exited the room in a hurry.

Early in her career, she'd discovered that being a female regularly tasked with supervising males typically resulted in one of two things: Either the men in her charge would try to humiliate her to conceal their own feelings of inadequacy, or they'd spend all their time staring at her longingly instead of doing their jobs. She found both insufferable.

With Lane's folder pinched tightly between her arm and side, she slipped into the interrogation room. Without an introduction or an acknowledgement of his presence, she began flipping through his files.

She'd long ago memorized them.

Her heart beat quickly, but she downplayed it as she casually slid into the chair across from him. For a moment, neither spoke. Finally, with a sigh, she raised her eyes from the file and stared at her captive.

"So you're Lane Bradley."

"Esquire, of her majesty's most honorable privy councilors," he said, faking a high-British dialect. Resting his hands on the back of his head, he rocked his chair on two legs. "And who might you be?"

"Agent Susara Eaves."

"Pleasure to meet you, Susara." He offered a handshake. She ignored it.

Letting his hand fall to the table, he continued, "I like your name. It's unique. So, how's your chest?"

She felt her face flush. "Excuse me?"

"Your chest. You were shot." He tapped his sternum. "I would have thought you'd remember that. I mean, every time I've been shot it's been...memorable, to say the least."

"My chest is none of your business."

He shrugged. "Sorry I brought it up. So which agency do you represent, Susara? The FBI? CIA? NSA? Some other acronym that instills fear in the lawless and the foreign?"

Susara glanced at the security camera in the room's corner. She always felt as though interrogations were like academic tests, and the professor was watching from over her shoulder to ensure she stayed on task. "New Era Recovery Office," she mumbled.

"NERO. Haven't heard of that one, though I can appreciate the reference to the Roman emperor, if that's what you guys were going for. It does seem a bit ironic to name a law enforcement agency after a sadistic, matricidal arsonist, though," he mused.

"It's just an acronym."

"It comes off as a tiny bit contrived."

Unfazed, she continued, "We'll see if you still feel that way when we hand you over to the FBI Art Crime Team, who, by the way, are *really* looking forward to meeting you."

"Hand me over…so you don't have the power to lock me up yourself, meaning this NERO is a private agency of some kind?"

"There are government agencies without arrest powers. The CIA, for instance."

He shook his head. "Yeah, I'm not getting that vibe from you. It's definitely a private agency you're working for, but man, it must have some clout for you to be in here right now."

She stared unflinchingly into his umber-colored eyes, glittering with a spirited playfulness. Unlike other prisoners, he showed no trepidation or rage. In fact, he looked as if he was enjoying himself.

"I'm not here to talk about me or who I work for," she said. "I'm more interested in what you've been up to. We've been hunting you for a long time, Mr. Bradley, following your tracks from the Simon Janashia Museum of Georgia to the

National Museum of Damascus. You've been busy. And fortunately for us, you finally slipped up."

"You're mistaken. I've never been to Georgia or Syria. Check my passport." He continued to rock on his chair, totally composed.

He'd subtly called her bluff. Admittedly, they only suspected it had been Lane who'd raided those museums—they had no evidence that put him there. No security footage or fingerprints were recovered. The entire robbery had been pulled off cleanly and neatly. Tidy. Which was why it could only have been him.

"We caught you in the middle of a sale of illegally obtained artifacts today," she continued, undeterred. "Your friend, Mr. Poldi, has already told us all about your little deal, and the mask of Shoshenq the Third is on its way back to Egypt where it belongs."

Brow furrowed and lips pinched tightly together, he leaned forward and began tracing his finger around the full-moon coffee stains on the laminate tabletop. "So I take it he told you about the Roman antiquities he requested, too."

"He told us everything," she said decisively.

A subtle smirk crossed his face, like a poker player who'd caught a glimpse of his opponent's hand. "No he hasn't, because we've never once spoken about Roman antiquities. I just wanted to see if you were really as bad a liar as I initially thought. You are."

If this interrogation had been a boxing match, he'd just delivered a staggering right hook. She paused, recovering, and then replied, "It doesn't matter. We've got enough here to lock you up for a long, long time." She emphasized her point by dropping his file loudly on the desktop.

"You mean for the FBI to lock me up for a long, long time, right?" There was humor in his voice. Irritatingly upbeat for someone facing grim criminal charges.

"You underestimate my agency's influence, Mr. Bradley. If you tell me everything you know about Poldi and any other clients you've dealt with in the past, I might be able to lessen your sentence. Maybe get you locked up back in the U.S. instead of some Third World prison. I've no doubt the Egyptians would appreciate such a goodwill gesture as our turning you over to them. I hear the jails there are especially brutal for a Westerner to be incarcerated in."

He shrugged. "They aren't so bad if you speak Arabic." Unshaken. Ice cold and impermeable. Either he was a practiced liar, or the agency's dearth of information on Bradley was more considerable than they'd thought.

"I want to know everything," she repeated.

His smile broadened. "I bet you do."

She leaned forward aggressively, hands gripping the edge of the table. "You're nothing more than a petty thief. A common criminal."

His smile vanished. "I've done more to preserve history than ninety percent of the world's academics and museum curators."

"For money."

"A guy's still gotta eat." His left hand wandered unconsciously toward his neck, his fingers toying with a small charm hanging from a silver chain.

She nodded toward his chest. "Something special you've stolen?"

Suddenly, his unflinching countenance changed. He covered the talisman with his hand and cleared his throat. "Do you have any relevant questions, or are we done?"

She smirked. She'd found a weakness. It wasn't much, but even the smallest chink in a suspect's armor could be leveraged to peel away his defenses until he was bawling and giving her his life story.

Before she could take advantage of her new find, her phone hummed in her pocket. She exited the room without another word, leaving the bundle of documents in front of him. She wanted him to stare at those long enough to get her message.

"Eaves? You still have Bradley in custody?" Her supervisor, Ruben Luis, was a Puerto Rican native who had recently been promoted to head of their small investigative team following the retirement of the previous director. He was the sort of man who spoke too quickly, laughed too loudly, and made no effort to conceal the fact that he viewed himself as the smartest man in the room. He'd formerly been one of NERO's field agents, like Susara, and was still getting used to the notion of overseeing what were, until recently, his peers.

"I do. Word travels fast." She hoped her impatience was evident.

"Yeah, well, he's a high-profile case. Listen, I want you to bring him back to the office with you. We might be able to use him to help us on another urgent case, particularly if we offer to commute his sentence in return for offering us his insight."

She tried to control her irritation. Rubbing her eyes, she spoke quietly. "What happened to locking this guy up?"

"He may have insider knowledge on others in the smuggling industry." His voice suddenly became distant, as if he'd set his phone to speaker and walked away. "If he's willing to snitch on those he's worked with, or even point us in their direction, we could return thousands of antiquities to their rightful owners and bring down entire networks of antiquities trafficking. He's more valuable to us in that capacity than in serving his time."

She knew better than to argue with him over the phone. The best she could do was to follow Ruben's orders, bring Bradley back to the U.S., and then subtly encourage her supervisor to hand him over to their point of contact at the FBI and have him locked up for good.

"I'll bring him."

"Excellent. Thank you. Oh, and are you all right? I heard you took a bullet." He said it as one would ask about a neighbor's family vacation—with only mild, casual interest.

Eager to get back to the interrogation room, she said, "I'm fine."

"Good. You're one of my best agents. I'd hate to have to replace you so soon after becoming your manager!" An attempt at a joke.

She didn't laugh. "I'll see you in a couple of days."

Ruben had said 'one of the best,' but even he knew better. She *was* the best the agency had to offer. When the director position had come available, she'd been the best choice for promotion, and everyone on the team knew it. But Ruben had connections with the right people and had spent far more time ingratiating himself with upper management than she had. She was too busy doing her job to kiss ass.

Walking briskly toward the interrogation room, she swung open the door and felt all the air leave her chest.

He was gone.

"Where's my prisoner?" She collared one of the policemen standing nearby.

"We got a phone call from Chancellor Merkel's office, ordering us to release him. His lawyer came and got him." The man's eyes nervously sought a bystander who might serve as a witness should Susara choose to put her balled-up fists to use.

Merkel's office? Who was this guy, and how did he have the clout to get a pass from the chancellor?

"And you didn't think to tell me before you did, you *draadtrekker?*" She spoke between clenched teeth, narrowly checking herself before assaulting the officer.

The man stared back at her with a bewildered expression. "Where did he go?"

"I don't know. But he left this for you." The policeman handed her a slip of paper torn from the corner of Bradley's file.

Susara—
Sorry I couldn't stick around to continue our conversation.
We should pick it up over dinner sometime.

Beneath the text, he'd hastily scrawled a phone number. She could trace it and track him down. Folding the paper in her palm, she muttered, "We're not done yet, Lane Bradley."

FOUR

Hopping over the door of his lawyer's BMW convertible and into the passenger seat, Lane rummaged through her glove compartment in search of a pair of sunglasses.

"So where are you off to now, sweet thing?" Dorothy King asked as she toddled toward the driver's seat. A short, thickset black woman with chin-length hair gone gray, Dorothy was the quintessential Southern lady: always sweet and polite, and seemingly impossible to upset. But beneath the charm and manners lay a ferociously intelligent mind. Known in the courtroom as 'the chess queen,' she was known to identify her opponent's strategy at the onset of a case and craft her argument to best counteract their approach, delivering it in a soothing Southern drawl that instantly put any jury at ease.

"The airport, darlin'." Lane mimicked her accent as he donned a pair of women's leopard-print sunglasses. "I'm Venezuela bound. Need to pay a visit to the late Hugo Chávez's progeny. Any Spanish phrases I should know?"

Dorothy giggled at her client as she turned the key in the ignition and coaxed the car into gear.

"How about *hasta luego*?"

"Sounds good to me." He reclined the seat and rested his hands on his chest. "How'd you get me out of there so quickly, anyway?"

"Oh, I know a few cabinet ministers who were willing to lend me their ear. I told them you were being held unfairly, you were an innocent bystander taken in during a police raid, and if you weren't released into my custody immediately, I'd have my friends at *Der Spiegel* run a special report on your captivity by suppertime. Lucky for you I also happened to be spending a long weekend in Paris, or you'd be hitchhiking your way to the airport right now."

He leaned over and kissed her cheek loudly. "You're a saint. I don't know why you stick your neck out for me time after time. You know I can't pay you what you're worth."

Slowing for a red light, she turned and spoke solemnly, "Honey, your parents were the best friends I ever had. Beautiful, sweet-hearted people. And you have all of their best characteristics combined. I love you like I do my own son, and I'll be damned if I'd let you get thrown in prison when it's in my power to keep that from happening." She patted his knee. "Speaking of loving you like my child, how's that sweet baby girl of yours?"

"Jordan's been in remission for a month, which is great." His voice became wistful. "But she was last time, too, before it came back and hit her so hard." His hands clenched his knees.

"Have you been reading her the Bible like I've been telling you to?"

He shuffled on the leather seat and began toying with his seatbelt. "Well, no. I mean, I've read it a few times. I figure the next time I'm in the West Bank, I'll pay a visit to Mount Quarantania in the Judaean Desert."

"To pray." It wasn't a question, but an affirmation.

"I had something else in mind. The devil taking Jesus to the Mount of Temptation, bribing him with all the kingdoms of the world and their glory, reads like a metaphor for a great big pile of riches. I'd bet the monks at the monastery there are holding out."

She swung around to face him, wagging a finger in his face. "First, you will not go robbing monks. Second, you should be reading the Bible for its meaning instead of as a historical text." She shook her head. "What am I going to do with you?"

He shrugged and rested his arm atop the door, letting the passing air tug at his fingertips. "One of these days I might come around."

"So I take it Jordan's still spending most of her time with her mother?" She turned up the car's heat.

He removed the sunglasses and carefully folded them in his hand.

"Yeah. Nicole's made it clear she doesn't want me around. Says I'm too unreliable, and my just showing up out of the blue is too hard on Jordan."

"A girl needs her father, though."

"I know. But she needs treatment more, and it doesn't come free. I'll empty every museum from here to Calcutta if that's what it takes to get her the best care available." His voice betrayed a steadfast resolve, but was laced with regret.

"Like any father would."

He shrugged. "Nicole gives me a hard time about it, but she doesn't hesitate to accept the money I send her, either."

She shifted hard, the car lurching violently. "Meanwhile, you're still living inside that old abandoned airport, aren't you? All moldy and dark...."

"Hey, it's quiet, and it's free. You'll have to come visit sometime."

She rolled her eyes.

He grinned. "Come on, when was the last time you went to visit someone and got an entire terminal as a guest house?"

FIVE

Washington, D.C.

S immering garlic wept through Susara's apartment door and blended with the omnipresent smell of cigarette smoke that clung to the hallway carpet no matter how often it got vacuumed.

She cursed.

Noah was home.

She'd hoped her boyfriend would still be at the office, or out for drinks with his coworkers—the only two places he ever seemed to be when not attached to her at the hip. Now came the inevitable argument that would erupt the minute she told him she'd only come home for a change of clothes and a shower if she could squeeze it in. Donning a plastic smile, she unlocked the door and stepped inside.

"You're home! Welcome back, gorgeous." Noah stood behind the kitchen island, apron and oven mitts on as he strained a pot of boiled pasta. Turning, he flashed his almost unnaturally white smile and tossed his head to clear the mop of hair away from his forehead.

God, he's young, Susara thought, slipping her shoes off and setting them neatly in their place on the mat by the door. Noah had wasted no time after Georgetown in his race to become an accomplished prosecutor, but despite his intelligence, there was no hiding his immaturity—his youthful, baby-soft features and puerile idolization of his girlfriend gave him away.

She dumped her bags and approached him.

"You made dinner," she said cheerfully.

"Well we haven't seen each other in weeks. I couldn't reach you on your cell, so I called down to your office and asked Ruben when you'd be back from Germany. When he told me you'd be getting in tonight, I thought I'd do something special. You catch the guy you were after?"

She felt a sharp twinge of irritation, like a biting fly on an exposed ankle. He'd called Ruben to check up on her. She wanted to rebuke him, explosively conveying that the number she'd left him was to be used in emergencies *only*. No doubt the other agents at NERO would hear about her clingy boyfriend calling her new boss for updates on her whereabouts, and would have a long list of jokes prepared for her next visit to the office. Swallowing hard, she forced a smile. Noah's adoration might have been smothering at times, but he was just trying to be sweet.

"Yeah. And then they let him go." Her mouth was dry, and she wondered if she was on her way to developing a cold. Those transatlantic flights always seemed to lead to that.

"Oh, I'm sorry." His brow furrowed with concern as he slipped off the oven mitts and dropped them on the stovetop. He leaned in for a kiss. She stopped him, moving the mitts away from the cherry-red burner before smiling and inviting him toward her again.

Their lips met. His breath smelled of spearmint—freshly brushed, as always. Noah was the sort who kept a toothbrush at his desk. He pulled her tightly against him in a passionate embrace. She winced.

"What's wrong?" he asked as she pulled away.

"Work injury."

"What do you mean?" Less a question, more a parental challenge.

She hesitated, knowing he would overreact. "I took a round to my chest plate. I'm fine."

"You've been shot?" He tugged his apron off. "We need to get you to a hospital."

"I'm fine," she repeated, patting his chest. "And, actually, I have to get going. I just came back to get some fresh clothes. My flight leaves in just over an hour."

Crestfallen, his features softened. "Flight to where?"

"Venezuela. We traced the suspect's cell number. I'm still on this guy's trail, and I don't want to lose him."

"Can't you catch a later flight? Just spend a few hours with me?" he pleaded.

"I really can't. This is the hottest lead I've had on him in years. I'm sorry."

Grabbing the pan, he slid it into the sink, metal ringing, bits of seared chicken scattering across the kitchen counter. Crossing his arms tightly to his chest, he said, "I can't keep doing this, Susara. I never see you. I just sit around worrying about you and hoping you'll come home."

"I wish it were different." Approaching him and touching his chest with her pointer finger, she seductively tugged at the buttons on his shirt. "How about I promise to take a week off when I get back, and you and I can go somewhere warm together. I'll bring that black two-piece you like. I promise it'll be worth the wait."

Tapping the kitchen island with his toe, he softened. "All right, but at least let me drive you to the airport."

SIX

Ajaccio, Corsica

Agapito Vicente waited outside the door of mafia consigliere Achille Musarde's office with the stiffness of a soldier at parade rest. Even as his adopted son of 40 years, Agapito felt himself battling the familiar timorousness that always overtook him when in his father's presence.

Though legally Musarde's son, Agapito was really more akin to an employee. Like a shelter dog, he'd been given a new name—one probably taken from a phone directory or someone Musarde had once worked with—when he'd arrived at the man's estate at the age of seven. That had set the tone. It had never been a father-son relationship; it was a purchase. Ownership. Musarde had needed a full-time errand boy, a role he trained Agapito to fulfill.

Sent to the finest private institutions, Agapito had faced regular beatings—sometimes by Musarde himself, usually by one of his hired hands when his father was busy—whenever he received anything less than the highest marks in his coursework. Musarde expected perfection, but not to encourage Agapito's well-being. No, it was only to ensure that his long-term investment proved worthwhile. Agapito had gone on to study archaeology at Oxford, and on the day of his graduation, was brought into Musarde's office, much in the same fashion as he came today, and was told simply, "Now, go and find me riches."

And he had. For decades. The cold, dark cellars below this estate housed thousands of relics Agapito had collected. Many of them had come at the cost of spilled blood. Blood he'd learned to scrub from his hands—and his conscience—each night.

Though he'd started out trying to be a legitimate archaeologist, dusting around dig sites and applying for grants with his peers, he quickly learned of his father's impatience, and more notably, the man's obsession with results by any means necessary.

After several hostile admonitions from the old man regarding his pace, Agapito's job became less about finding relics and more about determining which were worth killing for. Any love he'd once had for archaeology, for history's lost relics, had been extinguished the day he realized he had become little more than a mercenary. A gun-for-hire with a specialty.

"Agapito, come," Musarde grumbled, his voice low, smoky, muddied by a mystifying blend of Corsican and French accents. His accountant—a mousy little man wearing an ill-fitting suit jacket that billowed around the shoulders and hung low past his hips—skittered through the doorway, clutching a stack of binders to his chest. The man raised his eyebrows at Agapito and sighed before exiting in a hurry.

Agapito entered.

Hunched over his desk, Musarde looked like a weathered concrete gargoyle: his spine bent, nose and ears too large for his face, complexion washed out and gray. A patchwork of white scars intertwined across his face and neck where, decades before, the mafia's previous don had slashed him repeatedly with a box-cutter—punishment for advising him to expand the family's loan-sharking racket into a new area, a move that brought about one of the biggest law enforcement busts of the decade and landed the don's nephew in prison for 30 years.

"*Mon père*," Agapito said softly, waiting for Musarde's invitation to sit. He didn't give it.

"There's something I'd like for my collection. I want you to get it for me," the old man said bluntly, sliding a folded pamphlet across his desk.

Agapito cleared his throat. "You've been perusing auction listings again."

"Yes. Hugo Chávez's estate. A Minoan tablet. It looks promising." Musarde jerked open a desk drawer and withdrew a thick cigar, chrome lighter, and guillotine-blade cutter.

Agapito rubbed his eyes. "I've told you before, stealing from high-profile auctions is very risky—"

"Still a coward, even after all these years," Musarde spat, a fine mist of saliva showering his desktop.

"I'm not a coward, I'm cautious, and of much more use to you outside of prison. Why do you want this tablet, anyway?"

Agapito asked, twisting his face as he scrutinized the photo of the simple artifact. "Doesn't look like anything worthwhile to me."

Musarde leaned across the desk and slapped Agapito's face with an open hand. "When I tell you I want something, you get it. Don't question me."

Agapito kept his cool despite the insulting sting. Allowing his volatile temper to rise to the level of his father's would not bode well for either of them. He was suddenly very cognizant of the weight of the long-slide 1911 pistol stuffed into the leather shoulder holster beneath his coat.

Reaching into his desk, Musarde withdrew a yellowed, photocopied piece of paper and spread it out before his son. It looked to have been copied from a journal entry in which someone had drawn a likeness of the tablet featured in the auction. Below the image, a line of Italian scrawled across the page.

"Read it," Musarde ordered.

Agapito rubbed his cheek where he'd been struck. "It says something about the Phaistos Disc, a radiance of some sort, and a key. I don't know what that means." He leaned away from the desk, far enough to exceed his father's reach.

"Of course you don't, you imbecile. Luigi Pernier, the man who discovered the Phaistos Disc, wrote this in his journal—a journal that was stolen from me some time ago by Lane Bradley, that insufferable man you killed."

Agapito smiled with his eyes. "Lane Bradley. It's been years since I've heard that name. We never did find where he hid that journal."

Musarde grimaced, the resentment still fresh. "I have the crucial parts of Pernier's work here. He'd said the tablet, the one in the auction, is the key to reading the Phaistos Disc's inscriptions."

"Why is it so important to you to read the disc?" Agapito asked carefully. For all the years he'd spent hunting down things related to the disc on his father's behalf, knowing of Musarde's obsession with the artifact, he'd never really known why.

In a rare moment of apparent discomposure, Musarde looked down and began twirling the gold ring on his left pinky finger—the Ring of Mavro Spelio. Years before, convinced the ring had something to do with the Phaistos Disc given the spiral of symbols on its face analogous to the legendary artifact, Musarde had sent Agapito to take it from its owner in Switzerland. The man's eyes, wide and swathed in burst blood vessels as Agapito strangled the life from him on his kitchen floor, still haunted Agapito when he slept.

Musarde cleared his throat. "Pernier wrote of when he first found the disc; his hands when he touched it were healed and made beautiful."

"Surely that's a myth." Agapito slid the photocopy back across the desk toward his father. "The disc is in a museum in Heraklion right now. Don't you think every visitor would have experienced the healing power of the disc during the century that's passed since Pernier found it if such a thing were true?"

Musarde seized a small bronze bust of Caligula from his desk and hurled it across the room, leaving a triangular indentation in the plaster wall where the statue's base had struck.

"Don't you think I know that? That's why I need the tablet! Pernier never found a way to make the disc respond as it did when he first found it, but he knew the tablet held the key. It was stolen before he could use it. For the first time in a century, the tablet has been found. And. I. Want it." Musarde punctuated each word by stabbing the air with a letter opener.

Agapito glanced at his father's scars as he knelt to pick up the bronze bust. Musarde had lived a reclusive life since becoming disfigured. The wounds shamed him when in the presence of anyone from the family, and appeared as a hideous defect to anyone on the street. Although he had always been pragmatic when it came to his collection—how rare a given relic was and how much it was worth—this particular legend played to his vanity and desperate desire to be free of his humiliation.

Agapito scanned the text engraved in the statue's base before returning it to his father's desk.

Oderint dum metuant.

Let them hate, so long as they fear.

"You'll need me to steal the Phaistos Disc, too, then." Agapito spoke of it as though such a thing were merely a footnote, not the overwhelming logistical challenge it actually was. It wouldn't do any good to complain about the difficulty of such an assignment. His father had no regard for the struggle, only the result.

"First, the tablet." Musarde stared at the spiral of symbols on his ring. "Stealing the disc will invite pressure from law enforcement and other thieves. Everything else must be ready before we take it."

"Perhaps we can negotiate a pre-sale of the tablet. If it's going to auction anyway, the seller may be open to an upfront cash payment," Agapito suggested. Despite the callouses on his soul left behind by years of murder and violent extortion, he didn't relish the thought of shedding more blood for the sake of his father's misguided fantasies. If he could get what

Musarde needed peacefully, it would weigh less on his already burdened mind.

Musarde, calmer now, clipped the tip from his cigar. Pinching it between his lips, he swept the lighter's flame under the opposite end until it glowed cherry red. "Fine. You can try your way, first," he mumbled from the corner of his mouth. "Offer 50,000 American for it."

"If they refuse? They're Hugo Chávez's children—public figures."

"It would cost the same to cover up your taking the artifact and killing them all." Musarde let a cloud of acrid gunmetal smoke roll out from between his lips. "That's my only offer, in whichever form they choose to accept it."

SEVEN
Caracas, Venezuela

H e was just a tourist taking a late-night jog in a public park. To complete the charade, Lane wore a set of in-ear headphones, though he left them unplugged so he could hear if he was being followed.

Parque del Este had the same well-groomed appearance as a country club's driving range. A wall of lush, rolling mountains loomed in the distance, the air thick with humidity and the saccharine aroma of orchids. As much as he enjoyed the beauty of the towering palms and purple jacaranda trees in bloom, he was more appreciative of the fact that the public park could get him within just a few blocks of the *Residencia Presidencial La Casona*—the presidential estate.

The park was named in honor of Francisco de Miranda, a Spaniard from the 18th century who fought for American independence, then in the French Revolution, and finally, for the independence of Venezuela. He was a revolutionary in the truest sense of the word. He wouldn't mind, then, Lane reasoned, if Lane were to use his namesake as a launch point to steal from a despot's personal collection of antiquities.

The jog was the easy part. The moment he crossed over the estate's perimeter wall, things would take a turn for the serious. If caught, he knew there'd be no need for an alibi. He'd be dragged into the bushes, beaten until unconscious, and probably shot repeatedly in the face—a technique the Venezuelan police had perfected while dealing with government protesters. Obliterating a suspect's face was as purposeful as it was savage: It rendered a body so disfigured as to force a closed-casket funeral, and in so doing, eliminated the chance of photos of the deceased being used to fuel more protests.

Exiting the park, he hurried across the street, gliding into the trees surrounding the estate. Muscles tense, he silently ascended a hill overlooking the far reaches of the presidential compound.

Statues and fountains, fringed by manicured flowerbeds, peppered the ground between the estate's white adobe buildings. The compound dominated the area like a medieval castle—imposing and opulent, surrounded distantly by the destitute peasants who'd built it. Venezuela's socialist regime had made royalty of the Chávez family, but at immeasurable cost to the country's economy.

Kneeling, he surveyed his target, matching the layout of the grounds in his mind's eye to the satellite images he'd memorized in preparation for the heist. "Third building from the east wall," he muttered, scanning the complex. "That'd be…you."

A twig snapped. The soft soil underfoot betrayed no footsteps, but still, he sensed someone approaching. The careful, stalking movement. The softest brush of a pant leg raking against brush. He slowly raised himself to a crouch, holding that position until his thighs burned, listening. Internally, he rebuked himself for letting himself be seen. Where had he slipped up? Did the guards have dogs? Had they seen him in the park and followed him here? Ears straining, he closed his eyes as if to focus his energy on detecting this new unseen presence.

When he heard it, a final hesitant step, he wheeled around to face his attacker, prepared to launch himself at the threat. Finding himself face-to-face with the muzzle of a pistol, he instead took a long breath and dropped his fists. "I'm guessing you're going to be a whole lot harder to bribe than local law enforcement."

"Damn right. You're coming with me." Susara approached him slowly, gun thrust straight away from her chest, sights centered on the faded image of a surfer on Lane's T-shirt.

"And what happens when I don't cooperate? You really expect me to believe you'd shoot me, Susara?"

"It's Agent Eaves."

"But Susara's such a pretty name. Let's stick with that one."

She stood straighter, adjusting her grip on the pistol. "If I have to shoot you, I will. I'm beginning to think it would make my life easier." Shifting a hand from her gun, she reached for the handcuffs in her back pocket.

After a moment spent sizing her up, he smiled and shook his head. "Bad liar." He turned and carefully approached the estate's outer walls as if ignoring her presence entirely.

Shoving her sidearm into the holster on her belt, she followed him. Gripping his arm, she moved to force him to the ground.

He grabbed her wrist. Their eyes locked. A fist swung toward his abdomen and struck sharply. Using his body weight, he pushed her against the wall, broad forearms pinning her in place. "You surprised me the last time you arrested me, Susara. Gave me one hell of a bruise that started turning all kinds of iridescent colors this morning. I'm not looking to make it a matching set. Now, if you'll excuse me, I'm working." Snatching the pistol from her holster, he dropped the magazine, cleared the action, and before she could protest, field-stripped the weapon. Handing her back the frame, he dangled the pistol's slide in front of her nose. "You can have this back when I'm done."

Eyes wide, she stared at what remained of her sidearm. Kneeling, she recovered the magazine that had fallen into the grass. She changed tack. "Wait. Look, if you cooperate with us, maybe help us bring down other smuggling rings you might know about," she paused and pinched her eyes closed, shaking her head, "we could reduce your sentence."

"Or I could just continue what I've been doing for years without your help or permission. That's been working out well for me so far."

"Lane, please."

Angling his head toward her and placing a finger behind his ear, he asked, "Can you repeat that last part?"

She groaned, her hands tightening into fists. "I said *please*."

"The makings of humility. Now we're getting somewhere. Well in that case, I'd be happy to help you as a consultant. On one condition."

"You don't get to make conditions." She was obviously regretting her suppliant approach.

"I think I do. If you help me with this little operation I've got going here, I'll help you with yours. Call it a safeguard."

She chewed her lip, eyes tracing the walls of the compound. He could tell that this was uncomfortable for her, not being in complete control. Here she was, faced with either stealing from a foreign government's presidential estate with the man she came to arrest or going home empty-handed. Sure, she could yell for the police, but he had a strong hunch that she didn't have the Venezuelan government's blessing to be here. She'd be as likely to end up in prison or a casket as he would.

His proposition was ridiculous. Even he knew it. She had everything to lose by agreeing, and very little to gain. She didn't know if he would keep his end of the bargain, or if he was just looking for a way to get her off his back. But there was temptation there. She was actually thinking of saying yes.

After a moment of deliberation, she whispered, "I help you with this, you come back with me to D.C. Got it?"

He smiled. He hadn't seen that coming. "Deal. You can start by helping me recon this place."

He unclasped a rubber bracelet from his wrist, unfolding it to reveal an X-shaped device with a small, shielded plastic propeller on the tip of each extremity. With his thumb and forefinger, he gently swiveled a small camera lens outward from the center of the X. Placing his smartphone on a knee and swiping the screen a few times, he handed her the wristband device. "Go ahead and pick it up by its base. Make sure those wings are free, and when I start it, give it a gentle boost." He kept his eyes fastened on the phone, never turning to watch the small vehicle whir and lift off, up and over the wall.

"Cute toy. I fail to see how that's going to help you get in, though." She followed the small drone with her eyes as it vanished into the dark sky.

"Ordinarily it wouldn't help much," he agreed. "But the late Hugo Chávez never believed in fancy technology for protecting his treasures. He preferred lots of good old-fashioned armed security, which isn't the worst strategy: People may be less reliable than machines, but that also means they're less predictable."

"I would think that would open him up to the risk of an inside job," she said.

"Not when he had access to every one of his security guards' families. One thing about dictators: They understand violence better than most. I'm sure he made his men aware of what the punishment would be for stealing from him."

After a few minutes of scanning the compound from above and taking mental notes of the guard post locations, he piloted the drone into her waiting hands.

"Fortunately, it looks like Chávez's heirs' spending habits have forced them to scale back on the number of guards. This one's going to be a walk in the park." He dug a pair of wire cutters from his pocket. "Well, I mean, we literally walked in the park to get here, but I meant metaphorically—"

"I knew what you meant. What are you stealing, anyway?" she asked.

"You mean what are *we* stealing? Well that demands a little backstory. The current Venezuelan president, Nicolás

Maduro, doesn't actually live here—he can't seem to find a way to convince Chávez's kids to leave. Inside are thousands of priceless artifacts and artwork from the old man's personal collection. His kids are too busy partying to recognize just how impressive daddy's trove of relics really is."

She stood with her back against the wall and laced her fingers together to give him a boost up to the concertina wire-topped concrete walls.

Lane snipped the coil of wire and continued in a hushed voice as he clambered over the wall, his broad chest balancing on the ledge, and swung his feet to the other side. "That said, being a party animal is expensive. So, to maintain their lifestyle, the kids recently put the entire collection up for auction."

"And you're going to steal something before it can be bid on?" she asked.

"I'm going to appropriate it from people who deserve worse." He leaned over and extended his hand to her.

Taking a half step backward, she shook her head. "I could lose my job over this."

"Exciting, right? Come on. We won't get caught. Besides, you owe me one."

"Why?"

"I saved your life."

"I never asked you to."

"I'll keep that in mind for next time. Now, are you coming or not?"

She hesitated. He smiled sincerely and waved her toward him.

"Yeah, I'm coming." She leapt up and grabbed his hand. Together, they dropped into an open, neatly trimmed courtyard, and slipped toward the nearest building.

"Up we go." Cupping his hands, he nodded toward the building's gutters. She planted her shoe in his hands. As he lifted her up, he mumbled, "Excellent view from down here. You must work out."

"Eyes forward."

"Here's the thing: Your lower half looks pretty fit, but are you going to be able to pull me up with the other half?"

"I don't know," she said. "How were you going to do it if I wasn't here?"

"I guess I'd just jump."

She scoffed. "No way can a guy your height jump high enough to get up here without help."

He raised an eyebrow and smirked. "Everyone doubts the little guy." Taking two steps back, he leapt four feet off the ground to grab the gutter. The plastic squealed loudly under his weight as his fingers wrapped around the lip of the U-channel. A guard's voice echoed through the courtyard.

"¿Quién está ahí?"

Hanging from the gutters, fingers white as he struggled to pull himself up, Lane cursed. Susara gripped his wrists and leaned back, pulling him the rest of the way to the roof.

He gave her a nod. "Thanks for the help. You'd think that, with this being a presidential estate, they'd have sprung for some nicer gutters." He scanned the ground below for the approaching security. Shuffling quietly along the rooftop in the direction of the guard's voice, sneakers padding lightly on the ceramic shingles, Lane stopped at the far corner of the building. Below him, the guard, fumbling for his radio, edged cautiously into the open. Lane glanced back at Susara, winked, and leapt from the rooftop like a fearless child playing superhero. Only, instead of breaking an arm, he smashed into the guard squarely, knocking the man's radio into the grass.

Rolling the stunned man over, Lane expertly put him in a chokehold—forearm wrapped around the guard's neck, hand gripping his other arm's bicep. Slipping his free hand around the backside of the guard's head, he applied pressure, cutting off the blood flow to the man's brain. A few seconds of grunting and weak thrashing, and the guard slumped unconscious. Lane stood, dusted the grass clippings from his pants, and dragged the limp body into the bushes.

Rejoining Susara on the rooftop, he smiled. His breathing was calm and even despite the scuffle.

"Looks like you've done that before. Good work. Now we only have a few minutes to get whatever it is you're looking for before he wakes up," she scolded, staring at the man's unconscious form below.

"You're so negative. I bought us some time and didn't get either of us shot. Where I come from, that's a good thing."

Sidling up to a well-lit window in one of the roof's dormers, he paused. His mouth opened in silent surprise, eyes wide as he looked inside. Like he'd seen a ghost.

"What is it? She scooted closer for a better look.

A tall, bespectacled figure paced below. Wearing a tweed jacket, his brown hair speckled with gray and neatly coiffed, the stranger looked as though he'd just finished lecturing a university English class. He moved with a carefully calculated gait, his hands held behind his back.

"Lane? Who is that guy?"

EIGHT

Kamid al lawz, Lebanon
2006

Wind gusted through the dig site, shrieking over rocky outcroppings and deep, excavated pits like a child's breath through a toy whistle. A few miles away, the city of Kamid al lawz hid from Israeli artillery, lights out and shades drawn.

"Agapito, send the basket down. I've found something." The wind nearly drowned out Lane's voice.

Agapito's eyes darted across the desolate landscape, nervously observing the movement of shadows and rustling tufts of sun-bleached grass. "What? What have you found?"

"Tablets with what looks like cuneiform text on them." Lane coughed, the sound rough and dry. "Now I'm sure of it: This is a Hittite settlement."

"Trinkets," Agapito shouted down the darkened shaft. "Please tell me we didn't come all this way for some crusty stones. My employer will not be pleased."

A construction worker's helmet emerged from the hole as Lane climbed a rope to the surface. His eyes were bloodshot—irritated by blowing sand—his face smeared with dirt and sweat. "A few things I'd like to discuss. First, we've already had a busy night, OK? We filled the truck with all the easy stuff they left sitting out. You weren't happy with that. I entertained you and got my gopher on, climbing into these godawful pits. It's dark down there, Agapito. And very, very cramped. You know what likes spaces like that? Scorpions. I don't care for their company. They're stabby. Second, your employer should know by now that archaeology—the kind that doesn't involve ripping off museums—comes with a certain fallibility. The fact that we've found anything at all should be a relief to you. At least you won't have to go back empty-handed. And third, when I say send the basket down"—he reached for the wicker basket perched on the edge of the pit, tied it to the rope he'd climbed, and dropped it below—"send the damn basket down." The rope snapped taut as it reached the bottom, a trickle of gravel following behind.

"Find me something shiny," Agapito called after Lane as the latter eased himself back into the hole, lowering himself along the rope. "Something gold, or with precious stones, or even bronze. He likes shiny. And hurry up. I don't know how much longer we have until someone gets suspicious."

The report from an artillery position thumped in the distance.

"I'm sure they have bigger things to worry about right now," Lane shouted as he tugged the rope. "Go ahead, haul it up."

Agapito complied, drawing in the rope hand-over-hand. Cradled in the basket, propped atop a stack of cuneiform tablets, rested an intricate bronze icon—a carefully woven mesh circle with a series of mushroom-like figures mounted around its circumference, a pair of crudely fashioned birds sweeping up from its base.

"How's that for something shiny, Agapito? Your boss should be happy to see that. It's a Hittite sun disc. It's been 80 years since one of those has been unearthed."

Mesmerized by the find, Agapito stood and began slowly walking toward the truck, polishing the disc gently with his sleeve.

"Agapito, send that rope back down. I'm done down here. First round's on you."

Gently setting the sun disc inside their vehicle on Lane's seat, Agapito reached into the glove compartment and withdrew a pistol. He closed the door and returned to the pit.

"Lane, I'm sorry to have to do this to you. I truly am. You are a superb archaeologist, and a brave man. But you're also an inveterate thief. You stole something dear to my father, and he's demanded your death as punishment."

It was black inside the pit, but if there'd been any light, Agapito might have seen Lane wince visibly at the mention of Musarde.

"Wait. Agapito, don't."

"Tell me where you hid the journal, and I'll leave your fate in the hands of the Lebanese rather than taking your life myself. Perhaps they'll be kind and let you rot in prison for the remainder of your days." Agapito coaxed the handgun's slide rearward, checking for the shimmer of a brass cartridge inside the chamber.

"I don't know about any journal," Lane shouted back. "Come on, let me out."

"Last chance. Don't lie to me again," Agapito said, angling the pistol downward toward the dark hole. Silence. His finger tightened on the trigger until the mechanism broke. Nothing. No gunshot, no recoil. He cleared the round and tried again. Nothing. Those miserable black-market vendors had sold him a pistol with a broken firing pin.

"It's your lucky day." Flinging the handgun into the dirt, Agapito turned to leave. Lane would never make it out of that hole before the authorities arrived, anyway. He was as good as dead. A blistering wind stirred, and Agapito's voice was nearly lost in the din. "May we meet in another life as friends."

NINE

Residencia Presidencial La Casona
Caracas, Venezuela
Present day

N udging Lane's shoulder, Susara repeated, "Who is that?" He appeared completely lost, his mind in a different world.

"Agapito Vicente," he muttered. "The competition. A thief who works exclusively for a Corsican mafia consigliere—his father."

"I take it you two have a history?"

He looked at her somberly as he spoke, the cadence of his voice revealing his enduring resentment. "He left me behind on a job years ago. His betrayal earned me six long, cockroach-infested, starving, indoor plumbing-free months in a Lebanese prison." He sighed and returned his stare to his adversary below. "A man with limitless ambition, an absence of morality, and just enough intelligence to be dangerous. He must have seen the auction listing."

"What is it that you two are trying to take, anyway?" she asked. "You never actually told me, specifically, which piece you're looking for."

Ignoring her question, he held a finger to his lips as he nudged the window open.

"Mr. Perez, it's very kind of you to allow us an early look at your former employer's collection."

"Well, if you brought cash, it'll be worth my time." A dark-skinned man in his mid-twenties stood beside Agapito. Silk shirt open to his navel, the young man glittered with sweat despite the temperature-controlled room. His glossy eyes and wandering, open-mouthed stare suggested he'd been indulging in chemical entertainment only moments before Agapito and his men had arrived.

"Oh, rest assured, it's worth your time." Agapito looked around the room. "Where is the clay tablet with the *labrys* on it?"

"The what?" the man asked, distracted. A stereo thumped from somewhere in the compound, the DJ running a sound check before another night's festivities.

"An axe. The tablet had an axe on it," Agapito growled, his disdain obvious.

"Oh, that. Yeah, it's around here somewhere."

Gripping Perez's shirtfront, the Corsican slid his pistol from the holster beneath his jacket and jammed its muzzle against his neck. "Find it."

Lane reached into his pocket and fished out his phone.

"What are you doing?" Susara whispered.

"Creating a distraction."

"Just what kind of distraction is making a phone call going to accomplish?"

"This kind." He pressed *send*. A second passed before the rumble of an explosion echoed from the other side of the compound. Smoke wafted toward the horizon from the opposite end of the estate.

"I thought you said this place was secure," Agapito shouted at Perez as he and his men ran toward the sound, exiting the room below.

"Tell me that wasn't an explosive charge," Susara groaned.

"Why? Oh, right. You're with the *policia*. Come on, no one got hurt. It's a teensy charge. The Chávez family is only out a trash can."

"Where'd you learn to handle explosives, anyway?" she asked as Lane slipped through the window and dropped into the now-empty building. She followed, cursing as she landed awkwardly on the concrete floor. He caught her before she toppled into one of the displays, righted her, and promptly set to work searching for the tablet.

"Well, it started when I got into a little trouble in France way back when. The gendarmes were chasing me after a little run-in at the Carnavalet Museum—"

"And what were you stealing from them?" she interrupted, massaging her ankle.

"Why does everyone insist on using that word? I was returning a necklace belonging to Marie Antoinette to her heirs," he said with a flourish of his hand.

"For money."

"Yes. We've been over this."

"And you believed that your client was actually related to Marie Antoinette?" She cocked her head and raised an eyebrow challengingly.

He dithered. "Well, that turned out to be a lie. But it's all part of the learning process. There are worse things in life than being too trusting." Walking a serpentine path around the room's many glass displays, he glanced quickly at each one in search of the relic he'd come for. "I couldn't get out of the country without raising flags, I was flat broke, had no contacts—well, none that I could trust, obviously—so I did something desperate. I joined the French Foreign Legion."

"Really?" she asked. "You expect me to believe *you* were a Legionnaire? Mister nonconformist brigand, a member of one of the most legendarily disciplined fighting forces in the world? Come on."

"Well, historically the Legion was comprised of criminals and society's castoffs, which fits me pretty well," he said. "Anyway, I didn't exactly make a career out of it. I learned some French, stuck around long enough to pick up some basic demolitions and combatives training, and then went AWOL at first opportunity. They'd probably shoot me on sight, even after all these years."

As he continued his story—something about a cell phone trick he'd picked up from an IRA bomb-maker—Susara moved to the opposite end of the room, strolling leisurely from one display to the next as if visiting a museum on a rainy Sunday afternoon. The Chávez collection really was impressive. The man had amassed everything from golden Incan statues to crudely minted Spanish coins, all stowed carefully in what appeared to be humidity-controlled cases. Renaissance oil paintings on the walls, enveloped in UV-resistant glass, glowed in the light cast by custom halogen bulbs designed to prevent fading.

During her career, she had heard every excuse for stealing relics, and they almost always boiled down to a desire for money. Lane's argument that he was saving artifacts by moving them into the private market seemed typical of that mindset at first, but seeing now the attention a wealthy collector like Chávez had paid to preserve his pieces, and the ill funding many museums faced, she realized he might have a point.

"…which is hardly foolproof, because the lithium-ion cobalt batteries in those phones are unstable as hell. One short, and boom! No open casket for you."

"Lane, I think this is the one you want." She stopped before one of the vitrine cases. Inside rested a modest clay tablet the size and shape of a family Bible. A faint impression of an axe appeared in the slab's center.

Jogging to her side, he patted her shoulder. "Good work. You've got a keen eye."

Sliding an aluminum lock-picking gun from his back pocket, he set to work on the case's keyhole.

Subdued voices came from the courtyard.

"Lane, hurry up. They're coming back."

"The faster I try to do this, the longer it's going to take." He chewed his cheek as he worked at the lock. "Don't pressure me; I'll get nervous and won't be able to perform."

Distantly, sirens whined. Someone had undoubtedly called the police following the explosion. They were running out of time to make a clean escape.

Susara ran her hands through her hair. She looked at the door and back at the locked case. "I shouldn't be here. God, why did I agree to come with you?"

The men approached the door.

She had to do something. Setting her jaw, she tugged her shoe from her foot, stuffed her fist inside it, and struck the case. The glass shattered, alarms sounded, and the murmurs turned to shouts.

"Why'd you do that? I almost had it," Lane lamented, drawing the tablet through the case's broken frame. Grabbing her arm, he pulled her tight to the wall alongside the room's entrance.

"They were about to come in," she said, shaking the glass shards from her shoe and slipping it back on. "Besides, guilty by an inch, guilty by a mile. If I'm going to lose my job, I want it to be for doing something worthwhile—not just trespassing."

"That's adorable. You think they'd let you live long enough for you to lose your job?" he said, eyes fastened to the entryway.

The doors burst open. Agapito and his men flooded inside, crossing the room with their pistols held low. Waiting until they'd all entered, Lane and Susara slipped behind them, through the doorway and into the muggy night air.

Face to face with Perez.

Glancing back and forth between the two, and then to the tablet buried like a football against Lane's left bicep, the Venezuelan opened his mouth to cry out.

Lane's hand snapped against Perez's throat—a light but deliberate strike. Instead of a scream, only a deflated squeak came out as Perez gripped his neck, sliding against Lane, chin resting on the shorter man's shoulder. Gently guiding him to the dirt, Lane patted the man's head and followed Susara toward the perimeter wall. As they climbed toward freedom, Agapito stepped clear of the building, handgun at his side. His eyes followed them over the compound's wall. Before passing out of sight, Lane locked eyes with his rival.

Though his posture appeared poised, Agapito's countenance told a different story. He possessed the discomposed expression of a man caught in a lie.

TEN

The Gulfstream's stark white aluminum skin glowed in the darkness, with the exception of a few black identification numbers stamped on the craft's tail. The jet idled outside an unmarked hanger in a distant corner of Simón Bolívar International Airport, away from commercial traffic and prying eyes. Swinging into a plush leather seat, Lane gently placed the tablet at his feet and handed back the other half of Susara's pistol.

"As promised. Nice gun, by the way. Heckler & Koch P7, right? Haven't seen one of those in years. Has the cocking mechanism built right into the grip—safe to carry with one in the chamber. Squeeze to make it ready to go, and let off to put it back on safe. Takes a brave person to charge into a gunfight with a relic like that."

Reassembling the pistol, Susara nodded and ran a finger along the handgun's slide. "When I first started working for NERO, I was told to go buy any service pistol I wanted. Price was no object. I didn't know anything about guns; I went to school to be an archaeologist, not law enforcement. But this one caught my eye, and it's gotten me out of a few jams since then." Pulling the slide rearward, she checked the chamber for a live round before holstering the pistol. She still felt chagrined at being so easily disarmed, and wondered where Lane had received hand-to-hand combat training.

"That whole 'price is no object' thing seems to be a common theme with you guys," he said, bouncing his fists on his seat's leather-wrapped armrests as he glanced around the airplane's luxurious interior. "You definitely travel in style."

"The founder of NERO is one of less than 500 billionaires in the world, a man willing to drop enormous sums of money to preserve and protect antiquities. Spending a little extra on a private flight for me to capture an infamous thief like you was probably a no-brainer." She did little to mask the vitriol in her voice.

Lane's smile vanished. He leaned forward in his seat as Susara sat down across from him and crossed her arms and legs. "I get the sense you don't like me very much."

Here was an opportunity to assault him with an obscenity-laced polemic detailing all the reasons she didn't like him. But she held back. For some reason, in that moment, his dark brown eyes staring back at her with genuine concern, she felt her anger ebb. Because she wasn't really mad at him. In fact, if his name hadn't been Lane Bradley—the man she'd spent so much of her career hunting—she might really like the guy. No, she was mad that her agency had sent her after a man who, at least at first blush, seemed more decent than any she'd arrested, while painting him as the most conniving and malicious of them all.

He cleared his throat and looked at the floor. "Susara, why did you agree to help me back there? You and I both know you could have raised the alarm or called in backup to take me in."

The answer was simple, but difficult for anyone but her to understand. She'd come along because she had wanted to see her mystery man at work. Though she had spent years hell-bent on bringing Lane down, she still maintained a grudging admiration for his skill. This had been her opportunity to see how it was done, to observe the other side, spectate in real time the sort of robbery that would have landed as a manila folder on her desk on Monday morning. With her office door locked, she would stare at vague notes and blurry photographs shot by Third World policemen until she could envision the entire robbery from start to finish. Only, this time, she could live it out—see the entire thing through her own eyes. The thought alone of participating in such a crime had made her feel a peculiar nervousness verging on pleasure—like the first time a boy had unclasped her bra. You show me yours, I'll show you mine. Knowing it was wrong had made it that much more exciting and tempting.

"So what's so special about this clay tablet?" she asked, changing the subject.

Like a puppy caught destroying a throw pillow, he slid back in his seat meekly. The jet's engines grew in volume, the craft beginning its forward motion down the runway. He mumbled, "I suppose at this point we're essentially partners." Reaching down, he slid the clay tablet, its corners chipped and rounded with age, into his lap. "Minoan. Early Neopalatial. The axe, or *labrys*, was used as a symbol of King Minos's power." He withdrew a small, worn leather journal from his pocket and flipped it open, planting a finger along the spine to hold it open as he angled it toward her.

"What am I looking at?" she asked, accepting the journal.

"A journal belonging to Italian archaeologist Luigi Pernier. The same guy who discovered the Minoan palace at Phaistos. And that's his penned illustration of this very tablet. He found it beside the Phaistos Disc inside a temple depository."

Her brow furrowed skeptically. "OK. Worth getting shot at?"

"I think so, yes." He brought the clay tablet to his knee and snapped it in half.

"What the hell, Lane?" She let the journal drop and reached forward to stop him. "We risked our lives for that just so you could destroy it?"

"Calm down. It's not the tablet that's priceless. It's what's inside."

Carefully snapping the tablet halves into quarters, he began picking away pieces of clay with his fingernail, slowly revealing four stones, rounded and smooth like river rocks. Each was the size of an airport kiosk paperback and featured deep carvings on its face. Glyphs of some kind.

"Chávez never knew what he had," he whispered, concentrating on his work. "This tablet has been lost for over a century, and only someone who's read Pernier's journal would know what it was and why it's so significant." He leaned back and wiped at his eyes with the back of his hand. "I don't have my contacts in." He handed her the first stone. "Do these symbols look familiar to you?"

After a moment of scrutinizing the find, she said, "The symbols on the right side of each stone are clearly Egyptian hieroglyphs."

"Good. And on the left?"

Her eyes widened as she realized what she was holding. "My God, these are Linear A symbols."

Closing his eyes, he leaned back in his seat and smiled contentedly. "Now you understand why I had to take these, right?"

"Linear A text has never been deciphered."

"Not until now. These babies are like miniature Rosetta Stones. Only instead of Greek, demotic, and hieroglyphs, they show hieroglyphs and Linear A. With them, we can decipher one language we can't read using one we can."

"But why would the Minoans do this? And how the hell did you know those stones were inside?"

He nodded as though he'd been awaiting the question. "The Minoans were a seafaring people and were known to be close trade partners with the Egyptians. Whoever carved these stones must have been intimately familiar with both cultures' languages, and might have been trying to ensure the message on the Phaistos Disc was preserved, even if one of the two civilizations fell. Why did I know there was more to this tablet? Minoan tablets are rare, right? I mean really rare. We're talking 1921 Helica de Leyat, 1787 Chateau Margaux—"

"I get it. Rare."

"Right. Well, it's because they're fragile. The clay the Minoans used to make these tablets was never kiln-dried, only baked in the sun. The tablets were never intended to last. They were temporary records that would get pulped when they became obsolete, the clay reused. This tablet was fragile enough for me to break in my hands, but the message inside couldn't be if it was to survive the ages. Hence the stones."

"Wait, back up. What does this have to do with the Phaistos Disc?"

"The tablet and disc were found together. It only makes sense that these stones were meant to help decipher the disc's message." He cracked his knuckles. "It's one of archaeology's oldest enigmas. No one has been able to read the disc since its discovery. That changes today."

Plucking a wad of air-sickness bags from her seat back, she began placing each stone into its own bag.

"What are you doing?" he asked, brow furrowed as he reached forward in a halfhearted attempt to stop her.

"You come with me back to the NERO offices, and I'll give these back. Then we'll see about solving puzzles."

ELEVEN
NERO Headquarters
Washington D.C.

Accepting the change held in the cafeteria cashier's outstretched hand, Susara offered a croissant to Lane. He seemed preoccupied by the rows of Australian Aboriginal masks mounted on the walls.

"Aren't you going to leave him a tip?" he asked as they turned and walked toward the elevators.

"Why? All he did was hand over a pastry from behind the counter and run a register. That was the extent of the service he rendered. I'm not giving him extra money for that." She casually plucked a small chunk from her croissant with her pointer finger and thumb. "Left here." She nudged his shoulder to steer him down the adjacent hallway.

"The guy probably makes minimum wage."

She rolled her eyes. "He makes the amount his service merits. Do minimal work, get minimum wage."

"You're kind of a tightwad, aren't you?"

"I believe in hard work," she said. "I have no sympathy for those who choose the easy path through life, and I'm certainly not going to reward them for it."

He took a bite from his croissant. "What about those who are just trying to make a go of difficult circumstances? Working their way through school? Or trying to provide for their kid as a single parent? What if your stingy tip just took food out of some poor kid's mouth?"

She turned to face him, prepared to argue, but seeing his subtle smile, realized he was just trying to get a rise out of her.

"You should go back there and give him some money, then, Lane. Given all the work you've been putting in during the past few years, I would think you'd have enough to put sandwich guy's kid through college and buy him a Ferrari."

"You know how hard it is to make money in my business? Hell, I'm thinking about going back and asking the guy for an application."

Sharply dressed employees cast dubious glances at Lane as they passed by, looking over the stranger's holey jeans, faded T-shirt, and unshaven jaw.

Lane walked beside Susara cagily, like a distrusting bull terrier on a leash.

"This place makes me uncomfortable."

"Why wouldn't it?" she asked. "You're at the nerve center of the most powerful and well-funded artifact-recovery agency in the world. It must feel strange to be here without handcuffs on."

"It's not that. It's just…this building gives off a bad vibe. Cold. Industrial. Like the architect kept pictures of Gorbachev in his wallet and got sweaty at the mention of East Berlin."

"Well, it's built on a decommissioned missile silo, so you're probably not too far off."

They reached the end of a long concrete corridor and paused for the elevator.

"And in regard to that bit about wearing handcuffs," he said solemnly, taking a large bite from his croissant, "I'd like to remind you that we had a deal. I help you, you let me continue my work. I want those stones back by the time I leave here today."

"I'm true to my word. Don't get your panties in a twist."

The elevator doors parted slowly, and the two entered. She pushed a button for the second floor, but instead of being lifted up, the elevator suddenly plunged, causing Lane to stagger.

"So, what's the story about this place? You mentioned some mysterious billionaire created the agency." He cautiously placed a hand on the reflective surface of the elevator wall for support.

"I don't know who he is, and I'm sure he wants to keep it that way. So we just call him 'the founder.' We have a running bet on who it might be, though. Drop your guess and a 20 into the box in the lounge if you get a chance."

"I wouldn't have any idea. Not exactly the sort of people I run with." He dragged a finger along the collar of his shirt as though the temperature had suddenly become insufferably hot. "And that doesn't bother you? Not knowing who you're working for?"

"I'm not doing this for anyone but me and my father. I believe in my work, and I don't care who's signing my paychecks so long as I can continue to do it."

"Your father into archaeology?"

"He was. He's gone, now," she said solemnly.

He winced and quickly changed the subject. "So you guys work with federal law enforcement agencies to repatriate stolen artifacts, is that it?"

She nodded. "We're like INTERPOL in that way. We do the investigations and research, then turn over any pertinent intelligence to other nations' police forces to make the arrest. Sometimes field agents like me lead the raids and seizures. But we still don't have independent arrest powers." She smirked, shook her head as if contradicting herself, and said, "We are allowed *some* flexibility when it comes to apprehending suspects. We're encouraged to let the police make the actual arrests, but the exigencies of our work sometimes require the use of force. We have an excellent legal department, and word has it that the founder has some impressive political leverage."

"And for the longest time I was only worried about being pursued by the FBI," he said.

She leaned in. "This is just between you and me, but the FBI's Art Crime Team wishes they were as good as we are. To their credit, we don't have to deal with the bureaucracy they do, and we have unlimited funding. They call it an unfair advantage, but they know just as well as we do that it boils down to skill. And we just do it better."

Exiting the elevator, the two walked toward Ruben's office, one of dozens fringing a large central atrium illuminated by artificial light meant to imitate the glow of the noon sun. Daring a glance over the handrail, Lane took in the spiraling, hundred-foot drop to the bottom of the silo, where a meditation garden had been planted. Susara shoved her croissant, barely nibbled on, into his free hand.

"Not hungry?" he asked.

Flicking the crumbs from her hands, she straightened her blouse and her posture. "You look malnourished. Eat up." Entering Ruben's office, she cleared her throat to announce their presence.

"Oh, you're back. Did you get him?" Ruben asked, his back turned to them as he sorted through a cardboard box filled with office supplies and personal effects, still getting settled in the new office.

She cast a thumb over her shoulder at Lane, who had stopped to study Ruben's modest collection of Roman sculptures he had just placed on a corner shelf.

"Lane, this is my supervisor, Ruben Luis."

"Him? That's him?" Ruben asked skeptically, rising and scrutinizing him in much the same way Lane regarded the displayed antiques. "I expected him to be...taller."

"Why does everyone say that? I'm not that short." Lane instinctively moved to cross his arms, but with a croissant in each hand, decided against it.

"It's just...you're something of a legend." Ruben scratched his dark goatee. "For a professional thief, you have a cleaner record than some of the folks working around here."

The cuffs of Ruben's sleeves and the collar of his shirt had darkened from white to ochre, sweat-stained, his shirttail above the beltline set in a spiderweb of wrinkles and creases. A man too cheap to accept the cost of dry cleaning and in too much of a hurry to bother ironing.

Lane looked at Susara doubtfully. "I don't know what you mean by thief."

"You don't have to be guarded about it. We know what you do, and as I'm sure Agent Eaves has already explained, we're more interested in your assistance than arresting you."

Moving the croissants to free a hand, Lane spoke with a cautious tone, "Listen, both of you: As flattered as I am by all this talk of my reputation among you law enforcement types, I'm a small fish in the stolen antiquities world. I'd love to help you out here, but I don't know that I can."

"But you know who the big fish are." Ruben opened his desk drawer and slapped a file on the desktop. "And a big fish took these."

Lane leaned in to look at the photograph of a pair of flintlock dueling pistols, then shook his head. "I'm more of a Middle Eastern and Mediterranean antiquities kind of guy. Those look European or American. Wouldn't know the first thing about them."

"They're a set of Wogden dueling pistols." Ruben lifted an errant hair from his shirt sleeve and released it above the wastebasket. "They're special because this was the set used by Alexander Hamilton and Aaron Burr in their legendary duel that killed the former. They were sold to JP Morgan & Chase in 1930, but were stolen while on display at the New York Gallery of American History two weeks ago. If these disappear into the black market, a key representation of this country's history will be lost with them."

Tapping the toe of his sneaker against the heel of his other foot, Lane stood straight and released a deep breath.

"You've probably got a little time. Moving something of that notoriety is a hard sell, one that would attract too much attention for most buyers to be comfortable with, at least in the near future. Whoever took the pistols will probably wait until the pressure is off before trying to move them. Could be years."

"Well, who took them?" Ruben pressed.

Susara picked up on Lane's subtle frown. Her supervisor was often insensitively direct, and although most NERO agents working for him had learned to accept that, the approach was too heavy-handed when dealing with a restive suspect— particularly one with reservations about helping them in the first place.

Lane took a deep breath and glanced at her. After a contemplative pause, he responded. "I can't be sure. Could be a lot of people."

She met his eyes and gave him an encouraging nod.

He rolled his eyes and sighed, subtly agreeing to play ball. "But if you're looking for big-name players with the guts and the resources needed to pull this sort of heist off, there's one guy that comes to mind."

"Who?" she asked.

"Ali Hamza. Libyan. Gun fanatic. Lousy dresser. He's been in the business almost as long as I have. The guy specializes in procuring weapons, especially those with historical significance. Muammar Gaddafi's gold-plated Browning Hi-Power, Al Capone's Thompson submachine gun, that sort of thing. I went through him to sell a couple truckloads of Martini-Henry rifles I appropriated from a cache in Nepal a few years ago."

"Where would we find him?"

"Is this how we're going to do this?" Lane asked incredulously. "I can't do all the work for you. I would have thought"—his voice dropped dramatically—"'the most powerful artifact-recovery agency in the world' would have the resources for tracking a person down."

"No need to be snarky," Ruben said. "All right, I'll get some people working on locating his whereabouts. I want you two to be ready at a moment's notice. When we find him, I want you to bring him in."

"Wait a minute." Lane held up his hands. "You said you wanted me to consult, not work for you as some kind of mercenary bounty hunter."

Leaning against the wall with her arms crossed, Susara smirked. "What? Afraid to get your hands a little dirty?"

"No, I'm afraid that when I go poking around with a law enforcement agent attached to my hip, my reputation will be ruined," he said defensively. "I'll have very violent, very disreputable people—most of whom don't like me that much to begin with, I might add—wanting to kill me, and no client will hire or deal with me again."

"Call it an occupational hazard," she said. "You could always go to prison, instead."

Lane looked from Susara to Ruben and muttered, "Fine, you win. But I want a company car, a corner office with a window, and my own coffee maker—the fancy kind that glows and takes those little round cartridges."

"Or we'll keep you out of prison," Susara repeated.

"That's fine too, I guess." Turning toward her, Lane's expression darkened. "But I'm serious now: I want those stones returned to me when we get back. That part's non-negotiable."

"You'll get them back," she reassured.

"I'd better. I don't like how you guys keep changing terms after I've signed on the dotted line. I help you bring in Hamza, that's it, right?"

"Works for me," Ruben said, unpacking a desktop model of Newton's cradle, the chrome ball bearings clacking against one another as he placed it near his computer.

As they turned to leave the office, Lane stopped in the doorway and pointed toward Ruben's collection of sculptures. "Those are excellent fakes, by the way."

TWELVE

Washington D.C.

T he Happy Buddha, a dimly lit little hole in the wall on the southeast side of the city, was fronted by a neon sign Susara had never seen fully lit. The uninviting smell of rotting fish parts that greeted visitors as they approached the entrance typically chased away all but those who had once before braved the smell and tried the food.

The neighborhood was as repellent as the smell. On one of Susara's and Noah's first dates, a man tried to mug them just outside the front door. As Noah dug out his wallet in compliance, she'd shoved her .25-caliber Beretta in the guy's face. Noah said that was the moment he'd fallen in love with her.

Susara tugged down the waist of her shirt nervously as they went inside. In Noah's company, she always felt underdressed.

She'd thrown on a comfortable pair of jeans and a T-shirt she'd had since college. He wore one of his best suits. Looking around at the other patrons, she felt reassured that he'd simply overdressed again.

"Did you put in a vacation request?" Noah moved toward their usual spot and pulled a chair out for her.

"I haven't had a chance to yet. I will, though."

He made no effort to hide his disappointment. "It's just that you say you'll take time off, and then you forget. Pretty much every time. I really want us to have some time together."

"We're together now, aren't we?"

He forced a smile as he sat down, carefully navigating around a sticky spot on the laminate floor. "Yeah, we are." He reached for her hands across the table. "I've missed you."

"I've missed you, too," she lied. Though it stung a little to admit it, she hadn't even thought about him except in passing. She'd been too wrapped up in all the events at work to think of anything else.

Clearing his throat and sitting up straight, he said, "I got word today that I'll be a partner at the firm by the end of the year."

"That's great news!" she replied earnestly.

He nodded, his eyes glittering in the candlelight. "I know, right?"

"I'm proud of you." She leaned across the table and kissed him. She tousled his hair playfully, but he didn't smile. Instead, he drew a plastic comb from his pocket and corrected the mess.

When he'd finished, he returned the comb to his pocket and said, "I think maybe now's the time we should start looking for a house. You know, think about settling down."

Settling down? What could he mean by that except that he wanted to her to resign from NERO? She didn't like where this conversation was going. She felt it the way a dog senses approaching thunder, and suddenly she had the urge to hide beneath the bed. Shifting her stare away from her boyfriend, she focused on the reversed letters of the sign on the window behind him. *Please take a menu and seat yourself.*

He continued without noticing the change in her mood. "You could get a different job, one where you're home every night. Or not. You wouldn't have to work at all. I'd make enough for us to get by on one paycheck."

He didn't have a clue. It felt as though she was sitting across from a complete stranger—one who had never taken the time to understand her despite all their time together, all their intimacy.

"I don't want any of that," she whispered, staring at the tabletop.

"What do you mean?"

"I promised my father I would pursue my dreams as an archaeologist. I did him one better by becoming one of the few people in the world whose job it is to find stolen antiquities and return them to where they belong. That means everything to me. I thought you knew that. Now...what, you want me to just give that up so I can stay at home and make babies? Did it ever occur to you that a family life was your dream, not mine?"

Brow furrowed, he stammered, "But, all that talk about marriage...you met my parents for Christ's sake."

"That was always you talking about it. Just because I never said *no* doesn't mean I ever said *yes*." Even she was surprised at how calloused and cold that sounded.

He was crushed. Staring at the flickering candle at the edge of the table, fingers kneading the tablecloth, his lips moved, but no words came out.

Her phone buzzed in her pocket. Glancing at the text message from Ruben, it read simply, "Go-time. Dubai. Flight leaves in one hour."

"Dammit," she cursed. "Noah, I'm sorry, but—"

"Just go. I'll get a cab." He buried his chin in his palm and waved off the approaching waitress.

THIRTEEN

En route to Dubai

Without bothering to use a fake name or make payments in cash, Ali Hamza had thrown up a glaring red flag as to his whereabouts when his most recent credit card purchase showed nearly $2,000 in drinks bought at a nightclub in Dubai the night before. It gave Lane and Susara a good place to start.

Leaning all the way back in her seat, she stared at a copy of *Archeology Magazine*. Her eyes wandered over the blocks of text until they finally came to an uneasy rest on a photo of an Incan mummy—ashen skin shriveled, dark mouth agape in a permanent scream. It captured her mood. Her mind was fixed on what Noah had said at the restaurant, his expectations, and how she'd responded. She juggled anger, disappointment, sorrow, and regret, leaving little room for anything else.

Lane sneezed, jarring her from her reflection and reminding her to turn the page. Glancing out the Gulfstream's side window at the passing clouds, she asked, "Where were you in the summer of 2012?"

"Why?" He lay spread-eagle on the floor, an arm draped across his eyes. He'd arrived there after hours of pacing the plane's small cabin like a caged animal, spontaneously dropping down and doing push-ups, mumbling to himself in Arabic and Farsi, and periodically settling down long enough to read a chapter or two from a coverless, coffee-stained paperback copy of Arthur Evans's *Scripta Minoa*.

"There's an article in here about the Archaeological Museum of Mallawi and its robbery," she said. "I helped on that case. Someone took over a thousand artifacts from the museum in one hit. They gutted that place a week before the city's protests. Protests that led to the museum getting burned. A job like that has your name written all over it, especially since they still haven't found the guys who did it. You wouldn't happen to know anything about it, would you?"

He rolled his head lazily to a side, eyes meeting hers, and grinned. "Nope. Don't know a thing about it."

"One thousand artifacts out the door before anyone knew they were missing. Legendary," she chuckled, shaking her head.

"And if you only knew how much work went into pulling it off." He returned his arm to his forehead and closed his eyes. "Those passive infrared alarms are a pain. It takes real commitment to cloak yourself with a Mylar blanket in a place as hot as Egypt. Did that job in the buff."

"You did not."

"Hand to God."

They both laughed.

"And the National Museum of Iraq?" she probed. "I've been trying to figure out how you managed to jump from the edge of the vault to the case with the Sumerian gold jar inside without setting off the alarms. That's an incredible leap."

He took on a confused expression. "I didn't jump. I bribed the American security consultant who installed that system to tell me how to deactivate it. I walked in like I owned the place." Raising a hand defensively, he continued. "And before you start lecturing me about stealing from the museum, ISIS was on Baghdad's front door at the time. I thought it would be a matter of days before they'd taken the museum. You've seen what those guys do with historical relics. Sledgehammers, bulldozers, the works."

She shook her head. "I wasn't going to lecture you. I was going to say that I built an entire mock-up of that vault and spent days—days, Lane—trying to figure out how you'd done it, what kinds of insane acrobatics you must have used to get at that jar. Now you're telling me you just shut the system off."

His expression softened and he chuckled. "I'm sorry to disappoint."

"So where does a guy like you go to school?" she asked, trying to keep the conversation going. It was a pleasant distraction from the long flight and her inner turmoil about Noah. "There must be a two-year program on the art of thievery somewhere."

"No such luck. Everything I've learned, I've picked up the hard way."

"So you've become this renowned taker of precious artifacts, all without any academic background."

His face twisted in a sour expression. "I can read as well as the next guy. And I don't need a $200,000 piece of paper for validation, either."

"Strange. So you're a multilingual history buff and you can't see things up close without a pair of reading glasses on. You're a nerd by any other name."

"Those things aren't so peculiar."

"But then you're also this muscle-bound, rough-and-tough, risk-taking marauder. It's a weird dichotomy."

"Why is that weird?"

She carefully earmarked her place in the magazine before closing it and dropping it on the floor. "I don't know. It's just that, generally, people either behave in a way that's safe and boring, or they're insane daredevils."

"And which are you?"

"Probably more safe than daredevil."

Propping himself up on an elbow, he said, "I don't believe you. If that were true, you wouldn't have been the first one through the door back at Poldi's castle, you wouldn't have agreed to help me rob the Chávez estate, and you sure as hell wouldn't be on a flight to the Middle East to capture a gunrunner with a known criminal as a partner."

She absently chewed a nail as she looked back out the window, then, realizing what she was doing, and that Lane was watching her, placed her hands in her lap. "Maybe you're right. My boyfriend really wants me to be the homebody type, but I just don't think it's in my nature."

"Boyfriend." He said it thoughtfully, like he hadn't heard the word before.

"Yes, why? You said that like you were surprised. Why would that be surprising?"

Rising from the floor, he looked at her and smiled genuinely. "It's not surprising. He's clearly a very lucky man."

Their eyes met. She cleared her throat, but her voice still faltered when she asked, "And you? You must have some princess in your life that you've spirited away from certain death in a far-off land."

He took on a numb expression, eyes downcast. "Nothing quite so exotic. I'm the proud owner of a failed marriage and all the petty complications that come with it."

"Your idea or hers?"

"To separate? Hers. And I can't blame her, really. I'm not an easy guy to be married to, especially when what she really wanted was stability. As you'd imagine, it's tough to be home every night for dinner when you…do what I do."

"You still love her?"

He shrugged. "You never really stop loving someone when you've been that close to them. But you have to temper that with the realization, if it didn't work out the first time, it never will."

The pilot interrupted their conversation, his low voice on the intercom filling the cabin as he mumbled something about coming into their final approach.

Susara nodded toward the plane's small bathroom.

"We should change into our gear."

"Gear?"

Moving to a closet at the rear of the cabin, she withdrew a pair of garment bags. Pinned to one was a note written in Ruben's hand that read, *Don't trust him. Don't let him out of your sight.* She crumpled it and let it fall to the floor.

"Clothes that won't get us thrown out of an upscale Dubai nightclub. I had the agency pick up a suit for you. They had to guess your measurements. Hopefully they noticed that you're a bit of a busty lass." She shoved the bag against Lane's muscular chest.

Stepping into the plane's closet-sized bathroom, he jostled loudly in the cramped space. It sounded as though his elbows and shoulders were battering the thin walls with each attempt to remove or slide on a piece of clothing. He returned a few moments later, fiddling with his tie. Though not exactly slovenly before, the change in attire had accentuated his handsome visage, the cut of the suit emphasizing the broadness of his shoulders and framing his face—drawing the eye to his rugged features and expressive eyes.

"It's a little tight in the shoulders, but otherwise pretty spot-on," he said, fingers clumsily weaving the tie around itself. "I can't for the life of me remember how to tie this damn thing, though. It's been a long time since I've had to get dressed up. Only for weddings and funerals, and the kind of people I associate with these days don't usually invite me to either."

"Let me try." She stepped close and pulled the tie loose before starting over.

"See? Tricky."

After struggling with the tie for a minute, she pulled it free. "Ties are overrated, anyway."

"Your turn." He bowed and made a sweeping gesture toward the bathroom.

Susara emerged moments later, smoothing the hips of a form-fitting black cocktail dress and standing a little unsure on a pair of heels.

He leaned forward in his seat, hand over his mouth, fingers stroking the stubble on his cheeks.

She looked up and blushed. "Well? Be honest: Do I look the part?"

He leaned back and moved his pointer finger in a small circle. She spun around.

"Our cover won't stand up to scrutiny," he said finally, sighing as he leaned back.

She looked concerned. "Why?"

"No one will believe a guy like me could be with a woman like you. Got a cardigan sweater hidden away back there you could throw on?"

She smirked. "You're just sucking up so I'll keep you out of prison."

"Is it working?"

Her smile widened. "It's a start."

FOURTEEN
N'dulge Lounge
Dubai, United Arab Emirates

athed in neon blue light, the club sweltered, packed
with wealthy 20-somethings tossing around wads of
their parents' cash as though it were Monopoly money.
Like the city outside, this building was a playground for the
unimaginably and unimaginative wealthy. Conex shipping
containers still bearing original paint and company labels hung
from the ceiling by thick, braided-steel cables—an interior
designer's unconventional attempt to add a modern industrial
flair to the building while providing private lounge areas
overlooking the dance floor. Although the place strived for the
atmosphere of an upscale European nightclub, the pervasive
chrome and velour, phosphorescent stars on the carpet, and
cowboy hat-wearing waitresses—dressed as if on loan from a

nearby gentleman's club—made it appear, at best, a gauche facsimile.

"Aren't you going to buy me a drink?" Susara asked, leaning across their table so Lane could hear her over the relentless thundering of the club's sound system. She caught him struggling to keep his eyes level, away from her exposed cleavage.

"Aren't you on the clock?" His hand wandered to loosen his collar for the third time since they'd sat down. She reached across the table and batted his hand away.

"It's called 'cover.' Who goes to a nightclub and doesn't drink?"

"Mormons?"

"Cops."

"OK, what are you drinking?" He smiled uncomfortably at a young woman who had brushed a hand along his arm as she walked by.

"Doesn't matter. I'm not actually going to drink it. I'm on the clock, remember?" she teased.

"Can I have your company credit card? Something tells me the booze here will come with a higher price tag than most cars I've owned." He massaged the bridge of his nose. The acrid mixture of perfumes and colognes, thick on the air, burned. "Besides, I'm sure the 'agency that cannot be named' won't mind. It's part of our cover, right? I'm thinking something top shelf is in order for me, since there's nothing that says *I* can't drink. Working freelance has its benefits."

Unclasping her small leather purse and sliding the card between her pointer and middle finger, she held it toward him. "I can't believe I'm voluntarily handing one of the world's most renowned thieves my company credit card. It's too ridiculous for fiction."

He feigned offense. "I have never stolen a credit card in my life. That's beneath me. Too obtuse a crime: like stealing someone's newspaper from their stoop and leaving a burning dog turd in its place. Besides, I won't even leave your sight, and you can have it back in a minute."

He stood, but Susara pulled him back down by his wrist. Looking over her partner's shoulder, she said, "That's him, isn't it?"

Daring a glance at the club's entrance as discreetly as possible, he nodded.

Her eyes widened as they followed their target. Hamza, though shorter than his security, still stood a head above the crowd. He was overweight, with more hair on his face than clinging to the fringes of his skull, but he carried himself like a warlord—with a conceited swagger and an air of imperiousness one would expect of a man wearing a zoot suit and swinging a cane with an eight ball for a handle. He was the sort who was sure to own at least one gold-plated handgun and at least one Ferrari—one of those ugly, low-end models from the '80s with faded cloth seats and an automatic transmission. He strode behind his two enormous bodyguards as they moved toward Lane and Susara, ramming a path through dancing couples and groups of scantily clad women tottering drunkenly in the direction of the bar.

When Hamza got within a few steps of their table, Susara felt her stomach tighten. Although the gunrunner didn't know her, he'd worked with Lane before and might recognize him. Forcefully reaching across the table, she grabbed Lane by his shirt and pulled him across the table. Their lips met, and she placed her fingertips softly upon his temple, covering the side of his face. Though the performance required some degree of faux passion to come off as authentic, she found she wasn't acting—everything about it felt natural. Her lips pressed tightly to his, the faint taste of cinnamon gum on his breath. He made no attempt to pull away. She held tight for a moment longer, until she was certain Hamza had passed.

Coming up for air, she looked behind them to ensure Hamza was out of earshot. "He might have recognized you if he'd seen your face."

Flustered, Lane mumbled, "I've only done business with him through phone calls and wire transfers."

She looked away. "God, I'm sorry. That's really embarrassing."

"Hey, if that's the worst thing that happens tonight, I'll be very pleased with how this mission washed out," he said, his tone encouraging. "But I suspect things are about to get a whole lot less pleasant." He nodded solemnly toward the hallway into which Hamza had disappeared, which led to the club's exclusive private rooms.

Together, they slipped through the crowd, traveling along worn carpet impregnated with sparkling glitter, the heavy bass notes thrown by mammoth floor speakers vibrating against the soles of their feet.

"Stick with the plan?" she shouted into his ear.

He nodded, rubbing his hands together and blowing between them as though they were cold. "Hamza's a man with more money than scruples, but his biggest weakness is sex. You want to get in his good graces, hire him a Russian hooker for the night. So to distract him—"

"That's where I step in."

"I'll be right behind you."

"Deal."

"Good luck."

He stepped into an empty private room adjacent to the one Hamza and his men had disappeared into as Susara knocked.

One of the security guards opened the door a few inches, blocking the view into the room with his body. "What do you want?"

"I was sent here by the club owner. He said I was to be a complimentary gift to Mr. Ali Hamza, his esteemed guest," she said in the most seductive voice she could muster while trying to be heard above the music.

The guard looked her over, and satisfied with her appearance and explanation, swung the door open.

She entered a small room adorned with contemporary glass and steel furniture, garish animal skins, glowing LED lights, and feather boas. The space had the sweaty, shame-laden odor of Casanova's bedsheets. Hamza sat on a black leather couch, bent over a coffee table. His nostril skated along the blade of a knife coated in a drift of white powder. With a snort, he reeled back and looked at Susara with glossy eyes.

"Who the hell are you?" he grunted, his belly straining against the buttons of a shirt several sizes too small for his form.

"I'm yours for the night. Unless you don't want me. I can get back to dancing, and maybe the owner can get you a different girl. Or boy, if that's what you're into," she taunted, turning toward the door.

"Wait. Don't move." He stumbled as he heaved himself up from the couch and aimed the knife in his hand at her chest. "You're not going anywhere." After a moment spent trying to focus on her face, Hamza threw the knife across the room, the blade sticking in the drywall. "Leave us." He waved his security out. "And you: Start me out with a lap dance."

"Music?" she asked, wrapping her hair around her hands and bending her knees seductively.

"I knew it was worth the money to come here." The Libyan eagerly fumbled with the stereo. "You must be part of the club's A-lineup, with a body like that. You speak English pretty well, too. Not like those Russian whores they bring in by the truckload."

Dropping into a seat, he ogled Susara's shapely figure.

She wrapped her fingers around the room's chrome stripper pole. Rocking her hips in time with the music, she turned to him and winked. Arching her back, she lifted a leg and wrapped it around the pole, slowly spinning around.

He leaned forward, mouth open and eyes wide.

Twirling a shoulder strap of her dress around a finger, she tugged the fabric down her arm.

He never noticed Lane enter the room. Covering the big man's mouth with one hand, Lane slammed his knuckles into Hamza's temple before pulling a forearm tight across his throat. The gunrunner squirmed and tried to cry out, face turning purple. Lane pulled him back against his seat, using his body weight to keep him restrained.

"What do you know about the Wogden pistols?" Susara asked, dropping the seductress act, her voice low and serious as she reached for the stereo and turned the volume up to cover their interrogation.

"You scream for help and I break your neck, Ali," Lane whispered in the man's ear before easing his hold.

"I've never even heard of them," Hamza squeaked.

"Don't lie to me. You know what they are, and I'd bet you know where they are, too. Start talking or we'll break every one of your fingers and your...other little digit." She nodded toward his groin.

Hamza said, "OK, OK. I may have *heard* of them. Why?"

Lane poked a finger through the silver earring dangling from the gunrunner's right earlobe and tugged. Pensively sniffing the air as Hamza cried out, Lane said, "Ali, you should go easy on the cologne next time. It's playing hell on my sinuses."

"Stop, stop! OK, I had them, but I already sold them. That's why I'm here. To celebrate." Hamza angled his head to appeal to Lane.

"Hit him again," Susara said, leaning against the stripper pole.

Gripping Hamza's beard, Lane dragged him from his seat. Pulling the back of the Libyan's rhinestone-speckled shirt over his head, Lane began dealing uppercuts to his skull like a hockey player with the gloves off. The dull thud of his fists connecting kept a syncopated rhythm with the music from the stereo.

"Stop!" Hamza pleaded, scraping the shirt from his face, his nose bent and bloodied and his eye beginning to swell.

Lane paused, and then drove a knee into the man's gut, letting him drop to the floor, gasping for air. "You got blood on my suit, Ali. This was the nicest suit I've ever owned. That's really disappointing." Gripping his shirt collar, Lane cocked his arm back to deliver another strike.

Hands held before him as if begging for mercy, Hamza finally admitted, "I have them in my storeroom in Tripoli. I'll give them back. Just please, don't hit me anymore."

"You were right, Lane. He's our guy," Susara said.

Hamza went from pleading to incredulity to rage in only a second. "Lane? Lane Bradley? You! You sold me out, you pig!"

Lane delivered a quick strike to the man's throat to shut him up.

"Spycraft 101, lady. You just blew my cover."

"Oh come on. We've got him. No need for cover, now."

The door opened and Hamza's two bodyguards entered with female dancers hanging on their arms.

"Kill them!" Hamza snarled as he twisted out of Lane's grip and scrambled through the door.

"Kinda wishing you hadn't mentioned my name, now," Lane said, assuming a fighter's stance, prepared to brawl with the two larger men as the dancers ran from the scene. But they didn't attack. Lane looked at them suspiciously as they raised their hands in surrender.

Turning to Susara, he found she'd drawn a pocket pistol and had it trained on the two men.

"Where did you have that hidden?"

"A lady has to keep some things secret," she said with a smirk. "Now, if you want to keep your reputation intact, you'd better go get him."

Pushing through the dense crowd, Lane attempted to follow Hamza's escape. He burst through the front doors of the club, skin simmering in the cool night air. He scanned the busy street. The gunrunner was gone.

FIFTEEN

It might have seemed vain to Susara and Ruben, but Lane regarded his reputation in the stolen antiquities trade as sacred. All it took was one incident like this, just one black mark on his name, and no one would trust working with him or buying from him again. Involvement in international crime didn't engender trust between parties to begin with. There had been times when deals had fallen through simply because a client didn't like his face, or his name reminded them of someone who bullied them in grade school. And now, Ali Hamza was about to give them a very valid reason not to trust him. An uncomfortable heat flooded Lane's chest, his fingertips cold, heart pumping wildly. Don't panic. He couldn't have gotten far. As pedestrians strolled by, he glanced from face to face, looking for some indication they'd seen a large, bearded, and bruised bald man running for his life.

Fortunately, it didn't take long for Hamza to make his presence known. Rushing, stumbling, his ponderous form collided with other pedestrians on the sidewalk. Shouts followed.

"That man is bleeding from his face!" a man exclaimed in Arabic. Looking toward the sound, Lane caught a glimpse of Hamza regaining his feet, dragging a woman to the pavement to pull himself up. Taking off in pursuit, Lane slipped through the crowd, striving to keep an eye on the gunrunner.

Soon, the crowds thinned and the buildings lost their grandeur. They were nearing the waterfront. Hamza's breathing was so heavy, Lane could hear him from 50 yards back.

"Lane, do you have him?" Susara shouted from behind them. She'd kicked off her heels and was now at a dead sprint, barefoot, following the chase.

"He's heading for the water," Lane cried back, turning the corner. The smell of rotting fish and two-stroke engine exhaust met them as they approached the harbor. Arriving at the end of the pavement, Hamza dove headfirst into the water, paddling frantically through shimmering rainbow hues of floating oil on his way toward the Jebel Ali Free Zone—a nearby commercial district free from government sanctions. It was likely the home to one of his smuggling storerooms, and he undoubtedly had a boat waiting for him there. If the smuggler made it that far, they'd never catch up with him again. He'd disappear and stay that way until he was certain the heat was off. By that time, the case would be closed and the Wogden pistols considered permanently lost.

Lane and Susara hit the water in short succession.

Like a porpoise, the Libyan bobbed and paddled swiftly toward the opposite end of the channel—a natural swimmer. Quite the opposite, Lane's compact, muscular build may have been perfectly designed for climbing and fighting, but swimming was another thing entirely. Without the added buoyancy Hamza's body fat gave him or the reach of the taller man's arms, Lane began falling back. The distance between them grew.

He was going to escape.

"We're going to lose him!" Lane wheezed as he spat out a mouthful of brackish seawater. "Susara?"

She'd disappeared.

Hamza reached the far side of the channel. Reaching a hand to the edge of the concrete wharf, the big man pulled himself up. Turning to look back at Lane, water spilling from his shirt and pants, he shouted, "*Ah dena mukk*, Lane Bradley, you son of a whore. I'll see to it that you burn for this."

Behind him, a figure glided from the shadows, soaking wet. Approaching fast, Susara's shoulder met Hamza's spine. His head snapped back violently as he slammed against the concrete. Breath audibly left his chest. She bent his arm behind his back to the shoulder.

As Hamza wailed in pain, Susara flipped her wet hair from her face, eyeshadow running, and looked at Lane, still making his way across the channel. "I'm guessing the swimming part of the triathlon pretty much rules you out of the competition."

Reaching the wharf, Lane heaved himself up and wiped the water from his face. "Actually, it's the bicycling. Too much chafing."

SIXTEEN

Ith Hamza trading time bawling and attempting to bribe local law enforcement from inside his holding cell, Lane and Susara trudged into the lobby of the nearest hotel, saltwater pooling on the marble floors where they stood. The concierge looked at them suspiciously until Susara fished out her agency-issued credit card.

"Two rooms, please."

"I'm afraid we have only one room left."

"Two beds?"

The concierge cringed. I'm afraid not. One king-size bed."

"If it has a couch, we'll be fine," Lane said, his exhaustion apparent in his eyes. "In fact, even if it doesn't, I'll sleep in the tub, or on the floor. Or, hey handsome, you live around here?" He leaned over the counter and winked at the concierge.

They rode the elevator from the lobby to the tenth floor in silence. Swiping the keycard and entering their room—aglow in a soft incandescent yellow and smelling of fresh lavender—they set to work drying off using the stack of cream-colored towels in the bathroom.

"We make a strange pair, don't we?" He hung his suit jacket over the shower-curtain rod. "I mean, you make a living hunting guys like me. I never would have guessed we would end up working together. And you know what? I actually think we did really well tonight."

She nodded, rubbing her hair vigorously with a towel. "Have you ever thought about going straight? You could have a career doing this sort of thing."

"Don't get me wrong, it's been great working with you." He unbuttoned his shirt and tossed it in the bathtub. "I just don't see myself doing this sort of thing full time. I know you have your reasons for working for NERO, and though you may not understand it, I have my reasons for living the life I do, too. As crazy as it may seem, I really believe I'm doing the right thing."

She frowned. Part of her wished he would change his ways, come work for the good guys and renounce thievery. There was something about him that demanded a certain degree of admiration, and she agreed more with his comment about their cooperation than she'd let on. They did make one hell of a team.

Spotting the silver talisman hanging around his neck, she took the opportunity to change the subject. "So what's the story behind that necklace?"

He slipped it beneath his undershirt and looked away, embarrassed.

"It's…nothing. Just a good luck charm."

She stepped toward him. Gently reaching her hands around his neck, she slipped the ornament out from beneath his shirt. It was well worn, the silver tarnished by years of skin contact, the figure's once-crisp edges rounded until it became difficult to make out any of the fine detail.

"It's beautiful. You shouldn't be embarrassed by it. A gift from your wife?"

He chuckled as he stared at the ceiling, but hidden by the seawater still dripping down his face, tears had filled his eyes.

"My mother. She gave it to me just before she was deported to Iran. The little winged man is a *fravashi*—a guardian spirit," he said softly, as though he couldn't find the breath to project any louder.

"Deported to Iran? Why?"

He wiped at his eyes, struggling to find his voice as he revisited the painful memory. "My dad was an American military advisor to the Afghans during the Soviet invasion in the '70s. At the time, Iran was undergoing a revolution, becoming an Islamic republic. My mother and her family were supporters of the shah—the last Persian monarch." He dropped his towel, stepped out of the bathroom, and walked slowly toward a wall comprised entirely of glass overlooking the glowing lights of the city below. "When the revolution ended, she fled the country to Afghanistan, met my father, and they returned to the U.S. I was born shortly after." He paused, collecting himself. "You've heard of the Iran-Contra scandal, right?"

She nodded. "American hostages held by Iranian militants in Lebanon."

"Yeah, well the U.S. thought they could do some trading to get those hostages back—American guns for their lives. The part that never got mentioned was that those militants were members of Iran's Army of the Guardians—the same revolutionaries my mother and her family had fought before leaving the country. They knew that she and others like her had escaped to America, and demanded they be returned to them as part of the exchange." Lane's fingers rolled into fists, his voice trembling subtly with long-burning resentment.

"Normally, that trade would never happen. But my mother wasn't an American citizen yet. My parents had only a religious ceremony and were never recognized by the state as married. My dad, being his bull-headed, overbearing self, had pissed off someone in the upper echelon of the State Department during his time in the military. This was his punishment. They sent her back to sweeten the pot, knowing she'd be put to death."

She cleared her throat, uncomfortable interrupting him. "I take it there's no love lost between you and your father, judging by your description of him."

Fondling the charm, he turned and looked straight into her eyes. "It's his fault she's gone. How could I not resent him?"

"Have you two ever spoken about it?"

Pinching the window's curtains between his fingers until his knuckles turned white, he shook his head. "I haven't seen him in more than a decade. When he didn't show up at my wedding, I got the message. We'd said everything we needed to say to each other a lifetime ago. I would say it's a shame that he'll never get to know his granddaughter, but I think she'll be better off for never having met him."

"You have a daughter?" she asked, trying to conceal her surprise.

He nodded. "Jordan. The most beautiful girl in the world." Rubbing the back of his neck, shaking off the tired emotions that had kept him awake at night for years, he said, "So that's the story behind the necklace. Does this room come with a minibar? I could really use a nightcap."

SEVENTEEN

D r. Magnus Eaves stretched his back and smiled, nudging the glasses on his nose as he leaned away from the 'history of Cape Town' exhibit they'd been arranging.

"Susara, run out and grab us something to eat, will you?" The museum was almost entirely unoccupied, dark and quiet, as the city prepared for a parade that afternoon. The skies were clear and the air cool. No one wanted to waste a perfect day inside a dusty museum. "Maybe some *vetkoek* from up the street?"

"You always want *vetkoek*. Can't we get a burger, instead?" She stomped her feet playfully.

Her father stepped toward her, cradling her hands in his and spinning her around like a ballerina. "So beautiful. So eager to leave all this behind. I only hope America doesn't change you too much."

She looked down at her feet. "I'll miss you more than I will my country, Papa."

He clicked his tongue and spun her around once more before guiding her toward the museum's entrance.

"This is a good thing you're doing. Go to college, get your degree, and someday, after you get your fill of traveling the world, perhaps you'll come back and help your old papa run the museum."

"You're not that old," she teased, pushing the door open, the sunlight warming her face.

"But I am hungry." He withdrew a neatly folded 200-Rand note from his pocket and pressed it into her hand. "Now, *vetkoek* or burgers, it's your choice. But whatever you decide, bring it back soon. My stomach doth grumble in protest to its neglect."

She set out down the street, jogging toward Dyshiki's Eatery a few blocks away. She would settle for another lunch of *vetkoek*, as her father suggested, if only to please him. As the time of her departure grew nearer, the moments she shared with him grew more precious.

The thought of traveling halfway around the world, leaving everything she'd ever known behind, both excited and terrified her. But she'd been telling the truth: Leaving her father would be the hardest part of all.

As she paid for the paper bag filled with deep-fried dough and bowls of savory mince, the wail of sirens blared through the restaurant's glass front. At first thinking the parade had begun, she ignored the noise. But upon re-entering the street, she followed the sound as it blared from the direction of the museum. Flames licked at the sky, black smoke rolling out of the building's windows. Dropping the bag and sprinting to the museum's front steps, she stood fossilized, staring at the impassable wall of flames.

A crowd formed. She scanned the faces, looking for her father. The others began to mutter.

"Such a waste..."

"Apartheid over? Hardly."

"It's the unemployment. Damn kids have nothing better to do."

"Papa!" she screamed. "Papa!"

Someone shook her arm.

"Susara, Susara, wake up. You're having a nightmare," Lane said, one knee on the bed as he sat beside her. Moonlight painted the room in cold, monochromatic shades, reflecting eerily in his eyeglasses. Shadows painted deep ridgelines on his bare chest, dark valleys between tumescent abdominals and pectorals. A tattoo of a ring bursting with flame covered his right shoulder like a patch stitched to a sleeve, its placement mirroring the puckered scar left by a bullet that had long ago pierced his left shoulder.

She sat upright in bed, cheeks burning. Her chest, covered in a satin nightgown, rose and fell with heavy sobs as she tried to tame her breathing. Trying to keep him from seeing her tears, she hurriedly wiped her eyes.

"It's OK," he whispered, moving a hand to touch her shoulder. She slapped it away.

"*Gaan weg!* Get away from me!"

"Susara, it's me."

"Don't touch me. Just...don't."

He backed away. "I'm sorry. What'd I do?"

Blinking away the tears, her hands gripping the bedsheets like the edge of a cliff, she whispered, "They killed my papa. Tied him up and left him to burn alive in his own museum. Men like you, Lane Bradley. Men just like you."

EIGHTEEN
NERO headquarters
Washington, D.C.

The founder of **NERO** was allegedly a billionaire. But if he was, he was a real tightwad. Ruben's father, who'd spent his entire life working as a laborer in a Puerto Rican textiles plant, had always told him, "The rich don't become rich by being philanthropists." He was right. Ruben had figured his salary would have rocketed when he'd been promoted to director of field agents. He'd earned this position—kissed a lot of ass, bought a lot of expensive Christmas presents for the members of the board, and came in on more than a few weekends and holidays—but now that he was here, the position had proven lackluster.

There were those who would kill for his job, those who would appreciate it for the study of archaeology and the problem-solving skills each case required. But he had never been in it for that. He'd come to NERO because the pay was better, the risk lower, and the hours more reasonable than his job as a detective with the Washington, D.C. police. NERO had wanted him for his investigative skills, and figured he could learn the requisite archaeological knowledge along the way. He'd never really bothered with that part. There wasn't any point. He spent his days now as he did as a detective—making calls, handing out case files, and assigning investigations. He was still a detective in that sense: It didn't matter if the stolen goods were priceless antiquities or flat-screen TVs, the process was the same, as was the outcome. Someone either got their shit returned or they didn't.

He detested people like Susara Eaves who possessed such an inordinate enthusiasm for the work, as if she was doing something really special for mankind. At least on the police force, he could go home in the morning knowing he'd helped keep people safe. Here, well, antiquities theft was essentially a victimless crime. The insurance companies got the worst of it, and those pricks deserved everything they got. Leeches.

The phone on his desk blinked red but didn't ring. The number was unlisted, and Ruben dismissed it as a telemarketer or misdialed call. The call went to voicemail. Ruben went back to combing through a cold file he'd found stuffed away in his old office, debating whether he should save it or just drop the entire thing in the paper shredder. Moments later, the phone blinked red again. Unlisted. Now he was becoming irritated. He let the file drop in the recycling bin and picked up the phone's receiver.

"Director Ruben Luis, NERO."

"Señor Luis, my name is Agapito Vicente. I'm the Venezuelan minister of state for antiquities affairs, and as I understand it, you have something that belongs to us."

"What's that?" Tapping his keyboard to awaken his computer, Ruben logged in and began typing a search for the Venezuelan Antiquities Affairs Office. He wanted a photo and some background on whoever this guy was.

"A Minoan clay tablet that belonged to the late Presidente Hugo Chavez. It was stolen from the family estate a few days ago. My sources have informed me that you are currently in possession of the tablet."

The internet search returned no finds. Ruben leaned back in his seat.

"OK asshole, who is this, really?"

"I told you, I'm the Venezuelan minister—"

"You can call yourself whatever you like, but that office doesn't exist. What do you want with this tablet, anyway, and who told you we have it?" Ruben could only think that whoever this was wanted what Susara had placed in lockup after returning from Venezuela.

There was a long pause at the end of the line before the voice spoke, the accent transforming. "My name *is* Agapito Vicente. I'm a collector of antiquities, you could say, and I'm very interested in acquiring the tablet. Lane Bradley, who I believe you know, stole it, and I want it. What would it take in order for you to release it into my custody? I have significant monetary resources at my disposal."

Ruben stared at the computer screen, rolling the bristling hair of his goatee between his fingers. "Call me on my cell," he said, following with his personal number. He hung up and began walking briskly toward NERO's evidence lockup, nodding and smiling superficially at the other employees as he passed. His phone buzzed in his pocket, but he waited to answer until he'd entered the elevator.

"Ruben here."

"So to confirm, you do have possession of the tablet?"

"I know one of our agents was in Venezuela and put something in our evidence locker when she returned. I'd bet that's what you're looking for. What's it worth to you?" He tried to downplay the nervousness in his voice, but his hands shook. This was dangerous ground he was approaching, even just by speaking to this person.

"I'm prepared to offer you $50,000 for it."

"You want me to risk my career for 50 grand?" Ruben's voice dropped to a forceful whisper as he disembarked the elevator. Approaching the evidence locker, he scanned his key card and opened the room's steel door. He conducted a quick check to ensure no one was inside before locking the door behind him. "That doesn't even get near my salary. Don't insult me."

The voice on the other end of the line exhaled slowly, annoyed. "One hundred thousand, then, which is far more than the tablet is worth. I'll negotiate no further than that."

That was a lot of money. Ruben envisioned his elderly parents in Puerto Rico, sitting at the plastic folding table they'd found in a dumpster outside a restaurant when he was a child, bare feet on the peeling linoleum of their home's cramped kitchen. He'd always sent them what he could to support them in his absence, but once again, the salary of this new position wasn't what he'd thought it would be. This could be a life-altering windfall for his parents. They deserved it. He owed it to them.

Ruben spoke slowly and carefully. He couldn't afford to be misunderstood. "Paid in cash, and you'll make a big fuss when you arrive to take the tablet, playing up that whole Venezuelan minister thing, right? I don't want this coming back on me. I want to play this off like I was just returning this thing to its rightful owners."

"Absolutely. That's no trouble at all," Agapito said. "I'll be in tomorrow afternoon. You'll have half of the payment sitting in a suitcase inside your apartment when you get home tonight. When I have the tablet in my possession, I'll get you the other half."

"Wait, how do you know where I live? And my place is locked. How exactly are you planning to get inside?"

The line went dead. Ruben stared at his phone for a moment before returning it to his pocket and scanning the room's desk for the evidence log. In it, he found Susara's signature and the number of the drawer where she'd placed this mysterious tablet. A dehumidifier kicked on loudly from a dark corner of the concrete cavern, making him jump. He slowly walked the narrow alley between steel racks piled high with cardboard boxes and Tyvek envelopes. Fluorescent lights flickered overhead as he approached. Thumbing the stainless-steel lock to the side, he gave the drawer a tug.

A victimless crime.

NINETEEN

Following a short debriefing in a dark conference room—one Lane slept through entirely—he and Susara returned to Ruben's office. They hadn't spoken the entire flight home. He didn't appear angry, but confused and hurt. And he had a right to be. Comparing him to her father's murderers had been impulsive and untrue. The only parallel between the two parties was that the men who had killed her father had stolen a few things from the museum before they incinerated it. Investigators had written it off as racially motivated, the robbery more opportunistic than planned.

Having known this for years, she couldn't figure out what would have compelled her to say such a thing to him. Perhaps she'd subconsciously believed she was hunting the men who had killed her father when pursuing Lane, and the sudden

180-degree turn to working with him had just been too jarring to accept.

Ruben didn't look up from his computer as they entered his office. He'd finished unpacking his things, the only evidence of his recent transfer the pile of broken-down cardboard boxes stacked in the corner. An AM radio sports broadcast muttered softly in the background.

"Well guys, this has been...different. Definitely a new experience seeing things from your perspective." Lane extended his hand toward Ruben.

"Well, we owe you a debt of thanks for helping us track down the Wogden pistols," Ruben said without looking up or acknowledging the gesture.

Letting his outstretched hand drop to his side, Lane said, "So, if you could just return those stones that Susara was holding for me, I'll be on my way. Got a plane to catch."

Tapping a few keys on his keyboard, Ruben slid back in his chair. He flipped his tie carelessly over a shoulder. "We're going to hold on to those a while longer."

Lane looked as though he'd been punched in the gut. "Why?"

"Well, we've recently learned that those stones were stolen from Hugo Chávez's estate in Venezuela a few days ago. Wouldn't happen to know anything about that, would you?" Ruben shook his head in disbelief. "You really do think you're untouchable, don't you? You think you can just steal from anybody without consequence."

"How I got those stones isn't in question here." Lane turned to Susara, who up to this point had remained quiet. "You promised me I could have those back. That's why I came in with you. That's why I flew halfway around the world and risked my reputation. I trusted you."

"Reputation? You think you have a reputation to lose?" Ruben laughed. "You're a thief!"

"Yeah. I'm a thief," Lane said. "But I'm also a man of my word, which is apparently more than you can lay claim to."

"You don't think I'm honorable?" Ruben challenged, standing explosively, his office chair skittering into the wall. "I could have had your ass locked up the minute you set foot in here, understand? I'm letting you walk today, and I'm reluctant about doing it. Don't test me."

Lane moved closer to Susara and touched her hand, his expression pleading.

"You promised me you'd return those stones, and I know you're good for it. Don't let this happen."

Holding up a hand as if to interject, Ruben said, "Susara has no say in this at all. In fact, she's on paid leave for the foreseeable future depending entirely upon how this whole Venezuela debacle pans out. Those stones are going back to their rightful owners today."

Now it was time for Susara to be outraged. "You're putting me on leave?"

"The Venezuelan minister of state for antiquities affairs is on his way up right now. You'd better hope he's in a forgiving mood, Susara, for both our sakes."

Two security guards arrived outside the office door and knocked. Ruben pointed at Lane and nodded.

Lane struggled as they gripped his arms. "Venezuela doesn't have a minister of state for antiquities affairs."

"His paperwork was in perfect order. Besides, the dubious word of a criminal doesn't speak volumes against the man's legitimacy, does it?" Ruben gestured for the guards to take him and leave.

"I guess you're just like your organization's namesake, Susara," Lane growled as they dragged him out, "Nero—the emperor who fiddled while Rome burned."

Dragged down the hallway, still battling the two guards' hold on him, Lane stopped when he saw the approaching Venezuelan official and his entourage.

It was Agapito. So bold as to not even bother with a disguise, the Corsican had arrived with his men, prepared to take the cipher stones without lifting a finger.

"Oh come on, the guy's French. Not even the right continent!" Lane protested as they neared.

Agapito stopped as the two groups converged, leaned in, and whispered in Lane's ear, "Perhaps you should have stayed dead, old friend." The slightest hint of a smirk passed his lips as he entered Ruben's office.

TWENTY

The minutes that followed Lane's forced removal were torture to Susara. A condescending punishment, and Ruben knew it. He made no eye contact with her during the exchange with Agapito, didn't acknowledge her presence whatsoever, but it was implicitly understood she was to watch quietly, like a disciplined child, from the edge of the room. She was surprised Ruben didn't order her to apologize to the phony official for her role in the stones' theft.

After Agapito and his men had withdrawn, Ruben began to speak, but Susara cut him off. "I know you're getting off on this newfound position of power, but what you did just now was a huge mistake. Lane wasn't lying when he said that man wasn't a Venezuelan official. The guy's a thief."

"He had his paperwork in order. Your accusations are pure speculation, Susara. I expect better from you. You're letting your emotions interfere with your judgment. It's obvious you've gotten too close to Bradley, and now you can't see him for what he is. What he's always been. A thief and a fraud."

"How dare you call into question my professionalism?" she snapped. "You think because I'm a woman I must be blinded by my emotions? Would you speak that way to a male agent, you chauvinistic *poephol?*"

Stuttering for a moment, his skin reddening, Ruben aimed a finger at her. "That's it. You've gone too far. Turn in your service weapon with security on your way out. After you've taken a week off—an *unpaid* week off—to cool down and think about your role here, you can come back to work following a written apology to me and the other field agents for your behavior." Ruben lowered his eyes as he pointed a hand toward the door.

******

After spending a few minutes sorting through the day's mail, Susara trudged up the three flights of stairs leading to her apartment. She paused outside the door, listening for signs of life within. Being placed on leave, though it irritated her on principle, did afford an opportunity to finally spend some quality time with Noah. He'd be happy to hear that.

It would be good to decompress, anyway. Since meeting Lane, she'd felt her life, and her sense of priority, spinning wildly out of control. Time at home would help her to realign.

Unlocking the door, she entered her apartment. It was completely dark—the shades drawn. Noah must have already fallen asleep. Flipping the light switch, she felt her heart sink in her chest.

The entire apartment was empty, marked by neat, parallel vacuum lines in the carpet.

A piece of paper had been taped to the refrigerator door, but that was it. The walls were bare except for the nails where paintings and photographs had once hung, jutting from the drywall like errant darts. Stuffed in a corner of the living room sat a stack of hastily filled cardboard boxes overflowing with her things. Lifting the refrigerator magnet that held Noah's note in place, she took a deep breath before reading.

In bold black letters, it said, "I can't do this anymore. You know why. I've written this in permanent marker so it doesn't fade before you come home. Someday."

Turning the paper over in her hands, she realized he'd written the note on the back of a photograph of the two of them, taken from the frame she'd kept on her bedroom nightstand.

Returning the note—photograph-side-out—to the fridge, she moved into the living room and swept the window shades aside. Street lights illuminated the empty pavement below with streaks of white, shimmering on puddles of oil left behind by parked cars and rivulets of water from the lawn's sprinkler system. Folding her arms above her head, she leaned against the glass and wept.

TWENTY-ONE

Agapito didn't believe in ghosts, and he'd always considered law enforcement a very real threat to his business. Both presumptions had been proven wrong in the past few days.

Lane Bradley, the resilient *bâtard*, had apparently survived capture in Lebanon those many years ago. Agapito had to respect such a man not only for his unwillingness to die, but for his ability to keep his survival a secret for so long. Any respect that Lane had earned from Agapito, however, this mysterious agency—NERO—had lost. Some crudely forged documents making him out to be a Venezuelan official, a confident swagger, and a feigned accent had been all that was necessary for Agapito to march past their security. Convincing Director Luis to hand over the clay tablet—or the stones it had apparently contained—had required a little more effort. Mr.

Luis had the makings of a shrewd businessman. Agapito was none too happy that he'd been forced to spend money from his personal coffers, but if it pleased his father and kept him from unleashing his wrath, it would be worth every penny. He could make that money back easily enough.

Agapito had been genuinely surprised when he'd been handed the case filled with stones instead of the tablet. Seeing the confused expression on his face, Ruben had explained that the stones had been concealed within the tablet, and apologized profusely about the damage that had been done in the process of uncovering them. Agapito assured him with a wink that the Venezuelan government would forgive their American friends before making a hasty departure.

Now, followed by a small coterie of his men, Agapito made a beeline for the shipping container where he'd slept since arriving in the U.S. He found it more comfortable to be alone amidst the industrial backdrop of this dockyard than in a busy hotel, and hiding out amidst thousands of such containers all but eliminated the chance of someone tracking him down. What many others considered paranoia, he saw only as precaution. It had saved his life more than once.

Indicating to his men using only a raised finger, he stepped inside the steel container as they set about establishing a security perimeter. He switched on a battery-powered LED lantern and closed the door behind him.

Removing the cipher stones from their case and taking a look at them under magnification, all the events of the past two days became immediately transparent. Lane had historically been very particular about what he took, especially when procuring heavily guarded pieces like the one at the

Chávez estate. He would risk capture or death only for a piece worth the danger. And these, clearly, were worth the risk.

Although his father had ignorantly wanted the tablet only for its connection to the Phaistos Disc and its ridiculous legend, this time, he'd actually chosen a true prize. What Musarde had told him back at his estate, that Pernier believed the tablet held the key to the disc's power, had proven to be surprisingly accurate. These stones were the key to deciphering the disc. They were far more valuable to the archaeological community than the disc was, really, which excited him. After he'd entertained his father's absurd obsession, he would make a name for himself with these stones. That would be the supreme insult to Lane—stealing his discovery and taking full credit for it. And what amusing irony! Agapito, a violent criminal, credited with one of the most profound archaeological discoveries of the 21st century.

He now had no regrets about spending the money to bribe NERO's director. In fact, his assessment of the man as shrewd might have been hasty; Ruben clearly possessed little talent as an archaeologist and even less as a businessman if he let a find like this go for such a pittance.

Tapping a few keys to awaken his laptop, he contacted his father. Moments later, Musarde's face—made even more hideous by the distortion of his computer's small camera— appeared on Agapito's screen.

"You have the tablet?" His voice was garbled, the spotty internet connection making his already inscrutable accent that much harder to interpret.

"Yes, only, there were stones inside." Agapito held one of the stones before his screen.

"You destroyed the tablet!?" The picture shook as the old man slammed an open hand on his desktop.

"I wasn't the first to steal the tablet." He paused, knowing his next words would drive his father into a blind fury. "Lane Bradley, the man who stole your journal those years ago, had the tablet and shattered it, apparently." Quick to move on from that point, he added, "But, there's good news. These stones will give us the means to decipher your ring and the Phaistos Disc."

"You mean he lives?" Musarde's lips pulled taut as he scowled. Shoving a bulbous finger toward the camera, he yelled, "You told me you killed him!"

"He's apparently much more difficult to kill than I'd originally thought," Agapito said. "A mistake I won't make twice."

Momentarily appeased, Musarde slipped the gold ring from his finger and held it before the screen. "What does it say?"

"Give me a moment." Capturing a screenshot of the image, Agapito set to work using the cipher stones to decode the ring's meaning.

Musarde sat uneasily, his fingertips scraping across the wood grain of his desktop. A few minutes later, Agapito furrowed his brow, and Musarde leaned forward eagerly.

"What? What does it say? Speak, damn you."

Agapito spoke cautiously. "Hidden beneath the king's palace rests the Phaistos Disc."

Musarde remained quiet, waiting for more. When Agapito leaned back in his seat, the old man cried, "That's it? We already knew where the disc was." He strung together a list of expletives in his native tongue, punctuating each with a smash of his fist against the furniture.

When he'd finished, Agapito spoke quietly. "You needn't be so upset. We have the stones, and now, we only need the Phaistos Disc for you to find your *elixir vitae*."

That seemed to assuage Musarde's rage, the old man twisting the ring back on his finger.

Agapito shuffled the tweed coat from his shoulders and draped it over the back of his chair. "But first, I have some unfinished business to tend to with a ghost."

TWENTY-TWO

C old water ran from the bathroom faucet over Susara's knuckles, leaving behind a bloody swirl as it rolled into the drain. For the first time in ages, she had allowed her temper to go completely unchecked, and now had a lacerated hand and a ragged hole in the drywall outside their bedroom—*her* bedroom, now—to show for it. Steady tears had made her eyes ache almost as much as her hand.

This was her fault. She couldn't even be mad at Noah for leaving. She'd pushed him away. Part of her was glad it happened. They'd been fooling themselves thinking they could both get what they needed from each other.

She needed a drink.

Wrapping a towel around her knuckles as she scanned her phone's contact list, she realized that everyone she'd previously gone out with was at least as close to Noah as they'd been to her. She didn't feel like explaining why he'd left, or dealing with the discomfort that was sure to follow when those friends realized they'd have to choose between the two of them. Not tonight.

She stopped scrolling when she arrived at a newly entered number. The contact information read *Lane Bradley—track this number.*

Tossing the phone on her mattress, she paced before the foot of the bed for a few minutes, then picked up the phone and hit *send* before she could stop herself.

"Lane?"

"Who's this?"

"Susara." Silence. "You there?"

"If you're calling to apologize, don't bother."

She cleared her throat. "Actually, I was calling to see if you wanted to get a drink with me. I think we could both use one."

"Why? I mean, you've made it pretty clear how you feel about me, and I think you could probably guess how I feel about you right now. I expect to get ripped off by the guys I normally work with. Most of them would betray their own mother if they stood to gain something from it. But I figured you, supposedly one of the good guys, would actually stick to your word."

Easing onto the bed, she stared at the ceiling. The mattress felt harder than usual, and she realized that Noah had even taken the foam mattress pad beneath the sheets with him when he'd left. "Look, give me a chance to explain and to make things right." She could hear the soft, unintelligible voice of an NPR reporter in the background, and she wondered where he was.

He left a long pause before answering. "You're buying."

Two hours later, Lane ambled into the small, densely packed pub across the street from Susara's apartment. A large, nylon Union Jack had been stapled over the entrance and a soccer game played on a small TV in the corner, but in all other respects, the pub could easily pass for a typical American dive bar. The place smelled of stale fry oil and offered half-off shots of Jägermeister every time a police car or ambulance went by with sirens on.

Susara could smell fresh cigarette smoke on Lane's clothes from the pub's patrons loitering outside the building's entrance. He sat down across from her. Swiveling his hips, he scooted to the center of the vinyl-covered bench seat, cracked and barely padded.

"Took you long enough to get here," she said. "I thought we decided on seven."

"Didn't realize there was any urgency." He rested his arms on the seat back and stared at the bar impassively. The broad muscles in his arm and shoulder swelled and ebbed as he clenched and unclenched a fist.

"You look like you've had a rough day," she said gently, trying to get him to open up.

He slowly turned his head to look at her. When he spoke, his voice was low—crackling with electricity. "The find of a lifetime, gone. A mafia consigliere with no interest in archaeology beyond its price now has the keystones to one of the greatest mysteries in human history. As if that wasn't enough, I got manhandled by two very large, very angry security guards who dragged me in front of my lifelong adversary like a child, and then kicked me to the pavement. Yes, you could say that I've had a rough day."

"I know you think I had a hand in that, but I didn't. I'm upset about losing the stones, too," she said.

"I'm just surprised you guys didn't try to get me to continue running errands for you for at least a few more weeks before sticking the knife in my back," he deadpanned, leaning back and looking away, his fingers absently picking at the table's loose plastic edge-banding. Behind the bar, a glass fell and shattered. The bar-back cursed.

"That wasn't my idea."

"Doesn't matter whose idea it was," he shot back. "You still let Agapito take the stones, didn't you? That wasn't the antiquities minister back there, and you knew that."

"I was helpless to stop it. Ruben——"

"Is an imbecile?"

"Is still new to his position. He was just trying to cover his ass, and wouldn't listen to me. He thought I'd...." she paused and looked away.

"He thought you'd what?"

Pushing herself into her seat, she mumbled, "He thought I'd grown too attached to you to see you for what you really are."

He scoffed. "Well we know that's not true, don't we?"

She knew what he was referring to. "Look, Lane, I'm sorry about what I said the other night. About you being like my father's murderers. That's obviously untrue, and I still don't know what made me say it."

"I know exactly why," he answered. "Because you still think of me as a heartless thief with pliable morals. If I'm willing to steal, then I'm willing to lie. If I'm a liar, how can you trust anything I say? You'd never know the depth of my depravity. Maybe I'm a serial killer and habitual drowner of puppies, too.

I'll always just be another one of the criminals in your file, won't I?"

"No, you won't. You aren't, I mean." She tried to flag down the waiter. She needed a drink, pronto.

"I'm not what?"

A second passed before she spoke. "Just another criminal."

"So, is he right?" he pressed.

"Who, Ruben? About what?"

His voice softened. "Have you grown too attached to me?"

"I'd say you're like a loose thread I can't help but pull on, even though I know it'll just ruin my sweater."

He grunted and leaned back, his features relaxing.

She said, "I mean, I barely know you."

"Really? I feel like I've known you a long time. You have an old soul, I think. Maybe we knew each other in a past life."

"Aren't you supposed to wait until after you've started drinking to get philosophical?"

"That's only true for the first few. Rapidly diminishing returns after that," he said.

A waiter approached their table. "Can I start you two off with something to drink tonight?"

"I'll have two fingers of Glenmorangie, straight up," she said.

"Gonna be one of those nights, huh?" he asked. "Given the circumstances, I guess it's fitting. I'll have a double of Ouzo—straight-out-of-the-freezer, mother-in-law cold."

"A glass of what?" the man asked. "We only have a Merlot and a Chardonnay. People don't really come here for wine."

Susara snorted, covering her mouth as Lane glanced at her, eyebrows raised contemptuously.

"It's not a wine, it's a Greek liquor. Tastes like licorice. Turns cloudy when it's cold," he tried to explain.

"He'll take a Budweiser," Susara said.

As the waiter returned to the bar, Lane said, "That's the most creative you could come up with? Oh, we're out of filet mignon. Care for a hotdog instead?"

She gestured from one wood-veneered wall to the next as if to showcase the cramped interior of the bar. "That's what you get when you roll into a hotdog stand asking for steak."

As they waited for their drinks to arrive, Susara slid an envelope from her purse and set it at the edge of the table. Watching Lane's eyes as they settled on the fresh lacerations across her knuckles, she quickly returned her injured hand to her lap. "I brought you something. It's not enough to offset what happened today, but I hope it's a start."

He reached across to retrieve the package. Carefully slipping his finger between the envelope's flaps, he tore through the adhesive and withdrew the glossy papers inside. High-resolution photos of the cipher stones.

"I could kiss you right now." He ran his fingers along the edges of the photographs.

She plucked the photos from his hand. "I risked my job for these, and my job is about all I have left in this world. I'm putting it on the line for you."

"Why?

"Because I told you I'd give you the stones back, and I didn't. I may be a hard-ass sometimes, but I'm not a liar. Besides, I recognized that phony Vicente guy the minute he walked in. There's no way we're letting him get away with those stones."

Lane sighed, tipping over a glass tray filled with sugar packets, mixing straws, and coffee creamer. He began constructing a small fort. "This is probably the last thing you want to hear, but actually, at least for the time being, we're going to have to let him get away with them. Those stones are probably halfway around the world by now, anyway. Agapito's boss, Achille Musarde, keeps his stuff in the basement of his estate—an old vineyard wine cellar. But the place is a fortress. It's one of the most heavily fortified places I've seen that houses a private collection."

Positioning the straws to illustrate a floor plan and encircling it with round packets of creamer, he grabbed a sugar packet, and manipulating it to look as though it had dodged the creamer and made its way inside the room, continued, "Redundant, overlapping monitoring stations, a staff of on-site armed security comprised of seasoned private military contractors, a three-ton steel vault door with a seven-digit security code—that means 10 million possible number combinations—and an auto-lockdown function that traps any detected thief inside the vault, evacuates the air inside, and suffocates them without getting blood on Musarde's precious treasures." He flopped the sugar packet on its side, and then swept the entire exhibit to the edge of the table with the palm of his hand. "Needless to say, once he gets those stones inside, we'll have a hell of a time getting them back out without an army on our side. As far as hard targets go, this one is armor plated."

Their drinks arrived, and Lane looked at the waiter distrustfully, not speaking until he'd disappeared into the kitchen.

"So we're just going to let them go?" Susara asked, taking a sip of her drink. She didn't flinch as the Scotch seared a fiery path down her throat.

He drew short, vertical streaks in the condensation around the neck of his beer with the pad of his pointer finger. "I had hoped to keep Agapito from getting the cipher stones in the first place. Now he's got the same information we do. It'll be a race to get the disc."

"Wait, *get* the disc? You're talking about stealing the Phaistos Disc? From the museum in Heraklion? I can't even be hearing this, Lane." She slid back in her seat and crossed her arms.

"Well it's us or it's Agapito, but either way, that disc is getting taken."

"You just told someone whose sole job is to prevent crimes like the one you're describing about your intent to steal a priceless artifact. And you're asking me to help you do it. I'm beginning to think Ruben wasn't wrong about you: You really think you're untouchable." She took another drink, eying him over the top of her glass.

"I'm not that arrogant," he said. "But I do trust you. Like I said before, we make a good team. You saw that in Venezuela and Dubai. I wouldn't let just anyone in on what I'm doing." Reaching into his pocket, he withdrew Pernier's leather journal. Combing through the pages until he found the one he was looking for, he slid it across the table, waiting expectantly as she examined it.

"What am I looking at?"

"Luigi Pernier detailing the day he found the Phaistos Disc and the clay tablet."

"What does it say? I can't read Italian."

"He wrote of the disc's healing and beautifying powers. Pernier believed that it was the key to the Minoan people's legendary beauty and longevity—the root of a paragon civilization."

"Sounds like an entertaining legend." Though only a few sips into her drink, she could already feel a soothing warmth flooding her chest and her words losing their clarity. She should have eaten something before showing up.

Lane sat forward in his seat and whispered, "But what if it's not just a legend? What if there's something about the disc that makes it capable of initiating some kind of atavistic reaction in human DNA? A hard refresh of the human genome that eliminates genetic imperfections? Wipes the slate clean?" He leaned closer. "Pernier was crushed to death by a statue that fell from a block and tackle while he was excavating in Rhodes—a freak accident. He was sixty-two years old. Personal accounts from the dig crew said he looked no older than 30 when he died. He was 34 years old when he found the Phaistos Disc. The math works."

"Or he was one of those people who ages gracefully. *Omne ignotum pro magnifico.* One of my father's favorite expressions." She closed the journal and slid it back across the table.

"Everything unknown appears magnificent," he muttered, looking away.

"Exactly. Lane, a legend like that is beneath you. You have to know there are millions of stories just like that one surrounding every ancient artifact ever found, and they can always be traced back to some armchair researcher with a tinfoil hat and dubious credentials."

He shook his head. "No matter how small the chance of it being true, I need to see for myself. For Jordan."

She racked her brain for why he would need the disc for his daughter. "Why do you say that?"

He rubbed a finger against the worn leather of the journal. "Leukemia. It's been a rollercoaster. Remission, we take a breath and think it's over, and then it returns and the nightmare begins again. There's nothing I can do. I would tear the beating heart from my own chest to protect her, but I'm helpless. Except for this. The disc, if it does have the power to heal the way Pernier described, could save her life."

She suddenly felt ashamed, as though her dismissal of the disc's legend had been calloused or uncaring.

"Regardless of whether it's true or not, we have to steal the disc before Agapito does if only to keep it from disappearing into Musarde's vault forever," he said, the emotion leaving his voice as he straightened up. "Even if you don't believe the legend, as a NERO agent, you should come with me to keep the disc out of his hands."

She took another drink. Though outwardly composed, her mind raced. This was an opportunity for her to get her life back on track. By going along with Lane, she could arrest him the moment he stole the Phaistos Disc and get back into Ruben's good graces, making up for the Venezuela debacle. Lane would probably find a way to squirm his way out of incarceration, anyway, just as he always had. His daughter would be unaffected regardless; Susara knew the legend about the disc's healing powers was pure myth. Finally, she could apologize to Noah and maybe they could give their relationship another try.

She could fix this.

"So, you steal the disc. Then what? You try its mystical healing powers, and then just give it back when you're done?" she asked.

"That's my plan."

"I don't believe you."

"Look, I don't want the disc. I really don't. It's been perfectly safe at Heraklion for almost a century, and I'd like to leave it that way. I only want to save my daughter. Now, either you come with me to ensure the disc doesn't end up on the black market or in a lunatic's basement, or you get out of my way. I'm going to get it, regardless." His voice belonged to a man defiant and steadfast in his resolve. This wasn't a negotiation.

"You're really committed to seeing this through, aren't you?" The look in his eyes said everything his lips didn't.

She took a final drink, letting the last drops of the liquor tingle on her gums before swallowing. "Fine. I'm with you."

He looked relieved, and the makings of a smile crept across his face. "Good. There's just one more little thing standing in our way."

"That is?"

"Pernier never actually figured out what triggered the disc's healing powers. He suspected it had something to do with the temple in which the disc was found, but he wanted to read the disc to see if it gave more detailed instruction. The problem was, he never had the means to translate its symbols."

Tapping the photos of the stones with her pointer finger, she said, "But we do."

"Exactly. You were an archaeologist before you became a NERO agent, I'd assume?"

"Got a masters from Rutgers to prove it." She bit her lip, realizing how pompous that sounded.

"Well doesn't the archaeologist in you want to find out what the Phaistos Disc says? We've got the photos of the stones and there are plenty of images of the disc on the internet. We could put the two together right now and solve a mystery that's been tormenting the archaeological community for a century."

"Aren't you going to be disappointed when it only tells you how much grain King Minos kept in his royal storeroom?" She dragged her finger around the lip of her empty glass.

"Hey, if you don't want to help decipher it, that's fine. But let me take those photos back to my hotel to study. Just for the night."

"No way. You'll take them and be gone from the country before morning. No, I'm keeping them with me at my apartment."

"Fine then. Feel like pulling an all-nighter?" he asked.

She swallowed nervously, thinking about her empty apartment, the hole she'd punched in the hallway wall, her being alone with Lane late at night following drinks, and the loneliness that hung on her like a soaking rain after losing Noah. Despite her reservations, she said, "Sure. I don't care."

"Good. It's settled, then." Unscrewing the cap from his beer, he touched the bottle to her glass. "First, a millennia-old mystery. Then, we plan a robbery."

TWENTY-THREE

After drinking until their words flowed unchecked and their throats became dry, and then ordering *just one more* round, Lane and Susara stumbled back to her apartment.

"I like the minimalist look of your place." He followed her inside as she drew the key out of the lock.

"Nice of you to say that." She slipped off her shoes and set them neatly beside the door.

He kept his on, leaving faint shoeprints in the recently vacuumed carpet. She pretended not to care. "We need to get you some different shoes. Those things are ratty."

"Not a chance. They're lucky. And comfortable." He peeked between the window curtains to take in the apartment's view.

"Let me guess, size ten-and-a-half PF Flyers, rounded heels, faded tread on the inside arches."

He paused and lifted his foot to his knee to check. "That's quite the party trick. A little unorthodox—I mean, you expect people to open a bottle of wine with their shoe or guess your playing card—but still, I like it."

"It may seem strange to you, but those shoes are almost as familiar to me as they are to you. They're about all I've had to track you by. I've got a map in my office devoted to the places those shoes have left prints. It'd be the envy of many a world traveler."

Suddenly realizing Susara had taken her shoes off at the door, he stooped and began untying his laces. "I'm sorry. That was rude of me."

"It's fine. Actually, it's kind of comforting to have those tracks in my living room." Rubbing her shoulder uneasily, arm tight across her chest in a self-comforting posture, she added, "And before you ask about the empty apartment, my boyfriend moved out while we were in Dubai. It looks like I'm starting over."

"Sometimes that's all you can do." He seemed unsurprised by the news. "But you'll find that a fresh start can be a good thing. It creates opportunities for new adventures."

Something about the way he said it made her wonder what obscure part of his past had inspired the comment, and if he'd ever reveal it. It seemed a direct contradiction to his carefree nature. Nothing affected him, yet for a man who apparently couldn't be troubled, she sensed his suffering beneath the surface.

"You've done some starting over before, then?" she probed.

He placed his shoes by the door. "My whole life. My mom got deported, my dad and I started over. I dropped out of college, I started over. Joined the Legion..." he paused, his eyes drifting to the floor as sifted through old memories, "well, you get the idea."

"What made you leave, anyway? That tattoo on your arm, that's the Legion's symbol, isn't it?" She leaned over the kitchen island and ran a finger along her upper arm.

He slid his T-shirt sleeve up to reveal the bottom half of the tattoo, the once dark-blue lines faded like a photograph displayed for years on a sunny windowsill.

"What does it say?" she asked.

"*Legio Patria Nostra*. The Legion is our Fatherland."

"That doesn't fit with your story about joining up just to get out of the country, then going AWOL."

He let his sleeve down and absently scratched at the stubble on his cheek. "I actually enjoyed being in the Legion, in a way. I mean, aside from the fact that they gave us a really cool dress uniform with this white kepi and red epaulettes—quite the get-up; you should have seen it—it actually felt like I'd found where I belonged. It gave me this sense of, I don't know, elitism and fraternity, I guess, that I'd never experienced before. Those of us who survived training became part of a unique brotherhood."

"You mean figuratively survived, like, passed the requirements, right?"

"No, I meant survived as in didn't die," he said, his expression grim. "The Legionnaire's claim to fame is enduring punishing conditions and making do with nothing—sometimes even food and water. The Legion trains its recruits to fit that ideology. More guys have died training for the Legion than for any other military unit in the world."

"Not exactly a claim to fame to be proud of," she said.

"It kinda is if you manage to survive it," he replied. "Anyway, I got to travel, I became closer to my comrades than I'd been to any friend I'd ever had…it was a challenge, but a good one. I felt stimulated. Alive." He took a deep breath and shoved his hands in his pockets. "I don't know. One day it just fell apart."

She raised an eyebrow. "How so?"

Shuffling uncomfortably, he reached a hand to the back of his neck. "It's not really something I like to talk about."

"I won't tell anyone."

He stared directly into her eyes with an unsettling intensity. A vein in his neck throbbed as he worked his jaw. He began softly, "We were deployed to Côte d'Ivoire as part of a defense agreement with France back in...2004, I think it was. We were supposed to prevent a civil war from starting. We no more than got there and set up camp before the Ivorian Air Force bombed our base and killed a dozen of our men. We counter-attacked and destroyed every jet fighter the country had. But the damage had been done, and everyone was on edge from then on. It went from a peacekeeping mission to a war overnight." Approaching the fridge, he examined the photo of Susara and Noah. "That November, there were protests. Peaceful. A civilian march. One of our guys got excited and fired off a shot. Suddenly, everyone with a rifle was blazing away—a contagious shooting. Everyone just assumed we were under attack and that someone had a good reason for firing that first shot. All those unarmed protestors just mowed down in cold blood. The only thing that came of it was a few commanding officers got reprimanded and transferred back to France. I couldn't be a part of that. I'd endured all that physical suffering to become a Legionnaire, but this was more than I could bear. So I snuck out that night and paid a fisherman to smuggle me to Morocco. I met Nicole, Jordan's mom, while she was there on sabbatical. The rest is history."

"I find that easier to believe than you just deciding to quit," she said.

Exhaling slowly, he whispered, "I'm sorry, that was more information than you wanted to hear, I'm sure."

"Not at all." The more time she spent with Lane, she realized, the more layers he developed. He'd gone from being a two-dimensional criminal when she'd first met him to a human being—a man of flesh and bone struggling under the weight of a complex past, bearing deep scars.

He scrunched his nose and looked at her quizzically. "Why do I feel the need to spill my guts about my past to you? This is stuff I've buried for a decade."

"Must be the secret agent thing. I scare people until they tell me everything they know." Tugging open the refrigerator door, she withdrew two longneck beers from inside.

"I don't know about that. I've seen your interrogation techniques firsthand." Accepting the drink, he twisted off the cap and folded the thin steel between his thumb and pointer finger. "They don't exactly scream Stalinist gulag inquisitor."

"You vill talk, *tovarisch*, or face a Siberian vinter," she said in her best Natasha Fatale voice.

He laughed, then motioned toward the living room. "Still have those photos handy? Let's take a look at the stones."

She began apologizing for the lack of furniture and the pile of her things stacked in the room's corner.

He interrupted, "Hey, I know how break-ups go. No explanation necessary." Shuffling the images of the cipher stones out of their envelope, he spread them in a large semicircle on the floor, then began pacing. "Do you have a computer handy?"

She dug through the boxes until she found her laptop and an inkjet printer, nestled amidst an assortment of disentanglement puzzles that once sat on her coffee table. Picking out a Rubik's cube, she tossed it to him.

"Ah, I should have known you'd be a fan of solving puzzles." He spun a few of the multi-colored slides before handing the puzzle back. "I'm no good at these."

"Neither am I. But I still like them."

"You know, there's a known formula for solving Rubik's cubes."

"I know. But that's not really the point, is it?" She looked over the worn plastic toy. "I don't know why, but somehow, in disentangling the puzzle—the process of it, not just solving it—I feel as though I'm unweaving the things that are bothering me. It's therapeutic." She stared at the cube a moment longer, sighed, and dropped it back into the box. "Back to the big puzzle, right?"

"Yeah, right. Go ahead and pull up the Phaistos Disc. Print off both faces in the highest resolution you can find. I'm going to take my contacts out; my eyes are killing me. Bathroom down the hall?"

She nodded, but upon recalling the hole she'd punched in the wall, stopped him. "The, um, sink isn't working quite right. Why don't you just use the kitchen to wash up?"

He nodded slowly. "Sure."

Minutes later, handling the printed pages along their edges to avoid smudging the fresh ink, Lane slipped his glasses on. Sliding over until his shoulder touched hers, he held the photograph up where they could both see it. "Notice how the disc's symbols are divided into sections. The obvious answer is that they're divided into words or phrases. Some experts—and I use that term loosely—believe the Phaistos Disc is made up of logograms, like the stick figure signs on public restroom doors. But if that were the case, one look and you'd say, 'the symbol of the guy with spiky hair is meant to be a guy with spiky hair', and this whole thing would make absolutely no sense at all."

He cleared his throat and looked at her over his glasses to confirm she was following before continuing his theorization. "Others believe the symbols on the disc are part of a syllabic script—each image meant to convey syllables that comprise words. That makes more sense to me, but if that's the case, without other examples of the writing, there's no way to even guess at what the disc says—the reason this has stayed a mystery for so long."

"But the stones we took from the Chávez estate...."

"Exactly. Those stones show a direct connection between the symbols here," he swept a hand over the surface of the photograph, "and Egyptian hieroglyphs." He grinned and nudged Susara's shoulder playfully. "Centuries of tortuous speculation by academics, and here we are with our own personal copy of the *Idiot's Guide to Interpreting the Phaistos Disc.*"

"So it's as simple as marking the hieroglyphic parallel to each of the symbols on the disc and reading it," she said.

"Almost too easy, right? Care to do the honors?"

"My father would have loved this," she said quietly as she set to work, marking each of the disc's symbols with its hieroglyphic counterpart using a permanent marker. "He was never much for hands-on archaeology—he didn't like the heat or bugs, and there are a lot of both in South Africa. But he was fascinated with studying old things and loved to spend hours researching." She glanced at Lane, his eyes fastened to the photograph. "His museum was his world, his cocoon. Happily surrounded by his artifacts and books."

"I take it you two were close," he said.

"I adored my papa." She almost asked about Lane's relationship with his father, but upon recalling their talk in the hotel room in Dubai, chose silence instead.

She continued her work until reaching an impasse. Rocking back on her heels, she frowned. "This doesn't make any sense."

Staring hard at the interpretation, Lane dragged a fingernail along the edge of the page as he chewed his lip. Finally, he leaned back and sighed, rubbing his eyes beneath his glasses. "That should be it. We must be missing something."

"Maybe we should take these to an expert—"

"I *am* an expert," he shot back defensively.

"—linguistic anthropologist, is what I was going to say. Sorry Lane, but no one can be an authority on everything. Not even you."

"We don't need anyone else. We can figure this out." He rolled his shoulders and sat up straighter. She knew better than to try to dissuade him.

After a few long minutes of staring, she let out an exclamation. "I've got it! Hieroglyphs can be read from right to left. We were just reading it backward, from the outside in."

Regarding her interpretation with new eyes, she deciphered the script, the volume of her voice rising with her excitement. "Two palaces a sea apart. One, ruled by royal blood, the other, built beside the mighty river." She flipped to the next photo. "Within their temples, beneath the royal crest, hides the source of the kingdom's eternal beauty."

"This disc will guide the deserving to salvation," Lane finished. He wrapped an arm around Susara's lissome middle and pulled her tight against him, giving her an enthusiastic squeeze.

Leaping to his feet, he began pacing, pulling his glasses from his face and swinging them wildly as he narrated. "The Phaistos Disc was found in an underground temple depository, one destroyed by fire the night Pernier discovered the disc. But this indicates the existence of a second temple. A second temple capable of harnessing the disc's power."

Her smile faded. Like an excited child, Lane had become fixated on a fairytale, obsessed with the disc's lore. He'd lost sight of how ridiculous all this was.

"The city of Phaistos was ruled by King Rhadamanthus, Minos's brother. That's the royal blood mentioned here, and the first palace." He tapped the image of the disc with his pointer finger. "The other—a sea apart and built beside a mighty river—rules out King Minos's palace at Knossos. It must have been referring to a city on the Egyptian Nile—the mightiest of rivers—given the hieroglyphs on the stones. The Egyptians were allies at the time, so I suppose it's possible the second temple actually belonged to the Egyptian empire."

Reluctant to encourage his misguided enthusiasm, she asked, "But which pharaoh's palace? The disc has been dated to around 2,000 BCE, so the Egyptian pharaoh at the time would have been...."

He grabbed a handful of his hair as he attempted to recall his Egyptian history. "That would make it the beginning of the Middle Kingdom."

"Mentuhotep the Second," she said.

"And the capital city under his reign?"

"Thebes," they said together.

"Modern Luxor. That's got to be it," he said. "Beneath the royal crest—the symbol of the pharaoh."

"The ankh," she said, referring to the cross-like icon with a circle drawn in place of the topmost upright. "We find a conspicuous ankh—maybe made up of multiple structures orientated to look like one from the air—we find your second temple."

He touched her arm gently and smiled, eyes aglow with hope. She wanted to bring him back to reality, to convince him this was all just a fool's errand, a superstition dreamt up by a primitive culture, but those eyes kept her from saying a word.

"We should celebrate," he said. "You think that ignorant bartender knows what champagne is?"

A man's atonal whistling came from the stairwell, growing louder as he ascended.

"'*O sole mio*?" Susara said.

"Yeah, well he's no Pavarotti." Lane winced as the whistler projected a string of sour notes.

As the stranger reached the Italian tune's familiar chorus, Lane loudly sang Elvis' rendition. "It's now or never, come hold me tight…" he extended his hands toward Susara as if to dance a rumba, "…kiss me my darling, be mine tonight."

She laughed and stepped into his embrace, stepping in rhythm with him as she sang, "Tomorrow will be too late, it's now or never, my love won't wait."

The whistling stopped abruptly outside the apartment door. A throat cleared, followed by a light knocking.

Lane's expression went dark as Susara moved to answer it. "Wait," he whispered, grabbing her wrist. "Were you expecting visitors tonight?"

"It's fine. Probably just someone coming to pick up something Noah forgot."

"At 10 o'clock at night?"

Another knock, this one more insistent.

"Lane, you're being paranoid." She peeled his hand from her wrist.

Before she'd taken another step, a salvo of gunfire ripped through the apartment door.

TWENTY-FOUR

C opper-jacketed slugs ripped through the kitchen island, splintering plywood and upsetting pots and pans within as Lane and Susara sheltered behind it.

"Where's your gun?" he yelled, his countenance calm despite the holes appearing in the drywall only a few feet above his head.

She flashed back to the moment she'd handed over her service pistol to NERO's armorer. She shook her head. "Not here!"

A bullet slapped the refrigerator, punching a neat hole in the photo of Susara and Noah.

The door swung open with a booted kick. A masked figure stepped inside, sweeping the room with a CZ Skorpion submachine gun, a bulbous suppressor affixed to its muzzle. The gun instantly conveyed to Susara two things about the assassin: First, he was likely an amateur and a poor marksman. A small-caliber semi-automatic pistol or revolver in the hands of a trained assassin was an adequate and deadly tool. Whomever had sent this man knew of his inexperience, and had hedged their bets by handing him a gun that promised accuracy by volume. Second, it told her that their attacker was well-funded and well-connected. Suppressed, fully automatic weapons weren't cheap, plentiful, or legal in the nation's capital. There was money and influence behind this hit.

Before the assassin had time to take in his surroundings, Lane dove into the open and slammed his hand against the light switch, plunging the room into darkness. The whistler's gun spat orange in the black, then, the suppressed *thrump thrump* was replaced by a subtle *click* as the trigger tapped emptily against the frame—the Skorpion's bolt hanging open.

The man cursed, fumbling to remove the weapon's magazine in the darkness and swap it for a full one. Susara could hear hurried footfalls as Lane, taking advantage of the lull, rushed their attacker.

The muted thump of two masses colliding was followed by a crash as the men piled against the floor. She flipped the light switch to find the gunman pinned beneath Lane, his hand gripping a round metal object the size of a golf ball.

"Lane, that's a grenade," she warned, her voice low as she inched backward.

"A V40 mini-grenade. Yeah, I recognized it," Lane said, slowly leaning his weight away from the assassin, allowing the man to regain his footing.

The whistler kept one hand clenched around the explosive, holding it outright toward them as he scrambled for the door—leaving his gun smoldering on the carpet.

They stood in dumbfounded silence as their attacker's hurried footsteps, punctuated by a clatter and smash as he tripped and fell to the stair landing below, faded.

She mumbled, "So much for getting my deposit back."

The police arrived a short time later, the other tenants flooding into the hallway in hopes of witnessing an arrest or catching a glimpse of a corpse. A detective pulled Susara and Lane aside for questioning. The interview was brief, the detective's attitude largely apathetic. His demeanor changed abruptly when he looked over Susara's credentials. Suddenly, he became remarkably polite and attentive.

When the last of the police had departed, assuring her they'd be monitoring the building overnight, Lane rubbed his eyes and said, "You shouldn't stay here. Anyone who's *that* committed to killing you will be back again."

"I'm not running from anyone. They're going to have to try harder to scare me than this. Besides, how do you know they were trying to kill me and not you? Seems to me that your friend Agapito already tried to murder you once before. Maybe he's trying to finish what he started."

"They couldn't be after me. People love me," he joked, his half smile a subtle recognition that those bullets had undoubtedly been meant for him. "Regardless, I can't let you stay here alone. Let's get back to work."

******

Throw pillows from her bedroom littered the floor. Photos and topographical maps of dig sites and ruins in Luxor, defaced with pens and sticky notes, rested in crude piles that wandered the room. It'd been a late night. She'd spent most of it downplaying her shock at having her apartment shot up and her life very nearly ended, nodding vacantly when Lane would call out exultantly with some new revelation he'd had while scanning a book or scrutinizing a satellite photo.

She groaned, massaging the stiffness in her neck earned from the few hours of sleep she'd hungrily taken while lying on the floor. Looking around, her heart sank. Streaks of sunlight poured through the blinds, leaving vertical lines of shadow like prison bars on the wall.

He was gone.

At first, she didn't know why she found that disappointing. After all, she'd had every intention of betraying his trust following the heist of the Phaistos Disc, so how could she be upset that he'd played her first?

But there was something else. She'd felt, and perhaps it had been the booze or Noah leaving, that she'd found in Lane a kindred spirit. A social castaway misunderstood by society, fixated on a past no living being had seen. A student of archaeology who hadn't had his passion for history eroded by academia or extinguished by the stark realization that there was no real money to be made unearthing old things.

She'd been wrong about Noah, so it should have come as no surprise she'd been wrong about Lane, too.

There was a gentle knock on the door. The latch had splintered from the blow of the assassin's boot the night before, and even the lightest touch now caused the door to swing unsteadily on its hinges. Lane peeked inside. Seeing her awake, he took another step in, a tall cup of coffee in each hand.

"What's wrong?" he asked.

"Nothing," she said, pretending to rub away sleep. "Good morning."

He continued to look at her skeptically.

"I thought you'd taken the photos and left," she admitted.

He set the coffee on the kitchen counter and sat beside her on the floor.

"We're in this together, right? You've put your neck out for me by bringing these photos back, and I trust you. I expect you to trust me, too."

He extended his hand, palm canted upward as if to lead her somewhere. She shook it.

"Drink your coffee, then pack a bag. I got us a flight to Athens that leaves in a few hours," he said. "I figured it was safe to assume NERO wasn't going to provide us with a private flight for the purpose of stealing a national treasure from a foreign government."

TWENTY-FIVE

After scanning through every radio station twice, Lane settled for silence. He drove aggressively, weaving through the midday traffic, traveling 20 over the freeway's posted speed limit. The air conditioning blew at full power despite the cool morning, and though she was uncomfortable—crossing her arms over her chest and legs at her ankles—Susara stayed silent, eyes affixed to the digital clock on the dashboard.

The airport exit came and went.

She cleared her throat. "You missed our exit."

"I need to make a quick stop before we leave," he said. "It won't take long."

When she spotted the sign for Sibley Memorial Hospital approaching, she realized why he wanted to stop. He steered into the visitor's lot, and despite his apparent urgency to get there, sat quietly after they'd parked, staring out the windshield and listening to the soft knocking of the engine as it cooled.

"This is why you agreed to come back to D.C.," she said. "I didn't realize your daughter lived here."

He nodded. "You can stay in the car if you'd like. I won't be long."

"I'd like to meet her."

Tossing his sunglasses atop the dashboard, he stepped out of the car. She reached over, folded the glasses carefully, and slipped them into their case before exiting the car.

Together, they entered the building. The pervasive scent of disinfectant hung on the air. He led the way to the children's ward with obvious familiarity. Stopping outside a door with a cardboard cutout of a sparrow taped to it, he said, "You sure you don't want to wait in the lobby?"

"It's OK. Really." She reached past him and knocked gently. A woman's voice, soft and clear, invited them in. Nudging open the door, they entered. Susara felt her stomach churn the moment she stepped inside. A beautiful middle-aged woman, dishwater-blonde hair meticulously styled, stood at the foot of the room's only bed. Like a once-sunny plain suddenly shadowed by rainclouds, her demeanor darkened instantly upon seeing Lane.

A figure stirred atop the sheets of the hospital bed—a young girl, eight or nine years old, pale and bald. Despite her condition, the child emanated a defiant optimism.

"Lane, what are you doing back here?" the woman asked, clearly struggling to keep her tone calm. "You can't just keep dropping in without warning."

"I'm sorry I didn't call, Nicole. I just came by to see Jordan once more before I left for Greece. Guys, this is my associate, Susara Eaves. Susara, this is my daughter, Jordan, and her mother, Nicole."

Nicole gave Susara only a passing nod before resuming staring daggers at Lane. Jordan, however, looked up at her and smiled sincerely. Susara could see the family resemblance in her grin—definitely a feature of her father's.

"Can I speak with you privately?" Nicole asked, tears welling in her eyes, hands balled into fists.

"Sure." He pretended not to notice her fury. "But first, I brought Ms. Jordan a little something I picked up in Cairo. Forgot to give it to her when I stopped by yesterday." He withdrew a small necklace from his pocket and knelt by the bed, wrapping an arm around his daughter's body as she leaned toward him and kissed his stubbled cheek. His arm, tan and thick with muscle, only emphasized the girl's emaciated form and pallor when pressed against her.

"Thank you, Daddy!" she said, admiring the gold chain as he slipped it into her cupped hands.

He kissed her forehead, cradling her head tenderly. "Why don't you and Susara talk for a minute while Mom and I have a quick chat? Don't tell anyone, but Susara's a real-life secret agent. I bet she has some great stories to share." He winked at Susara before leading the way into the hallway. Nicole followed, giving Jordan a forced smile as she closed the door behind them.

The shouting commenced instantly.

"How can you keep doing this? Just show up out of thin air, acting like nothing is wrong? We go for months without knowing if you're even alive, then it's all Daddy, all the time, for two weeks. Then, *poof.* Gone again."

He attempted to soften the volume of the argument, but Susara could hear his every word through the thin wall. "Jordan has enough to deal with without hearing us fight. And you know why I'm not around as much as you'd like. Her bills don't pay themselves."

"Of course you'd say that. As if that's the only reason you go skipping around the world stealing things—for her. You do it because you enjoy it and because you're incapable of behaving like an adult. I suppose that necklace you gave her is something you stole, too."

"I bought it from an airport gift shop, Nicole."

They both took a breath.

"And that woman in there—you called her an 'associate'. New girlfriend, I'm guessing?" Nicole whispered harshly. "That's an all-time low, even for you. Looking to introduce your daughter to her subtly?"

"Not that it's any of your business since you made me sign the divorce papers, but I only met Susara a few days ago, and we're working on a job together. That's it." He paused, his voice dropping. "You liked me once, you know. Not just loved me, you *liked* me. And you trusted me. I don't know when that changed, but it hurts every time I see you."

Jordan cleared her throat and touched a hand to Susara's wrist. "This happens whenever Dad comes home."

"I'm sorry," Susara said, unsure of what else to say. She tried to mask her discomfort, wishing she'd heeded Lane's suggestion to wait in the lobby.

Jordan shrugged, adjusting the angle of her bed using the remote at her side. "That's just what they do now. It didn't used to be like that."

"That's got to be hard."

"Harder for them, I think." Jordan turned on the television mounted in the room's corner. "I think they still love each other, but you can't tell because they argue so much. Even if I was better, I think they'd still be like that."

"You're very mature for a young woman."

"Thanks. You're very pretty."

"Not as pretty as you or your mom."

"I don't feel very pretty. But I'm sick, so it's OK. Someday, maybe I'll be as pretty as you are. It's still nice of you to say that."

"How are you feeling?"

Jordan sighed. "I've had better days."

"I bet you learned that expression from your dad."

Jordan smiled and kicked her feet playfully. "Yeah."

"You must miss him when he's gone."

"I wish I was better so I could go with him and travel. He tells me about it sometimes—the places he's been, all the things he's found. Are you going to help him find artifacts on your next trip?"

"Just one very special one."

"Will you bring it back for me to see it?"

"I'll try."

Lane and Nicole, having reached an impasse in their argument, returned to the room, both feigning smiles.

"Honey, I've got to go if I'm going to catch my flight. I'm sorry I can't stay longer, but I promise I'll be home soon," he said, leaning over Jordan's bed. "You, me, a couple of gigantic bowls of cereal, and Saturday morning cartoons, right?"

"It's a date." The young girl smiled and hugged her father tightly, her eyes closed and her nose buried in his neck, taking in his scent once more before he departed.

"Oh, Daddy, don't forgot your lucky charm." She dug into a bag beside the bed and produced a stuffed animal—a sparrow, the painted metal eyes scratched, the fabric worn thin.

He accepted it like a gift from royalty, cradling it gently. "I'll bring it back first thing when I'm home." With a smile, he gently kissed her forehead. He turned to Nicole. Stepping near her, he cradled her fingertips in his palm and whispered, "Take care of my girl."

Wiping at her eyes with her free hand, Nicole nodded, staring at the beige wallpaper. "Yeah."

Susara waved goodbye to Jordan as they left the room. Before closing the door, she glanced at Nicole and gave her an apologetic nod.

"I'm sorry about that," Lane said, taking a deep breath as they stepped into the sunshine outside the hospital. The five minutes they'd spent inside looked as though they'd aged him years. "I should have known I wasn't getting out of there without a fight." He kicked a crushed soda can into the parking lot.

"No, it's fine. I'm sorry about your daughter's health. I'm sure it's been hard on you all."

He nodded and walked toward their parked car. "Seems to get harder every day."

TWENTY-SIX

An inquisitive pigeon perched on the wrought-iron railing separating the bistro's outdoor patio from the street. It examined Agapito with a canted head as the man awaited his meal. Inside, a cellist adjusted his seat—the man already red-faced and sweating, as if just the thought of playing his instrument had caused him to labor. A waiter with a napkin-wrapped wine bottle tucked against his arm breezed by. The building's glass door swung open as a young man, trying so hard to look calm that he forgot about masking his obvious limp, entered. Scanning the faces of the restaurant's patrons, he settled on Agapito and hobbled with urgency toward his table.

"Mr. Vicente—"

"Before you say another word, sit down and behave as though you haven't just committed a crime." Agapito sipped at his tea, fingers toying with the string anchoring the tea bag. "Perhaps you'd like a drink?"

"Yes, sir, I'd like that very much."

Flagging down a passing waiter, Agapito said, "My friend here would like a cup of tea when you have a moment."

"I'd prefer wine," the young man said with a thin, pleading smile. "It's been a...difficult day."

The waiter paused for confirmation. Wearing a scowl, Agapito nodded reluctantly. The waiter departed for the kitchen.

"Why are you here?" Agapito asked. "Perhaps there was some confusion regarding the proper etiquette of a man in your line of work? I could have gone my entire life without seeing your face."

"I'm very sorry, Mr. Vicente, but I didn't know what else to do. I've...I've failed."

Agapito closed his eyes and breathed in hard through his nose. "Were you seen?"

"Not by the authorities. But my gun—"

"*Your* gun?" Agapito whispered, leaning across the table.

The waiter swept by, leaving a glass of dark red wine on the edge of the white tablecloth. The whistler eyed it thirstily.

"What happened to *my* gun that I *loaned* you?" Agapito pinched the wine glass by its stem.

"I had to leave it behind." The whistler licked his lips. Shuffling an object from his pocket and holding it to the side of the table, he continued, "But I still have the grenade—"

Flinging the wine into the assassin's face, Agapito hissed, "You imbecile. Why don't you do me and the world a favor by pulling the pin and stuffing it down your miserable throat? You bring such a thing back to me in a public place?"

The man hastily returned the explosive to his pocket and began wiping his face with his shirtsleeve.

The waiter returned and placed a steaming bowl of *coq au vin* before Agapito while eyeing the fresh wine stain on the young man's shirtfront. "Will monsieur's guest be eating this afternoon?"

Agapito shook his head. "He has another appointment and won't be joining me." Staring at the assassin until he stood and limped toward the exit, Agapito tasted his soup. The spoon clattered to the tabletop. Grimacing, he slid the bowl toward the waiter.

"A culinary felony."

TWENTY-SEVEN
En route to Crete

Only the monophonic rush of blowing air filled the commercial airliner's cabin. Most of the passengers had disregarded their seating assignments and, upon spotting clusters of empty seats nearby, had sprawled out—heads buried in thin pillows the size of tissue boxes they'd found crushed in dark corners of overhead storage. Cabin window shades were drawn, as the cloud cover made anyone who bothered looking outside feel as though they were staring at a white bedsheet.

After half an hour spent fighting sleep, chin bobbing against his chest, Lane succumbed—his head sliding from the cerulean faux-leather headrest and resting against Susara's shoulder. She smiled, reaching to his lap and returning the bookmark to the pages of his book before closing it.

He was trusting. Sweet. Already, she felt an almost paralyzing doubt taking hold. Anxiety, uncertainty, apprehension, she struggled with these daily. It had always been like that. Just a part of her personality. With age and maturity, she'd learned to govern those sensations. Harden her façade and forge ahead. But the past few days had brought about a return to old feelings of insecurity, and she couldn't seem to overcome them. Everything about this journey to steal the Phaistos Disc felt misguided. Reckless. That wasn't her.

It wasn't even the notion of stealing the artifact that bothered her. It was the motivation and the inevitable result. She knew Lane was wrong about the Phaistos legend, and she'd already made up her mind to arrest him following the robbery. But then there was Jordan, his dying child, and his obvious commitment to getting her care. His pursuit of the Phaistos Disc, and his mistaken conviction that it would heal his daughter, further reinforced her belief that this man was decent—too benevolent and compassionate to betray, no matter how justified she might be in doing so. Was her commitment to arresting him less about doing her job and more a selfish attempt to fix her own mistakes at his expense?

Leaning her seat back, she sighed, releasing the air from her chest slowly. Only in a dream would Lane's vision of the Phaistos legend come true, but what a dream it would be! Her heart glowed with the thought of slipping into a dusty, lamplit crypt, pulse pounding, watching the Phaistos Disc in her hands begin to glow with a celestial white light, the wrinkles and scars vanishing from her skin.

Of course, even if by some bizarre twist the legend proved true, it wouldn't be anything like that. They'd decided after the hours they'd spent researching and scouring satellite maps that

Luxor Temple was the most intuitive choice for the second temple. It was located near the Nile and had been built in approximately the same time period as the Phaistos Disc. But the temple had been excavated centuries before. It was a tourist destination, now—hardly the lamp-lit crypt of her imagination.

Not that she would let things get to that point, anyway. Their first stop was Crete, and that would be Lane's last stop before his arrest.

She only hoped it would end there. Agapito Vicente had made clear his intention to kill them both, and as with any conflict, just because one combatant refuses to fight doesn't mean the war is over.

TWENTY-EIGHT

Heraklion Archaeological Museum
Crete

Footsteps reverberating as they passed through the museum's cavernous foyer, Lane and Susara shoved through a set of metal turnstiles into the first exhibit. Marble floors gleamed beneath rows of track lights and glass skylights. As she took in the dozens of artifacts on display, she noticed Lane scanning the building's walls, his eyes following them to the second story, ignoring the exhibit entirely.

"Funny thing," he said, still following the walls, "this building used to be a Roman Catholic monastery before it was destroyed by an earthquake. They rebuilt it with anti-seismic properties to keep that from happening again."

"Yeah, fascinating," she said distantly, not really paying attention to him so much as trying not to make eye contact with a pair of museum guards watching them. Wrapping an arm around his, she leaned in close, put on a fake smile, and whispered, "Try not to be so obvious that you're casing the place."

"No law against looking around," he said as they walked on. "Besides, in order for things to go smoothly tonight, I need to find all the best points of entry."

An elderly couple turned to look at him.

"Honeymoon," Lane explained.

The woman gave him a disapproving frown and shook her head in disgust. The man nodded and winked.

Fidgeting with a pair of sunglasses hooked over his shirt collar, Lane continued to scan the room as they walked to the next exhibit. "It also wouldn't hurt if we could take inventory of every motion sensor and camera location, air ducts, open skylights, that sort of thing."

"Do you go through prior to each robbery, just like this, and memorize everything?" she asked.

Nudging her and tapping the sunglasses, he shook his head. A camera. He was recording everything to review later.

"I don't usually have that luxury," he said. "Sometimes, when tanks are rolling down the street and people are shooting it out in the museum parking lot, you sort of forego these kinds of formalities. This is actually a fun change of pace for me."

Entering a small room apart from the primary exhibit, her fingers tightened on his arm. The Phaistos Disc sat behind glass in the center of the room, glowing in the lamplight. One of the preeminent relics from the dawn of human civilization, now an anachronism isolated in modernity. It was humbling, this piece of terracotta crafted by simple island dwellers. It embodied the struggle of a nascent civilization to evolve, to move away from basal savagery. This was a symbol of mankind's first clumsy, glorious steps. The Minoans were artists, and like all artists, they had a message they felt the need to articulate.

"It's marvelous," she said, stepping close.

"I'm guessing the case has wireless seismic sensors, plunger or biased magnetic switches, maybe even an environmental sensor for temperature changes." Scratching the tip of his pointer finger, he began scrutinizing the case like a 3D puzzle.

"Can you take a minute to just enjoy it for what it is?" She punched his shoulder playfully. "You're beholding a 4,000-year-old piece of human history. Act like it."

"I plan to pay it its due respect when this is done. But until then, it's still behind glass, and I've still got a job to do."

"All right, well, how do you intend to do that job?"

He shrugged. "Don't know yet."

"You could hide here until the museum closes," she offered. "Seems like 90 percent of the cases that cross my desk are inside jobs pulled off by janitors or people with after-hours access."

He shook his head. "I'd bet money this place has saturation motion detection to prevent that. Mixed infrared and microwave detectors covering every inch."

"What about a false fire? Triggering the alarm unlocks all the security doors. You could steal the disc and exit while everyone else leaves." She swallowed hard at the thought of a museum fire. She let go of his arm, remembering her father's death, her duty as a NERO agent, and her ultimate objective of arresting Lane following the disc's theft. This was no time to lose focus. It was all too easy to let his enthusiasm drag her in deeper, the appeal of this challenging puzzle—no different than the Rubik's cube on her coffee table—blinding her to what was really at stake.

He continued to stare at the display solemnly. "I like where your head's at, but that's an old trick, and one they're going to anticipate. They'll have protocols in place that require herding everyone into a waiting area where they'd cavity search the whole crew before releasing them. This museum's been here a long time and has experienced plenty of attempted robberies—key word being *attempted*. This isn't their first rodeo." He glanced at her. "What's the cleverest robbery you've ever been assigned to investigate?"

She thought for a moment. "Don't let this inflate your ego, but your stint in Mallawi is probably at the top of my list. Or the Damascus Museum. I spent three days sorting through security footage you'd replaced with clips from Wile E. Coyote and The Road Runner."

"You grasp the symbolism?"

"It was very clever."

"It's funnier in hindsight than it was at the time. I got shot on that job." He reached a hand to the scar on his shoulder and rubbed it tenderly. "Anyway, flattering as it is that you chose two of my cases as your favorites, it doesn't offer much change in perspective," he said. "I was hoping you could spark my imagination for tackling this one."

"Well, most robberies I see are either just violent smash-and-grabs or opportunism due to negligent security measures. Understaffed security teams, dysfunctional or dummy cameras, pieces displayed in the open, fire exits propped open to make smoke breaks easier, that sort of thing. Everything looks very secure here. Plenty of cameras, sensors, locked cases, monitored fire exits…." She bit her lip and slowly shook her head. "Since you're not the type to go in shooting, I don't have any good ideas."

He leaned over the railing surrounding the exhibit and waved a hand over the top of the vitrine display case. A loud chirp warned him of the motion sensors above.

"I might have an idea. If I can infiltrate the building undetected and get to the security office, which will probably take disabling a couple of hardwired motion sensors and wearing a signal jammer for the wireless ones, I can incapacitate the guards and shut down the whole system. From there I would have full run of the place."

"You make that sound so simple. Assuming you do get inside without being seen, and assuming you can take out the guards, you think they're going to just give you the passcodes necessary to shut the system down? I doubt that."

"Already have them."

"Really," she said skeptically. "Found them on the internet, did you?"

"Not exactly. Our mutual friend, Herr Poldi, gave them to me. Shutting the system down is the easy part. This case could be a bit of trouble, though." He eyed the wood molding supporting the glass. "The wood frame is just a veneer— there's nine-gauge steel under there. And even with the sensors disabled, the polycarbonate case is bullet and impact resistant."

"You could cut through it," she suggested. "A diamond blade works. I've tried it."

"Takes too long and makes too much noise. It'd be easier to get at the disc through the alarm technician's access door, which is probably going to have concealed hinges and a captive key. Hidden security screws hold the whole thing together...maybe I can bring my kit to get those out. I won't have long to do it, though. No doubt they have some sort of notification sent out when the system goes down." He leaned back and scratched his chin. "Frustrating. Always makes me just want to blow it open."

She pinched his shoulder. "You go on and on about saving priceless antiquities, but your fallback plan is to strap explosives to them?"

"I didn't say I was going to, but it sure would be simpler," he said.

From behind them, a baritone voice said, "Admiring our security system, I see."

TWENTY-NINE

A white-haired man in a crisp blue security guard's uniform stood nearby, hands behind his back.

"It's a thing of beauty," Lane said without skipping a beat. "Lane Bradley and Susara Eaves—we're with the New Era Recovery Office. NERO for short. No connection to the Roman emperor."

Susara felt her throat tighten. She didn't know what angle Lane was playing at, but dragging her into this and using her credentials could only mean trouble.

He continued with the charade. "We've been hearing rumblings of an attempted theft of the Phaistos Disc. We thought we'd drop in and take a look at your system to ensure the disc would remain safe."

The security guard didn't blink. "I hope you don't mind if I ask to see some identification."

Lane looked at Susara, eyes pleading. Reluctantly withdrawing her agency-issued employee identification card, she extended it to the security guard.

The guard accepted it, stared at the card carefully for several seconds, and then returned it—his features softening. "You should have called ahead."

"We wanted to see your security as it typically is," Lane said.

"Well, does everything appear satisfactory?" The guard's voice betrayed his contempt.

"Decent, from what I can tell. We wouldn't say no to a more in-depth tour of your system, though."

"Do you really feel that's necessary?" Susara asked, staring at Lane as if to silently communicate her disagreement with his continuing to press their luck.

"Only if they want to avoid the negative press that comes with losing one of the world's most priceless antiquities." A look of playful defiance. Lane was enjoying himself.

The guard licked his lips, then turned and spoke in rapid-fire Greek into the radio on his shoulder. Waiting until he received a short response, the man nodded and waved them along.

"You may have noticed our many overlapping security cameras—none of them dummies—saturation motion detection, and—"

"Mixed infrared and microwave detection?" Susara asked.

"Of course. Thieves are like clever rodents: Leave one crack and they'll find a way to squirm inside. We've spared no expense in preventing that."

Susara looked at Lane with a knowing smile. *You clever rodent.*

"That's all very good," Lane said, ignoring her. "But I have some concerns about the design of the building itself. The architect was no doubt more concerned with its anti-seismic properties than with the security of the building."

"I assure you, all security protocols were followed in the building's design. It's impenetrable while all systems are online."

"You mean it has been impenetrable so far," Lane corrected. "If it's not too much trouble, I'd very much like to take a glance at the architect's blueprints."

"You can request them through the city registrar."

Lane shook his head. "No, I mean the originals. The ones you don't show to the public.'"

The guard hesitated, clearly trying to think of a means to dissuade him or deny the claim.

"Of course, it's your prerogative to keep those records sealed," Lane's voice was lofty, his body language demonstrating his indifference. "But imagine the fallout if someone does manage to steal the Phaistos Disc, particularly following your lack of cooperation with our agency's attempts to bolster your security."

The man sniffed imperiously. "Wait here, please."

When he'd moved out of earshot, Susara leaned toward Lane and whispered, "You going to tell me what the hell you're doing?" She felt her face flush. "What happens when he calls the NERO offices and learns I'm on suspension?"

"He won't. You underestimate how lazy people are. Look, it's simple social engineering. Manipulating the human element of a security system to gain access. Appealing to vanity, greed, or fear of punishment to get what we need. A talented thief doesn't just rely on gadgets or sleight of hand to get the job done. Just stay calm and let me show you how I work."

The guard returned moments later with a copy of the blueprints rolled inside a cardboard canister. Slapping the tube against Lane's open palm, he said, "Here. If we can be of further service, please don't hesitate to ask. I'm afraid I must get back to work. Please return these to the front desk when you're through with your examination." He turned on a heel and marched into the nearest exhibit, grumbling "pompous Americans" as he departed.

Unraveling the blueprints, Lane laid them on the floor, putting a large display between him and the nearest surveillance camera. "I can't tell you how many times a heist's success has come down to the tenacity, or lack thereof, of underpaid security guards."

"You realize that if the disc is stolen now, we're the first ones they're going to come looking for," she scolded. "We were anonymous before."

Slowly, he passed his camera sunglasses over the blueprints. "They had our faces the second we walked through that door. Now, we just have an excuse for being here. Hell, we warned them about their security and told them exactly what we thought would be stolen. When it is, it'll just look like we had really good intel. You get that guard's last name?"

"Alexopoulos."

"Good. I'll get in touch with my IT guy and see about dropping a few thousand Euros in his bank account. That'll put the attention on him when all this washes out."

"Your sacrificial lamb?" she asked, still doubtful of his brazen approach.

"He'll be fine. It's only a tenuous link to the crime. Just enough to throw the authorities off the trail. Besides, I'm sure the guy could use a couple extra bucks. The economy here sucks."

Returning the blueprints to the security office—with many thanks and assurances that everything looked secure—they reentered the main exhibit.

"This has got to be killing you to walk through here without pocketing things," she teased as she admired the thousands of Greek artifacts on display.

"Contrary to what you might think, I'm not a kleptomaniac," he said under his breath. "I don't get off on stealing things. I do it because I care about preserving our species' history. Unlike other people who sit comfortably at home and lament the destruction of artifacts by dictators and invading armies while they read their newspaper, I'm actually doing something about it."

"I don't see any armies around here," she said.

"OK, yeah, this is more preventative than the work I usually do. Typically, I'm pulling stuff off the racks as the building's burning down around me. Kind of a deadly version of *Supermarket Sweep.* You have no idea how many times I've escaped with singed eyebrows."

"Tough life," she mocked.

Turning to Susara, suddenly giving her his full attention, his eyes narrowed. "Your job is *way* easier than mine."

"Oh, is that so? Ripping off a building is difficult work, huh? Where I come from, it's usually those who can't function as a contributing member of society who turn to theft."

"OK, maybe my job isn't *more* difficult than yours, but it is less forgiving," he insisted. "The same way the fox's job is more difficult than the hounds'. You and the rest of your pack carry none of the risk. If I manage to escape during your pursuit, your master goes home disappointed that night and vows to try again another day. If I slip up even this much"—he held up two fingers a quarter-inch apart—"even once, it's an all-expenses-paid one-way trip to Club Fed."

"Good. I'm glad your job is hard," she said. "That means I'm doing mine well. If it was easier, imagine how many more people with less honorable intentions than yours would start stealing antiquities. It'd run you right out of business."

"A little competition is healthy. Or at least entertaining." He held the door for her as they stepped out into the bright sunshine. "New guys always make the most comedic mistakes, and they keep your docket full so you have less time to worry about me."

THIRTY

Theodore Roosevelt Island Park
Washington, D.C.

Ruben shouldn't have bothered to bring a sandwich along. It was a futile attempt to make his lunch outing feel casual—literally a walk in the park. The surface of the Potomac glinted in the midday sun as the water rolled lazily by. Chickadees hopped along the concrete walkways snaking through the lush verdure of the park before being scattered by playing children. Vomit tingled and toyed at the back of his throat.

The phone call he had finally resolved to make had weighed heavily on him, and now, minutes away from dialing Agapito Vicente's number, he was experiencing doubts. Stronger than when he'd first deliberated this decision in the shower, while shaving, while eating breakfast. It had been just a thought, then. Just a random, innocuous thought. But as soon as he made this call, it would become real, and he would own it. He would be just as guilty of killing Susara Eaves as the man he was about to ask to pull the trigger.

He should never have taken the money for those stones. The cash would help his parents, but ultimately, it'd been an excuse. He'd agreed to the deal out of spite, just to make her look bad.

Susara had brought in Lane Bradley and made it look easy. The white whale that had topped their team's target deck for years, and she just went out and got him. And to prove that wasn't just a one-off, she'd brought the Wogden pistols back, too. The other agents under his command adored her. So did Ruben's boss. And now, by putting her on unpaid leave, he'd made himself into her enemy. She'd come back twice as ambitious and motivated, on a mission to ruin his reputation at every opportunity. Knowing her, she'd succeed, too. He couldn't let that happen.

His stomach shuffled in pace with his footsteps as he abandoned the pavement of the memorial plaza and sought privacy in the woods. He withdrew his sandwich from a pocket, placing it beside him on a park bench, and tugged the plastic wrapping until it laid flat—squaring the bread that had deformed in his pocket during the walk. Teeth pinching his lips, he took a deep breath, withdrew his phone, and pressed the numbers hurriedly—before he could talk himself out of making the call.

"Mr. Vicente? Director Luis here, from NERO."

"What can I do for you, Mr. Luis?" Agapito sounded distracted, and for some reason, that amplified Ruben's nervousness. He was about to cross a moral threshold he'd never before dreamed of considering, and Agapito sounded as though his golf game had been interrupted.

"I'm ready to accept the second half of the payment for the stones," Ruben said.

"I'll have one of my men bring the cash by. Goodbye, Director."

Ruben nearly shouted as he desperately tried to keep Agapito on the line, "I've been keeping tabs on Susara Eaves, tracking her phone. I don't know what she's up to, but she's not in the country anymore, and her boyfriend is still here— she's not on vacation. My guess? She's gunning for those stones. I'd watch your back."

"Don't worry about my back, Mr. Luis. It is well and truly covered."

Ruben swallowed hard, fingertips scraping his phone's aluminum carapace. "Mr. Vicente, may I ask a favor?"

"No, you may not. I don't deal in favors. I consider exchanges of both goods and services, but favors are by definition done only out of good will, and as such, are useless to me."

"Would cash be more acceptable?"

"I assure you, whatever service of mine you'd like to enlist is beyond the scope of whatever pittance you may have to offer."

"How about this? You can keep the other half of the amount you owe me—" he swallowed again. Cleared his throat.

Agapito sighed. "If you need more time to contemplate your thoughts, please feel free to hang up the phone and call me back when you're more capable of articulating them."

"Sorry, it's just…" Ruben whispered, "I want her gone."
"Who?"
"Susara Eaves. I want her gone. For good."

Ruben could hear a smile forming as Agapito answered. "It just so happens your needs and mine align, Mr. Luis. Otherwise, the remaining half of the money I owe you wouldn't so much as begin to cover my work."

"So you'll do it?"

"Certainly. Though I'd like to know why the sudden interest in her demise. I've seen more stalwart men than you give in to monetary persuasion, but assassinating your subordinate? That's an entirely different breed of malfeasance."

Staring through the trees at the verdigris-coated likeness of Teddy Roosevelt standing proudly in the center of the plaza, Ruben mumbled the president's famous quotation, "Get action. Seize the moment."

"I don't follow," Agapito said.

Ruben continued, his words coming quickly, his resolve hardening. "This is a matter of self-preservation. I like my job, and I intend to keep it. If that takes removing Susara from the picture, so be it."

"I see. Well worry not. I'll take care of your little problem." Agapito abruptly ended the call.

Ruben, slowly returning his phone to his pocket, eyes still fastened to the stoic, frozen effigy of the past president, reached for his sandwich.

THIRTY-ONE

Heraklion Archaeological Museum
Heraklion, Crete

It was dark enough now. Susara stopped the car at the corner of a street adjacent to the museum, parked before a jumble of Greek letters spray-painted on the stones supporting the building's front gate. The savory smell of a closed gyro stand filled the car as she rolled down her window. In the moonlight, the cream-colored museum walls glowed with an eerie luminescence, crackled paint peeling away from the concrete like flakes of dead skin.

"Are you ready to go?" she asked, more to herself than to Lane. She shivered, gooseflesh rising on her arms as a cool ocean breeze rolled through.

A small flashlight held between his lips, he grunted as he looked over the printed copy of the museum blueprints in his lap once more. He'd spent all afternoon poring over them, cross-checking them against the footage he'd taken inside the museum. Although she had come to know him as one who got bored easily, with an almost volatile energy totally unsuited to long hours of study, he'd surprised her by going completely silent upon their return to the hotel room, his focus anchored to the task at hand.

Letting the flashlight drop into his lap, he said, "Our security guard friend wasn't lying: All points of ingress, even the ductwork, are covered by cameras and motion sensors. I'll have to move slowly." He squirmed in his seat. "I don't know, Susara, something just doesn't feel right about this one."

"You've been planning this for months. Years even, right? Just treat it like any of your other jobs. You'll be fine. You're the best in the business." It felt as though she were convincing a friend to jump off a bridge. Her every word sounded disingenuous. Duplicitous. Thankfully, he was too preoccupied to notice.

Slipping a pair of nylon shooting gloves over each hand, he snugged the cuffs tightly around his wrists.

Looking over his attire critically, she tugged his sleeve. "Do you own a single clean shirt?"

"Not one."

"Is it so hard to do laundry?"

"It is when you don't own a washing machine and live in an abandoned airport."

Someone from the next block over laughed. A window slammed shut.

"And here I was expecting some kind of black, skin-tight monkey suit or a maintenance guy's uniform. I'm a little disappointed you didn't even dress up for this," she said.

"That whole ninja, wearing all black, *Mission Impossible* thing is for the movies." He scanned the street, watching for pedestrians or passing cars. "If you're careless enough to move into someone's line of sight when you're breaking and entering, camouflage isn't going to help you. And when you make your escape, a guy running away from the scene wearing a ski mask just shouts, 'I'm a criminal.' As for the building maintenance get-up, it isn't worth the trouble here. CCTV networks are almost never monitored in real time, and I intend to flush the footage as soon as I'm in." He stepped out of the car and opened the trunk, stuffing the pockets of his cargo pants with lock picks, a wireless signal jammer, a multi-tool, a length of nylon rappelling rope, and a can of women's hair spray. "Besides, when you're wearing street clothes, you can always claim you were just looking for the restroom." He stepped around to the driver's side of the car after gently closing the trunk, eyes fixed to the front of the museum.

Not a light on in the place.

A cat slinked along the top of the security wall outside the museum, pausing to eye Lane before flicking its tail and continuing on.

He leaned in through the window. "Should you see something I should be concerned about, call me. Otherwise, I want you behind the wheel. This car had better be running, in drive, your foot on the clutch, ready to blast out of here There's no telling how close it's going to be or if I'll be getting shot at as I make my escape. Plan for the worst." He rolled his shoulders as he sized up the building. "Boat's at the docks with a full tank of gas. We ditch the car when we get there, and we're home free."

Her fingers kneaded the steering wheel. "You really have been planning this for a while, haven't you?"

"Was it the boat that gave it away? Or the fact that the car you're driving had its serial numbers ground off and may or may not have been purchased with cash from a guy named Vinny who runs a chop shop on the mainland?" He chuckled, but there was no humor in his voice. "Yeah, I've been working on this for a while."

Before they'd left, she'd watched him check the vehicle's headlights, taillights, and brake lights. He wasn't going to risk getting pulled over for a minor infraction. Every detail, even those that most would have considered unnecessary, had come under scrutiny in his preparation for the heist. That was what made him so good, what set him apart from the rest. He prepared for each job like it was a science, but conducted it as though it were an art form.

She extended her hand.

"I hope it works out," she said, though she knew it wouldn't. The second he walked out of that building holding the disc, she would have him in cuffs. That was the plan, and she was sticking to it. She envisioned her father's face, brow furrowed as he peeked over his glasses at one of his displays, his kind eyes aglow in the museum's dim light. He would have wanted her to stay the course. After all, Lane was a thief. She'd put away hundreds of them over the years. One more could save her career, a career she'd worked her entire life, from the moment she'd left South Africa, to reach.

"I'm sure it'll be fine," he said distantly, shaking her hand gently before jogging toward the museum. Scaling the property's wrought-iron fence, he climbed onto a rolling dumpster for a boost to reach the building's exterior fire escape. Cautious, placing his hands and feet slowly and deliberately to avoid making any noise, he climbed to an adjacent window's balconet. Nimbly swinging his lower body to build momentum, he bounded to the next window, skirting the rooftop until arriving beside a tarnished copper gutter pipe he could scale to the rooftop. Hand over hand, with the confidence and proficiency of an ape climbing a tree trunk, he ascended to the building's apex.

With a final pull, the sinewy muscles in his back churning beneath his shirt, he heaved himself atop the rooftop before disappearing into the shadows.

THIRTY-TWO

With no regard for time, Lane carefully unfastened the screws holding the roof's air-duct cover in place. He wouldn't rush himself until he'd disabled the building's security system. That was when things needed to move with some urgency; he had no idea what kind of automated notifications might be sent out when the system shut down.

Tying the end of the rappelling rope around a roof vent to anchor himself, he tested his weight against it, then carefully lowered his body into the narrow ductwork. Spider webs wrapped around his shoes, his shoulders scraping against the thick layer of dust and bird droppings on the tunnel walls.

Reaching the first elbow in the vent system, he moved into a seated position and began pulling himself forward until he had room to lie prone. Slowly, snakelike in his movements, he shuffled toward the jagged streams of dim moonlight coming up through the first ceiling vent.

"Least. Favorite. Part," he groaned as he tried to control the increasing squeeze of claustrophobia stealing the breath from his chest. Crawling to the vent, careful to avoid making excessive noise, he rolled to his stomach, lifted the grate, and scanned the opening.

A small plastic box had been mounted to the ceiling a few feet away. An infrared motion sensor. Withdrawing the can of hairspray from his pocket, he doused the screen with thick layers. The film would insulate the sensor from his body heat, ideally long enough for him to input the security codes he'd gotten from Poldi and shut the system down. From there, he'd take the guards down individually as he encountered them on their patrols.

He scanned the room for any other sensors he might have missed. Slowly, muscles tight, he lowered himself through the opening.

That's when he saw it.

He'd missed one. Another sensor partially hidden behind an exit sign.

But there was no piercing scream of alarms, no flashing lights.

Something was wrong. Not a single light from a clock radio, computer monitor, or two-way radio charger shined in the security office. Only the softest glow of moonlight illuminated the interior of the museum. Someone had already disabled the security system and every electronic device in the vicinity.

He slid the rest of the way inside, dropping quietly to the floor. His steps were cautious as he moved through the dark, listening as his shoes squelched on the tile floor. Wet. His foot bumped a large mass. He explored the object with the palm of his hand. Warm. Motionless. There was something slick, a viscous fluid, on his gloved fingertips. Blood. Feeling his way up the fallen man's chest, he discovered two weeping knife wounds in his left pectoral. Lane slipped off a glove and checked for a pulse. Nothing. He tugged the nametag from the guard's hip and moved toward the museum's central atrium, angling the laminated card into the moonlight.

Alexopoulos.

He cursed, pocketing the name tag. Exiting the security office and entering the museum proper, he stepped among the rows of pearl-white statues on his way toward the Phaistos Disc. The place was nightmarish in a way; many of the stone figurines were missing limbs and had been strung together with steel rod, or had been reduced to only a head on a stand. They stood frozen, bathed in the moonlight flooding through the skylights overhead. Like crucified corpses on the Appian Way to Rome.

He approached the area where the Phaistos Disc had been displayed that afternoon. The case had been pried open with a hydraulic jack, the tool left on the floor at the foot of the display. The disc was gone. Agapito had beaten him to it.

Just as he sensed the presence of someone else in the room, Lane felt the cool dance of piano wire against his neck. Instinctively reaching a hand to protect his throat, he felt the cutting tension of the wire as it snapped taut across his gloved palm. A knee jammed against his back. Yanked backward into the atrium, he was swung around to face the museum's glass front. He looked up, face red, fingers contorting to keep the wire from cutting off his airflow. The rows of statue heads watched apathetically—impartial observers of a contemporary gladiatorial battle for survival.

Blood trickled from his palm, the wire shredding the fabric of his glove. His attacker grunted as he threw his weight back, driving his knee deeper into Lane's spine.

He couldn't even cry out in pain. The back of his hand pressed tightly against his windpipe. Shoes, slick with the guard's blood, provided no traction. He scrambled for a foothold, his vision blurring. Ink black smothered the edges of his sight. He had to act quickly, before he passed out. Summoning the last of his strength, he turned his hips and drove his body into his attacker, taking away the man's leverage. They both crashed to the marble tile floor, the garrote slipping down Lane's forearm, freeing him to strike back against the assassin. His elbow struck the man's face, bone smashing cartilage. Desperately, his fingers probed for the man's eyes—anything to force him to release the wire chewing the skin from his arm. Finally, the man relented, abandoning the garrote and allowing Lane to get distance. Peeling the wire from his flesh, he tossed it away.

The dark-clad man raised himself from the floor and shed his ski mask, snorting out a crimson mist from his crushed nose. Despite being covered in blood—both men's—it was easy to see that the assassin was a local, of dark complexion and with Mediterranean features. Definitely one of Agapito's hired guns. Lane shook his head and wheezed, "Don't. We can both walk away from this."

The man gave no indication he'd understood. Wiping at his nose with the back of his hand, he slid a thin blade from a sheath at his hip, the steel glinting in the dim light. He charged. Lane sidestepped the lunge, the blade carving through the fibers of his shirt along his ribcage. Gripping his attacker's wrist, Lane struggled to move the point of the blade away from his guts. His free hand found his assailant's neck. Slamming the man's wrist against his knee, Lane attempted to disarm him. It failed. He tried again, and together, the two men staggered, driving headlong toward a nearby display. Glass shattered. A beseeching whine rose from a dying man's chest.

Exhausted and still desperate for air, Lane tugged off a glove and reached a hand inside the case, sweeping aside glass shards as he touched two fingers to his attacker's neck. A shard of broken glass had seated itself deeply in the skin, piercing the man's carotid artery, dousing the display case with his lifeblood. There was nothing to be done for him. Drawing back his hand, Lane wiped the blood from his fingers against the man's shirt and picked up the bag at his feet. Reaching inside, he withdrew a padded case and opened it.

A spiral of symbols glowed in the moonlight.

The Phaistos Disc was his.

THIRTY-THREE

Susara felt a wave of relief and a jump in the tempo of her heartbeat as Lane's shadowy form appeared near the door and slipped outside. She felt for the handcuffs in her back pocket as she approached him.

"I thought I told you to wait in the car," he said, his voice hoarse. Narrow, symmetrical bruises had begun to form on both sides of his neck, darkening along the excoriated skin. A steady drip of blood trickled from his palm.

She paused, suddenly concerned. Rushing to him, she began examining his wounds. "Are you OK? God, Lane, that's a lot of blood."

"It's not all mine." He ripped off his gloves and shoved them in a pocket. "Typical Agapito. Doesn't even have the stones to kill me in person. He'd prefer to let everyone else do his dirty work. It's the only way he's stayed in the game so long; he doesn't take risks, he pays others to take them for him."

"What happened in there?" she asked, incredulous.

Circling a finger, motioning for them to get moving, he walked at a hurried pace toward their idling car. "Agapito beat us to the punch. His guy must have used some kind of EMP generator to knock out all of the building's electronic security measures. Killed the guards." He withdrew the security guard's blood-spattered nametag, glanced at it once more, and let it fall to the pavement. "Ham-fisted way of doing it. Completely unnecessary waste of life."

"I'm sorry, Lane." She meant it, too.

"Well, for what it's worth, it takes the heat off of us. The authorities will look into the dead guy's history and start tracking down former accomplices who may have betrayed him. We won't even be on the radar."

As they arrived at the car, she stepped close to him. This was it. If she was going to arrest him, this was the time to do it. He was wounded. Weakened. Unsuspecting. But instead of reaching for the cuffs, she moved her hands to touch the chafed skin on his neck.

He looked bewildered. "I'm OK. Really."

She reached for his wrist, turning his hand until the bloodied palm faced her. "We need to get you to a hospital."

"There's no time." Unslinging from his shoulder the backpack containing the Phaistos Disc, he gently set the bag in the car's back seat. "We need to get moving before the authorities arrive. I've got fishing line and a needle in the boat. You can stitch me up on the way out of here."

She slid behind the wheel. Hopping into the passenger seat, he reached into the back seat and removed a spare T-shirt from his bag, wrapping it around his hand and pulling the knot tight with his teeth. As the car began moving, he leaned back in his seat and gazed out the window at the passing streetlights.

She tried not to stare at him, to instead focus on their escape from the island, but she struggled to look away. There was something off about him, as though a different man had emerged from the museum—someone darker, someone colder. He'd killed a man, taken his bag, and walked to the car as if he'd been expecting such a roadblock all along. Sure, he was upset that things hadn't gone to according to his plan, but he seemed mostly unshaken. That troubled her.

"Watch it through here." He nodded toward an approaching alleyway. A car bumper protruded from the shadows. "More guys have been caught by speeding away from the scene than by committing the actual crime."

After an hour and a half spent following the serpentine roads winding along Crete's jagged, boulder-strewn coast, they arrived at a small marina. Along the docks, yachts and sailboats bobbed peacefully at their moorings. Despite the increased risk that came with lingering on the island with the stolen disc, Lane had been convinced the authorities would first search Heraklion's major port and airport before extending their search to other parts of the island. So far, it appeared he'd been correct.

The car's headlights illuminated the corrugated siding of the marina's administrative building.

Lane gestured toward a sleek form bobbing low on the water. "There's our ride." An onyx black rum-runner glinted in the moonlight like a giant floating spearhead.

"A go-fast boat? Your version of the middle-aged guy's sports car?" she teased.

"A Saudi horse breeder reneged on our deal for a Sumerian statuette, so I took his boat as payment." Exiting the car, he handed her the backpack containing the disc and their bags. "I didn't learn until later how much these things sell for. I may have overcharged him a little."

"Lane." She nodded toward his blood-spattered shirt. The blood from Agapito's hired gun, still wet. Then she pointed to the cloth wrapped around his hand—already sodden. There was DNA plastered all over this vehicle, and the crime scene investigators, when they found the car, would be able to draw a direct line between him and the robbery.

"Yeah," he said simply. "I'll take care of it." Drawing a deep breath, he grabbed the cigarette lighter from the dashboard and unwrapped the bandage from his hand.

She disembarked, grabbing their bags from the back seat and carrying them toward the waiting vessel.

Exiting the car, he unscrewed the car's fuel port cap and stuffed the bandage inside. As gasoline crept its way toward the exposed end of the fabric, he pressed the lighter's striker and ignited it.

Sprinting along the pier, he untethered the boat and jumped in beside Susara just as the car erupted in flame.

THIRTY-FOUR

Nicosia International Airport
Nicosia, Cyprus

Dawn broke slowly, the rising sun burning off the thick fog obscuring the horizon and painting the abandoned airport in lavender and golden hues. Earthy petrichor had replaced jet-fuel fumes, nature slowly reclaiming its hold on the artillery-scarred buildings. Strands of tawny grass stretched skyward as they emerged from fractal rifts in the pavement.

Lane parked his Jeep at the base of a hill covered in a cluster of hangars.

"Welcome to the humble headquarters of Baseborn Archaeology Inc.," he said, hopping out of the vehicle. He planted a shoe on a strand of rusty barbed wire so Susara could pass over it. "It isn't much, but it's home." His hair and shirt were still soaked from the spray of the choppy Mediterranean, but he was too enervated to care.

She scoffed. "You incorporated your robbery business?"

"It's Cyprus, baby," he joked, feigning a New York mobster's parlance. "Everybody's got a business around here, and almost every single one is a front for some illegitimate Eastern European enterprise. Mine's probably more aboveboard than most of them."

"Why 'Baseborn', though?" She kicked a small stone in front of her as she strode up the red clay slope leading to the shattered asphalt runway. As Lane joined her, he took a turn, the stone hopping ahead of them as they walked side by side.

"It means ignoble. Contemptible. Plebeian. Seemed fitting given the character of my employees." He pointed a thumb at his chest.

"It's an ill-fitting name. You're not any of those things." She paused, leaning against a rusty post supporting a curled-up length of security fence.

A sleepy look in her eyes, shoulders relaxed, she seemed to have abandoned, if only for the moment, her impatient, rigidly goal-driven bearing. It suited her well, he thought.

"I can't picture you living anywhere but here," she said, cupping a hand over her eyes as she admired the vista.

He ran a hand through his hair, down the back of his neck. "It fits my needs." He gave a small smile. "Wanna see my pad? I'm expecting one of those reality shows to call one of these days, asking for a tour."

They walked a short distance to a nearby hangar, its large door partially ajar.

Inside the cavernous space, an enormous World War II-era bomber rested, its rubber tires flat and aluminum skin covered in a thick layer of dust. Scattered indiscriminately along the walls of the hangar stood stacks of rusty barbells, old safes with their sides cut away, welders, plasma cutters, and clusters of oxyacetylene tanks.

"Looks like your housekeeper's been busy," she said.

"Not to your standards of cleanliness, Sergeant?"

"What? I like things neat."

Nudging an angle grinder out of the way with his foot, he said, "Neat terrifies me."

Approaching a workbench covered in a snarl of electrical wires, she asked, "What's this?" She palmed a small plastic box the size of a tablet computer.

"It *was* an infrared transceiver. Great for copying keyless entry signals. It slipped out of my pocket and fell from a rooftop last year when I was running a job in Macedonia. Never worked quite right after that."

Dumping the device onto the workbench, she turned and stared at him. "You know, we arrested half a dozen guys in the process of robbing the Museum of Macedonia."

"Which reminds me, I've got some apologetic letters to write and a cake to bake with a metal file inside." He sniffed indifferently and approached the airplane. "Say hello to Malvina." Running a hand along a wing's front edge launched a thick cloud of dust into the still air. "When the Turks invaded Cyprus in the '70s, the Cypriots left everything behind—even this old Avro Lancaster bomber. Now, this entire place is a U.N. protected area, a buffer zone between the two countries. Needless to say, I don't get many visitors." Squeezing through a narrow aperture under the craft's glass nose, he grumbled, "She's a little…cozy." He flicked a light switch in the bombardier's quarters before pulling himself into the cockpit.

Following him inside, she stared with wonderment at the cramped interior, illuminated by strand lights running the length of the aircraft. The space smelled faintly of old leather and motor oil. Piles of books had been stuffed in every shooting port and gunner's station. The dim light illuminated a small kitchenette in the navigator's compartment and an army cot piled high with blankets in the fuselage.

Setting about making the bed, he said, "I don't know what food there is in the pantry—uh, bomb bay—or how much of it is edible now since it's been a few weeks since I've been home, but you're welcome to it. I'll get clean sheets on the bed, and you can get a few hours of sleep before we set out for Luxor."

"Aren't you going to rest?"

"There's only one place to sleep." He gestured to the cot as he pulled the sheets taut. "Besides, I've got to get back to the boat and get it fueled up and ready for tomorrow. We have the lead on Agapito, but he's tireless. He'll try to find a way to get the disc from us."

Sliding the pillow into a fresh case, he patted the sheets. "I'll be back in a little while."

As he turned to leave, she grabbed his hand. His eyes moved slowly from her fingertips to her torso, finally settling on her lips.

For a moment, he contemplated pulling her tight to him and falling onto the cot. He envisioned the two of them making love in the dim light, the intimacy of the space amplifying the closeness of their naked bodies as they messed the sheets he'd just changed.

Then, abruptly, he forced the thought from his mind. She was a beautiful woman. Smart, strong, and fearless. Everything he'd loved about Nicole when they'd first met. But he'd seen the other side of that passion, when the pendulum inevitably swung the other direction. It was impossible to forget the shouting, the accusations, and the tears. He'd resolved years ago not to let himself be drawn in by such magnetism again. Besides, even if Susara was different, now was not the time to let his guard down. His focus had to remain on the disc and saving his daughter. He didn't need any distractions, no matter how tempting this one might be.

"Your hand looks like it's already beginning to close up," she said, looking over his wound.

Exhaling slowly, reluctant to let go of the air in his chest, he gave a small nod. "I heal quickly. All this calm, healthy living, you know? Anyway, try to get some rest." Squeezing her hand, he turned, ducking his way into the cockpit before dropping through to the bombardier's quarters. He'd suddenly found the air inside hard to breathe.

THIRTY-FIVE

Washington, D.C.

Reclining in the driver's seat of a gloss-black Cadillac sedan parked on the second floor of a downtown parking garage, Agapito flipped through a copy of *Golf Monthly* he'd found in the glove compartment. He read by the flickering light of the fluorescent bulbs overhead. Clearly, the man to whom this car belonged—now bound, gagged, and bleeding through the upholstery in the vehicle's trunk—was a golf enthusiast. The sport had never appealed to Agapito. Something about the apparent futility of repeatedly striking a miniature target with a stick. Not that it would matter if he had wanted to try the game; Musarde had never let him play sports, deeming them a waste of time, lacking real-world applicability. He wouldn't know where to start.

Glancing out the window, he scanned the structure's elevator well, then checked his watch. Any minute.

One of his men, tasked with reconnaissance in the days leading up to Agapito's arrival in the States, had followed Susara's boyfriend to his work, learning his schedule and relaying that information to Agapito as a possible point of leverage should he need it to get the Minoan tablet back. When recovering the stones had proven such a simple task, he'd dismissed that information as unnecessary.

But following the news that his man in Heraklion had failed to steal the Phaistos Disc, and had been killed in the process by a man Agapito knew could only be Lane Bradley, he'd revisited the information. Doubtless, Lane and his rogue-agent accomplice had stolen the disc to keep him from it.

This didn't worry Agapito. They'd done the hard work for him, and they'd soon hand over the disc in exchange for this young man's life. He didn't know much about Susara Eaves, but Lane was predictably soft. The people's thief. A gentle soul. He would give up the disc to save Susara's boyfriend— that much was certain.

Fortunately, this Noah James took no precautions whatsoever. He never varied his routes to and from work or his time of arrival or departure; walked with his head down, looking at his cellphone; and never checked the back seat of his car before entering. A typical American, blissfully unaware of his surroundings and confident that no one would be hunting him.

As easy a mark as the young man might be, Agapito was taking no more chances. His men had failed him twice already, once in killing Susara and Lane, once in recovering the disc. This time, he'd do the work himself, and do it correctly.

Noah left the elevator two minutes later than his usual departure time. He set out at a leisurely pace, briefcase swinging from a strap on his shoulder, his face anchored to his phone's screen. Approaching his vehicle, parked adjacent to where Agapito sat, Noah rummaged blindly in his suit pocket for his keys. As he unlocked the car and leaned inside to place his briefcase in the back seat, Agapito planted the muzzle of his pistol where Noah's topmost vertebrae met his skull.

"Into the driver's seat. Now."

"You can have my money." Noah raised his hands. "There's an ATM in the skywalk. I'll give you whatever you want."

"I don't want your money. Get in the car and drive to the airport. Try anything heroic, and I'll send a jacketed hollowpoint through the back of your seat and into your pelvic region. Do you plan to have children someday?"

Noah nodded. A whimper escaped his lips, his eyes pleading in his reflection on the glass.

"Get in."

The young man complied, sitting in the driver's seat and planting his hands at 10 and two.

"That's a good boy," Agapito whispered, slipping into the back seat, his pistol held below the window, hidden beneath his golf magazine.

THIRTY-SIX

The Jeep's worn-out suspension groaned and squeaked with every pothole in the narrow, sun-bleached asphalt road leading back to the airport. Lane drove slowly, not to spare the rusty vehicle, but to give himself a little more time to process things alone. Killing Agapito's man the night before had shaken him. Not out of some sense of guilt for defending himself, but because, if the Phaistos Disc's healing powers turned out to be little more than a figment of Pernier's imagination, he'd stopped a man's heart for a piece of old clay. Worse, he'd spent years chasing this legend, assembling the lost pieces of a puzzle he wasn't even sure could be solved. Precious years that could have been spent with Jordan during a time when she'd desperately needed her father.

He braked as a flock of sheep meandered across the road and into the arid hills, stopping to feed on desiccated gray-green brush. Allowing his eyes to follow the cracked vinyl of the dashboard to the window, where the distant Troodos Mountains rose as looming shadows against the horizon, he felt in his pocket for his phone. He tapped the screen. Stared at her number. A minute passed, then five. He stuffed the phone back in his pocket, waited until the sheep had passed, then drove on. He wasn't ready.

Arriving at the airfield, he eased to a stop and shoved the shifter into park. He hoped Susara was still sleeping. It would be hard enough to keep it together when talking to his daughter; he didn't need an audience. He stared at the phone in his lap for a moment. He never knew if calling home would make things better or worse. If Nicole had it her way, he'd never call. Just feign dead and let Jordan forget about him. He'd lost Nicole years before, but he was determined not to lose his daughter. With a deep breath, he dialed the familiar number and listened to the ringback tone, phone tight to his ear.

"Hello?"

"Nicole? It's Lane. Is she awake?"

"It's five in the morning. No, she's not awake yet." Her anger had subsided since they'd last spoken. Now, she only sounded tired.

"Do you think you could wake her up for me? I promise I won't keep her up long." He bit down hard on his lip to keep his voice from quivering. She heard it anyway.

Her voice softened, "Lane, are you OK?"

He pinched his eyes shut and lied. "I'm fine. I'd just really like to talk to Jordan, if I could." Hot tears forged a fresh path down his cheeks. In the background, he could hear Nicole enter Jordan's hospital room and gently close the door behind her, the latch clicking into place.

She whispered, "Lane, you know how much I hate all this, what you do, but I would never want to see you get hurt. Please take care of yourself."

Rummaging through the glove box in search of tissues or napkins, he mumbled, "Thanks. I will."

Nicole said goodbye, then gently roused Jordan. "Honey, it's Daddy on the phone. He really wants to talk to you."

He could hear bedsheets being cast aside as his daughter eagerly sat upright. "Hi Daddy!"

That voice, sleepy but excited, innocent and pure, cut him to the core. He pounded a fist against his thigh to force himself to stop crying. For her. He only had to feign strength for five minutes. He didn't want her to know how badly he was hurting. To hear him at his weakest.

"Hey honey! I'm so sorry to wake you up. I won't keep you long. How are you feeling?"

"I'm good. Where are you?" Such a tough kid, more interested in her dad's travels than in talking about the pain that ruled her life.

"I'm on Cyprus. It's going to be hot here today. I wish you could be here with me. We'd go to the beach and collect seashells. It's a good day for that."

"I'd like that."

"Do you have a big day planned?"

She yawned. "Not really. We were going to walk around the courtyard for a little bit. The last time I got really tired when we did it, so we came back and I napped for most of the day. Maybe today I can stay out longer."

He could picture her frail body gingerly shuffling around the small hospital courtyard, blinking away the sunlight. He should be there, be the one she'd lean against while she walked. Her shade. Her rock.

No napkins in the glove box. He wiped his eyes against his shirt sleeve.

"I'm sorry sweetheart. But those naps are good; sleep is the body's way of fighting back. I want you to fight this with all you've got."

"*Invictus maneo*, right Daddy?"

He smiled. "That's right, sweetheart. Who taught you that, anyway?"

"You did. That's the only one I remember, though. The other ones are harder."

"Let's learn some more together when I get home."

"OK. When are you coming home? I miss you."

Like a dagger to the heart. He winced, resting his forehead against the steering wheel, his chest heaving with silent sobs.

"Daddy?"

Forcing a sharp breath, he whispered, "Soon, honey. Soon. You hang in there until I do, though, OK?"

"I will. Promise."

"Thanks, Sweetheart. I love you."

"Love you too, Daddy."

When he heard the click of the call ending, he lost it. Blinded by tears, he hurled his phone into the windshield. Slammed his palms against the steering wheel until fresh blood soaked through the bandage on his injured hand. Threw his elbows into the seat back and kicked the floorboards. The vehicle shook. Finally, too exhausted to fight anymore, he slumped over and sobbed quietly into his crossed forearms.

THIRTY-SEVEN

The persistent tapping of a seagull hopping along the roof of the Lancaster woke her. Though the hangar remained mostly dark, the narrow strip of sunlight between the door and frame gave Susara the impression it was mid-afternoon. Clutching at her phone to see the time, she sighed and let her head drop back to the pillow.

What was she doing here? She'd only come along on this ridiculous pursuit with the intent to arrest Lane after the robbery of the Phaistos Disc. Well, he had it now. And last night, she'd resolved not to bring him in. So what did that leave? She still didn't believe the legend of the disc, and now she was on the other side of the world, still on probationary leave from NERO, still on the rocks with Noah, only now she had no way to fix any of it.

Everything about this was illogical, yet she stayed. Maybe it was her curiosity that kept her following Lane. Or loyalty. They had gone through a lot together in a short time. Or perhaps it was the sense of danger—or freedom—that came with shedding her responsibilities, for the first time in her life abandoning all the mundane trappings of daily life that weighed her down.

She looked up at a photo taped to the turret gunner's glass bubble overhead, a black and white image of Lane and his daughter dancing in a pile of fall leaves.

Perhaps the reason she stayed went beyond all that.

Slipping on her shoes, she crawled out of Malvina and strolled onto the tarmac, approaching the Jeep. The vehicle was in a sad state of disrepair. It had no tail lights, a single headlight, and no sign of an exhaust system. The hood was the dissonant note—rust-free and vivid white, cannibalized from a newer model.

She found Lane slumped in the driver's seat, face hidden by a grease-smeared ball cap. One hand, resting on his chest, was covered in a clumsy wrap of bandages—crusty and stained carmine. In the other hand, he held the stuffed sparrow Jordan had given him. Susara tapped lightly on the vehicle's door.

"We should probably get going."

Starting awake, he looked around, momentarily unsure of his surroundings. His expression calmed once he'd figured out where he was.

"You sleep OK?" he asked.

"The best I've slept in months." She stretched her slender arms toward the sky and let out a satisfied hum. "I was exhausted."

"It's a good bed." Placing the stuffed animal on the passenger's seat, he ran a hand beneath his hat, through his hair.

Pointing at the bird, she asked, "Your lucky charm, right?"

He poked the toy softly with a finger. "It was Jordan's favorite as a baby. I used to hold it above her crib and pretend it was flying. God, she'd just laugh and laugh. Now, she gives it to me whenever I leave for a job, to remind me of her and for luck. I return it to her as soon as I get home, every time. It's just one of our traditions." He paused, staring at the toy. "Reminds me of a better time. Back when we were all just...authentically happy."

"What happened?" she asked.

He shrugged, staring out the window morosely. "Lots. And at the same time, not enough." His eyes wandered toward his injured hand. Peeling back the bandages to examine the ragged wound, he sighed and gingerly put them back in place. "I'm sorry this has been such an ordeal and there's been so little time to rest. But I can't shake this feeling that I'm racing time here. If something were to happen to Jordan while I was gone, I'd never forgive myself."

She patted his shoulder and smiled reassuringly. "Nothing bad is going to happen. It's easy to see how strong she is. Just like her dad." She unlatched the door and gestured for him to get out. "Come on. We need to get some breakfast and some fresh dressing on that hand."

He tossed his hat into the back seat of the Jeep. Together, they strolled toward the hangar.

"You didn't have to sleep out here last night, you know," she said, trying to sound casual.

"I didn't plan to. I spent most of the morning trying to fix one of the boat motors' drive belts. Must have snapped on our ride over last night. No belt, no charge to the alternator, and no water pump. We're going to have to find a different way to get to Egypt; I'm not limping us into open water with one working motor."

"Can't we get a new belt?" she asked.

He shook his head. "Around here, if it isn't something you can find at a souvenir shop, then no, not in a hurry."

"So what do we do?"

He placed both hands on the hangar door, and with a forceful pull, slid it fully open. Sunlight flooded inside, a gentle rain of dust glittering as it fell. "We go see Yuri."

******

Following a short drive, they rolled to stop outside a weathered, bunker-like concrete warehouse camouflaged by its unremarkable similarity to all the other buildings nearby. Two hirsute men, dripping sweat as they took turns trying to pull-start a chainsaw, stopped in their work and stared at the newcomers.

Lane turned to Susara with a look of consternation. "Don't take this the wrong way, but please let me do the talking when we get inside. Yuri is a little...unstable. He's a product of the Cold War, and still distrusts Westerners. As far as he knows, I'm Iranian. If my accent suddenly seems a little...off, roll with it."

"I understand," she said. "Do I get a cool nom de guerre?"

"Knock yourself out. But it's probably best if you don't get any lines this time. You'll see what I mean in a minute."

Taking a step toward the first of a dozen of the warehouse's loading docks, he stopped and turned to her again. "He may offer you a drink. Politely decline. The last time I agreed to *one* drink before I left, I woke up three days later on a barge headed for Istanbul."

"Noted."

Ascending a short stairway into the building's cramped, subway tunnel-like entryway, the two were met by the earthy aroma of sawdust. Lane leaned over and pressed a button below an intercom on the wall. "Paging Yuri Pedropofich, please come to de front disk," he said, instantly transitioning to a flawless Persian accent—stressing every syllable.

"Eh? Who is it?" A voice crackled in reply.

"Lane Farrokhzad."

"Lane who?" the voice came back.

"It's Lane Bradley. I was just messing with you." His fake accent disappeared and he turned to grin at Susara.

She pulled his hand away from the intercom button. "What happened to him thinking you were Iranian?"

"What? Some Iranians speak English better than others. He's not the most astute assassin I've come across, anyway."

"Assassin?" she hissed. "You failed to mention we were dealing with a contract killer."

"That's a common profession around here. Besides, he's retired," he reassured. "He deals in smuggling illegal timber now."

"Oh, well suddenly I'm entirely at ease, Lane."

An electronic buzzer sounded, and the locks securing the mesh door before them snapped open. Entering the central staging area inside the warehouse—piled high with stacked mahogany, ebony, and Brazilian rosewood—Lane and Susara looked around for Yuri.

"So he illegally exports wood?" she asked, raising an eyebrow. "Hardly seems profitable as far as illegal activity goes. I mean, guns, drugs, prostitutes…lumber?"

"Actually, it's enormously profitable," he corrected, lifting the topmost board from a stack on the floor and sighting down its length. "These are critically endangered species, and you know better than most how much people want things no one else has."

A lumbering bear of a man, coal-colored hair curling down to his shoulders to balance the thick beard bouncing against his sternum, stepped down a steep galvanized stairway, each ponderous footstep making the open steel grating underfoot ring. Spotting Lane, he let a slice of bologna sausage he'd been devouring fall over the railing.

Lane spread his arms wide as though inviting a hug. "Yuri! Long time, old friend. How's the family?"

The big man ignored the gesture, stomping his feet as he came closer.

Lane's shoulders slumped.

Grabbing a handful of Lane's shirt, the big man delivered a thunderous right hook, driving him to the floor.

Reeling from the blow, Lane cried out, "Why?"

Massaging his pie plate-sized mitt, the Russian spat. "You told me you'd send Mother an icon worthy of her *krasny ugol*. It showed up looking like it'd been run over by a truck. After I loaned you my diving boat for your trip to the Black Sea—one you returned with bullet holes up and down the hull—that was the best you could do? A ruined icon?"

Lane shook his head in an attempt to clear his vision. Slowly regaining his feet, he said, "I had no idea the icon showed up damaged. But in my defense, have you seen how much Russian helicopter pilots drink? It's lucky it made it to her at all."

"I'm unclear," Susara said. "You're talking about a religious icon, I'm guessing?"

"A Byzantine copper engraving of the Trinity I picked up outside Istanbul last year." Lane tenderly rubbed his temple, then checked his fingers for blood. "Yuri's mother wanted it for her *krasny ugol*—a kind of corner shrine kept by Russian Orthodox Christians. Yuri here was kind enough to trade the use of his very nice boat in exchange for the icon. As for how the boat got damaged, I came under fire when bandits—"

"Bandits? You mean authorities, don't you?" she interrupted.

Yuri chuckled. "I like her. She's like me—sees right through your storytelling."

"Still, it wasn't my fault the boat got shot up," Lane concluded. "I'm 100 percent certain I was outside Turkish territorial waters when they opened fire."

"I want another icon for Mother," Yuri said plainly.

"It doesn't work like that. I can't just generate artifacts on demand."

The big man crossed his tree-limb arms and swept a finger toward the building's entrance. "Then feel free to let yourselves out."

Lane ruffled his hair and pinched his eyes closed. "Fine. I'll see what I can do. I'll try to find her the biggest, best damn icon ever crafted by the hand of man. But I need your help, first."

The Russian rolled his eyes and began walking away.

"It's not much!" Lane shouted after him. "We just need a ride to Port Said. That's all."

"Take a water taxi."

"We kinda need to do it under official radar. No passports. We've got a guy hunting for us right now who has a way with easily persuaded government officials, and we want to throw him off the trail. We came to you because you have a reputation for being one of the best for this sort of thing," Lane carefully maneuvered, trying to stroke the big man's ego without coming across as spurious.

The big man puffed up, looking from Susara to Lane and back again. "One of the best? I am the best. Smuggling two people into Port Said? Child's play. The Egyptian authorities are a joke. I can have you there by nightfall." He leaned in toward Lane, balling his calloused fingers into a fist the size of a grapefruit, and growled, "And in return, you'll get me *two* icons for Mother."

THIRTY-EIGHT

Off the coast of Egypt

Yuri's container ship, as long as a football field and piled high with Conex containers, trundled along the Egyptian coastline heading toward Port Said. Although Susara had reservations about being left alone in the ship's bridge with the swarthy Russian assassin-turned-smuggler, Lane had assured her he was perfectly trustworthy.

As far as hardened criminals went.

Below them, Lane—shirtless and dripping sweat in the heat of the midday sun—did wind sprints in the open passages between freight containers. Susara divided her time between watching him during his workout and staring at the distant shoreline, so unmoving it seemed as though their ship had made no forward progress in hours.

"How well do you know him?" Yuri asked abruptly, breaking the rhythmic clicking of his chewing. He dexterously wrangled another pickled mushroom from the jar and popped it into his mouth.

"As well as one can get to know someone in a week." Her toes curled inside her shoes at the strong smell of vinegar. Reaching overhead, she adjusted a small fan—the only thing keeping the cabin bearably cool—angling it so it would keep the smell at bay.

"You a lover, then?"

"Not that it's any of your business, but no. We're...business partners."

"I suppose you're an Iranian too, eh?" He glanced at her and gave a knowing chuckle. "As I said before, I see through his storytelling. Everything about him screams American."

She felt her stomach tighten. If Yuri knew Lane was American, and hated Westerners, did he have something insidious planned for them when they reached port? Would they even make it that far?

He wiped a dribble of juice from his beard with the back of his hand. "I'm guessing his parents were Iranian? Farsi isn't typically taught in American schools."

Eyes locked on the big man, waiting for him to make a move, she said, "Mother."

He nodded, but continued to stare straight ahead impassively. He toyed with the chrome captain's wheel, sliding a finger around its polished surface without moving it.

"So you know Lane's an American. He said you don't...care for Westerners." She shifted her weight toward the door. But what would they do if they had to escape? They were trapped aboard a ship in the middle of the Mediterranean, after all.

He rolled his eyes. "Of course, big scary Yuri, just because he worked for his country's Federal Security Service a lifetime ago, must hate Americans." He made a sound like a deflating balloon with his lips. "Westerners buy 90 percent of my product."

"You worked for the FSB?"

"Worked. Past tense. I left that life behind." He absently rubbed his pinky finger against a white scar bisecting his left eyebrow. An old injury, but one that apparently still made itself known. "I may not look cute and cuddly, but I'm not a bad man. As if someone with a history like Lane's could judge my character."

She let her guard down somewhat. "What do you mean?"

With a grunt, he slapped the lid back on the jar of mushrooms. "Just be careful with him. He's always so cheerful and self-assured, but there's a side of him you don't know. I've seen it. There is a ruthless man beneath that calm mask. He'll do anything to get what he wants. Anything."

She looked out the window at Lane as he paused, hands on his hips, broad chest rising and falling with each breath. He leapt up, grabbing the edge of a container, and churned through a series of rapid pull-ups. Though he'd added an extra layer of fabric to the bandage covering his wounded hand before he'd begun, he still appeared to be favoring his uninjured side during the exercise. On the final repetition, he heaved himself up to stand on the Conex, then resumed his sprints—this time leaping over the open spaces between the containers. He wore a smile the entire time, like a winded dog still eager to chase the Frisbee.

"There's a little of that in each of us, isn't there?" she asked, glancing at Yuri.

"Not like him." Gently placing a meaty hand on her shoulder, he leaned in and whispered as though passing a secret. His breath was warm and acetose. "I once dropped him off in Alexandria during the coup to remove President Morsi. The country was in chaos, the army raiding Muslim Brotherhood camps, the Brotherhood burning down churches and police stations, that sort of thing. That's the kind of place where Lane works. So I dropped him off, and I stayed offshore to pick him up again when he'd finished. I listened to the police reports on the scanner as they were happening. There was a firefight at a museum. A white man killed half a dozen guards and as many protesters who got between him and some mask."

"The death mask of Shoshenq the Third," she said, feeling a tightness in her throat as she recalled the artifact recovered from the raid on Poldi's castle.

"So you've heard about this?"

"No. Well, yes, but how can you be sure it was Lane the police were talking about?"

He looked confused, as if unable to comprehend why she would doubt his story. "How many white men do you suppose go lurking around Middle Eastern museums during riots? Tell me you haven't seen glimmers of violence in him. I'm just saying, Susara, be careful. Please." His voice was grave, his expression sincere.

"Don't you trust anyone, Yuri?"

He looked away and wiped a hand over his mouth, then drew his fingers through his beard. "When you spend 20 years working for an intelligence agency as ruthless as the FSB, you learn the importance of being distrustful."

The big man turned his attention back to the wheel as Lane climbed the steel stairs to the bridge, wiping the sweat from his face with his balled shirt. In his other hand swung the backpack with the Phaistos Disc inside. He hadn't let it out of his sight since he'd taken it from Heraklion, carrying it around like a child with a security blanket.

"There's a boat approaching on the port side," Lane said, still breathing hard from the workout. His smile had vanished. "Looks like port authority. You wouldn't know anything about that, would you? Huh, Yuri?" Hurling his shirt at the big man, he stepped forward, chest out, hands tightened into fists. Susara stepped between the two men.

"I get that you were upset about your boat and your mother's icon, but this? I trusted you," Lane said.

Yuri kicked his shirt away. "It's probably just a random check. Perhaps you shouldn't be so quick to accuse your friends."

Fuming, Lane scowled and aimed a finger at the rapidly approaching boat raking a white trail across the surf. "I don't like coincidences, Yuri."

The big man nodded, following with his eyes the craft's bounding path as it moved to intercept them. "Neither do I. Get to the deck and get inside one of the containers. I'll do the talking."

Lane and Susara complied, Yuri following behind. The Russian tossed a case of bottled water inside and slammed the door behind them. The steel box was a black oven, the heat stifling and the air hard to breathe—thick with sawdust.

"I really hope I'm wrong about him," Lane whispered, tearing two plastic bottles from their binding and handing her one. The water was boiling hot. "You just never know in this business. I've had people I trusted betray me more times than I'd like to admit."

She cleared her throat nervously, glad it was too dark for him to see her cheeks flush. "Lane, tell me about the death mask of Shoshenq the Third. How you got it out of the Museum of Egyptian Antiquities."

"What do you want to know?" he asked, his tone insouciant.

She decided to take the direct approach. "People died there. They blamed a white man for murdering the security guards and some bystanders."

"I wouldn't know. I'm more palomino-beige than white. They must have been talking about some other guy." He said it as one would a joke, but there was no humor in his voice.

She sensed his reluctance to talk about it, which only made her want to press the issue harder. He was hiding something. To a seasoned interrogator like Susara, it was blood in the water. "Lane, to any Egyptian, you're white."

"So you think they were referring to me." A statement, not a question.

"I don't know. When we were in Washington, I would have said you couldn't possibly be a killer. But the way you handled that other thief in Heraklion? You were so cool about it, so unshaken."

A pause.

"I've done things in my life I'm not proud of, but I'm not going to apologize for surviving when I've been forced to fight for my life," he said.

"Were you the man they were talking about in Cairo?" Although she already knew the answer, she wanted to hear him say it. To admit he'd killed for the mask. To mercifully dash the fragile hope she had for him.

"Probably. But I didn't kill those people."

He shuffled, and she heard him wince as the bare skin of his shoulder touched the blistering container wall.

"Things were completely out of control by the time I reached Cairo," he explained. "I snuck into the museum, which wasn't hard. There were plenty of distractions for the security guards to worry about—those who hadn't abandoned the museum already. I got inside just as a mob of teenagers pushed through the entrance. They started smashing and burning anything they could get their hands on."

She heard him unscrew his water bottle's cap, but he continued without taking a drink.

"One of the security guards lost his cool and opened fire on the kids. They got ahold of him and beat him to death. It was just a mess, so I grabbed the mask and got the hell out of there. I'm not surprised someone saw me leaving and assumed I'd done it."

The right words wouldn't come when she tried to think of a response. Maybe she should say something about her being sorry for mistrusting him, or feeling sympathy for those who had died. Before she'd whispered a word, he began again, his voice building to an emotional crescendo.

"I made it down the block around the time the building started burning. There was nothing I could do but sit down and watch it smolder. And the rest of the world watched, too. They stood by and admired it like a neighbor's bonfire—from behind the glass, in the comfort of their homes. And they only said, 'Wow, that's one hell of a flame. Smell that smoke, son? That's the sweet, sweet bouquet of our species' history being annihilated.' Lost forever to ignorance and violence."

Ignorance and violence. The same forces that took her father those years ago.

A muted voice broke the silence that followed.

"You don't mind if we have a glance at your cargo, do you, Mister...Petropovich?" asked one of the port inspectors. Their boots made a dull *clunk, clunk* on the deck as they neared, the men no doubt weighed down by body armor and rifles.

Susara tensed, her hand grasping for Lane's in the darkness. She tipped over one of the water bottles, instead. As it rolled across the floor, an inspector asked, "What was that?"

THIRTY-NINE

The port inspector gripped the lift handle on their container and pulled. Steel scraped loudly against steel as the door slowly opened, the shrieking cry of the metal embodying the panic felt by those inside. A razor's edge of sunlight shot through the dark.

Yuri hurriedly explained. "Typical poor packing by the monkeys in my warehouse."

Even without seeing him, they could sense Yuri's fake smile as he spoke. "Laborers. Dumb bastards expect to be paid like doctors but can't be troubled to stack boards with any care. You know how it is. I appreciate your concern, but I don't want you to have to waste your afternoon in this hot sun just to check my goods. Would you honor me by letting me buy you and your men something to drink, inspector?"

"I appreciate your thoughtfulness," the Egyptian official laughed. Yuri must have slipped him a wad of cash. "Yes, it is rather hot out. Perhaps we'll go get that drink now."

As the clank of the officer's boots on the steel deck grew distant, Lane let go of a long breath and whispered, "You feel that?"

"Feel what?"

"The last layer of the skin on our teeth being shaved off. You were *this* close to learning the subtleties of the Egyptian prison system's dietary regimen. Let me tell you, it's not what the brochure promises."

"I meant to ask you about that when I had you in interrogation back in Germany." Legs aching, she stood up and tried to orient herself in the darkness. "How'd you end up in an Egyptian prison? We had no record of that."

He wiped a hand along his arm to clear the layer of sweat beading on his skin. "You remember that job at the archaeological museum in Mallawi you were so impressed by? Well a few pieces didn't make it on the trucks, and not wanting to spoil a perfect heist by leaving anything behind, I threw them in the trunk of my rental car. A guy takes one wrong turn and ends up at a police checkpoint. That's my luck. Well, anyway, I managed to convince them I was an archaeologist operating without a concession and had just dug those artifacts up. They fined me and stuck me in prison for a week. Fortunately, they never put two and two together between me and the museum theft."

Equal parts skill and luck. No wonder he'd eluded authorities for so long. "You're impossibly lucky, you know," she said.

He laughed. "Luck? No. I owe it all to my charm and good looks. I'm not too proud to admit it."

Half an hour later, the doors to the container swung open and Yuri stuffed his head inside. "It's dark enough now to get ashore without being seen."

As Lane and Susara stepped onto the ship's deck, they turned to each other, squinting even in the low light, and laughed. They looked as though they'd been inside a sauna, their skin and clothes soaked with sweat.

"Hey Yuri, thanks for your help." Fishing into his pocket, Lane withdrew a wad of cash and stuffed it into the Russian's hand to cover the port inspector's bribe. Contrite, he said, "You were right. I shouldn't be so quick to accuse my friends."

Handing Lane his shirt, Yuri smiled, then delivered a genial slap on his bare back. Grimacing as he stared at his hand, now covered in sweat, Yuri wiped his palm on his pants. "And don't forget—"

"How could I forget about Momma Petropovich? A new icon. Got it."

"Make it two," Yuri corrected with a smirk, nodding toward the cargo lift in the rear of the ship and the rigid-hulled inflatable boat used for going ashore.

By the time Yuri had delivered the two Americans to the docks, the sun had set on the streets of Port Said. Though the temperature of the night air lingered above 90 degrees, compared to the sweltering heat of the shipping container, it felt invigorating. Overhead, a pair of motionless ship-to-shore cranes towered like skeletal colossi over docks lined with old rubber tires, swarmed by thousands of watercraft—humble dinghies and ponderous merchant vessels alike. The streets hummed with life despite the late hour, bathed in the yellow glow from headlights and streetlamps, filled with the rhythmic tapping of tambourines and the droning buzz of men playing traditional stringed *rebabs*. Across the Suez Canal, the parallel spires of Port Fouad Grand Mosque pierced the sky with radiant white light, diffused by the clouds and glinting on the lapping waves.

"Let's find ourselves a ride." Approaching a dark alleyway between a convenience store and a stall packed with wire racks of belts, sandals, and sunglasses, Lane began looking for an unlocked car or minibus. Nearby, a pair of disheveled men rooted through an overflowing garbage bin, stuffing rotted fruit and bits of moldy bread into a plastic bag. Coptic Christian pig farmers looking for cheap feed for their livestock.

"So where do you think the Heraklion job will rank on your list of heists?" Susara asked. "I know it didn't go as planned, but you still got what you were after and without leaving any evidence you were involved."

Without turning to look back at her, he scoffed. "Not even top 10. That was about as close to true catastrophe as I've come on any job." Picking up a loose brick from the sidewalk, he glanced at a nearby pickup truck's passenger window, then back at the brick in his hand before reconsidering and letting it drop. "You may not believe this, but my skills aren't really in the actual theft. That plays a part, but social engineering is everything. I happen to be very good at what I do because I can read people very well."

"Prove it."

He glanced around before his eyes settled on a man inside a nearby restaurant, seated beside a street-side window. "OK, take a look at that guy in the corner booth. What if I told you I know exactly who he is and what he's doing there?"

"I'd say you're full of it."

He chuckled. "First, tell me what you notice about him."

"He looks kinda dirty, so I'd guess he's poor or works a manual labor job."

"OK, that's a good start. What else?"

She considered the man for a moment. "Well, he looks like he's nervous. Waiting for someone or something. He's tapping his finger on the table and he keeps looking over the bar at the clock."

A playful smile crossed his lips. "Is that all you've got?"

"Let's have your little theory, then."

He rubbed his hands together. "OK, you said he's a laborer. I agree. But this restaurant isn't where the locals go to get a drink after work and unwind. It's a high-end place tailored to tourists coming in off the cruise liners in the harbor, and it's smack dab in the middle of a hotel district. He's uncomfortable with that, but he's also uncomfortable because he's meeting someone to do something naughty."

"Oh really?" She smiled and crossed her arms.

"His hands. You said he's dirty, but just look at him. He washed up for this meeting. He's wearing a button-down shirt and he's combed his hair. His hands aren't dirty, they're stained. What could leave a stain like that?"

Her eyes narrowed and her voice lost its joviality. "OK, I'm intrigued. What would stain his hands?"

"Let me see your phone."

"Hey, that's cheating. If you want me to believe you're really *so good* at this, prove it without looking stuff up."

"I'm not going to look anything up. I'm just trying to make a point."

She complied.

He flipped the phone over in his hands before handing it back. "That looks like a new model. Very streamlined and small for how powerful it is, right?" he asked.

"OK, yeah."

"Part of what frees up space for better processors and cuts down on bulk is what's called a tantalum electrolytic capacitor. Tantalum has excellent capacitance for its mass, so capacitors manufactured with it can be made very small without sacrificing how much electricity they'll hold. Illegal mining and exportation of tantalum in Congo has been compared to the blood diamond trade in terms of the number of people killed and the hunger of the modern world for the stuff. Egypt has one of the largest tantalum reserves on the planet. I'd bet you anything that man works in a tantalum mine."

"That explains the stained hands, but who's he here to meet? And why?"

He waited a moment for her to think of it herself.

"You're thinking he's either selling insider secrets on the mine or he has plans to sell smuggled tantalum to a foreign national. Hence the restaurant."

He snapped his fingers. "Not bad, right? Now, if I wanted to manipulate that man, I'd pretend to be someone from a regulatory body or law enforcement who was on to him and his scheme. I'd blackmail him into complying with my needs. He'd go away relieved that he got off the hook without prison time, and I'd get exactly the information I needed without being forced to abduct him and interrogate him in the back of a soundproofed box truck."

"Harsh."

"Exactly. I think my way's much kinder. And less messy."

An urgent vibration tickled her leg from inside her pocket. Out of habit, she answered her phone directly without looking at the caller.

"Eaves."

"Susara, it's Noah."

Glancing at Lane and pulling the phone tight to her shoulder, she cleared her throat. "Lane, I need to take this."

Nodding, he walked to the end of the alleyway to give her privacy, humming to himself as he casually tugged on car door handles.

"Hi," she said, running her fingers through her hair. "I didn't expect to hear from you."

"I'm in trouble," Noah said bluntly.

"What kind of trouble?"

There was scuffling at the other end of the line, and another voice—a deep, intense one—came on. "Agent Eaves?"

"Who's this?"

"My name is Agapito Vicente. I believe we met in passing in Venezuela and in Washington."

His words gripped her stomach and twisted. "You brazen son of a—"

Agapito clicked his tongue, interrupting. "Let's keep this civil. I have something you want, and you know you have something of mine. When my contractor didn't check in yesterday, I suspected something had gone awry. The police are reporting several dead bodies were discovered in the Heraklion Archaeological Museum. I can only assume that's the handiwork of our mutual acquaintance, Lane Bradley. You should be more careful with the friends you make, Agent Eaves. He's not who he pretends to be."

"Let Noah go," she said, chewing her fingernail anxiously as she walked in a tight circle.

"When you bring me the Phaistos Disc, I'll release him into your care. But I'd caution you not to keep me waiting long. For every hour that passes, I intend to take one of his fingers. We're at Heraklion International Airport, in a private hangar."

She struggled to recall the one class she'd taken at the academy on hostage negotiation. Only one point came to mind: Make the hostage-taker work for everything by demanding a concession in return. Never give anything without getting something back.

"It would take us hours to get there. You come to us. You can begin the timer on Noah's fingers as soon as you arrive in Port Said. That's a fair compromise," she said, fighting to keep her voice steady.

Agapito paused, contemplating the counteroffer. "All right. Port Said. We'll select the meeting location. Standby for my phone call." He hung up.

"We good to go?" Lane asked, returning to her side. Noticing her perturbed expression, he asked, "Everything OK?"

Pretending to be interested in one of the leather purses on display, she clasped and unclasped the buckle. "That was Noah—you know, my ex. He's, um, well he's wanting to talk, and I don't want to hold you up."

"It's not a problem," he said. "I'll wait. After all, the temple's been waiting to be found for 3,000 years. What's another hour?" He hadn't meant a word, she could tell. It physically pained him to have to wait, especially now that he had all the puzzle pieces and was so close to the temple.

She knew she should just tell him the truth. But from everything she'd seen, and knowing Lane's and Agapito's history, there was more to the assassin's demands. He wanted the Phaistos Disc, but if Lane came along, there could be no doubt that Agapito would kill him. She wasn't willing to trade Noah's life for Lane's. She'd rescue Noah herself.

"Well, actually, I…." Though she worked frantically to come up with a believable excuse for staying behind to rescue Noah, she was too distracted. "I just need a little time alone. Just a few hours. You go ahead. We'll meet up later."

He looked as though he'd just heard an off-color joke at a funeral. "Susara, we're *this* close to uncovering one of history's most coveted secrets. And you're bailing now? This isn't about the whole Museum of Egyptian Antiquities thing, is it? I told you the truth."

"No. It's nothing you did, I promise. I just need to work this out, that's all." She could tell he didn't buy it, but she also knew she'd left him with no other choice than to go on without her. He'd waited years to get to this point, and nothing, especially her boyfriend problems, were going to stop him from seeing it through.

"All right. If that's what you need. Just take the train to Luxor and give me a call when you get there," he said. "And be careful. The culture's a little different here, especially regarding single women, dressed like you are, alone at night."

"I've been here before," she replied. "Don't worry. I've got it handled."

"Good. I'd hate to have to negotiate with your new husband for your freedom. You look like you'd be an expensive purchase. You have such lovely teeth."

"Very funny."

His expression became serious. "Good luck with all this, Susara. I hope it works out for you." He offered her his hand, and she shook it.

"Likewise, Lane. I hope you find what you're looking for."

He approached a dirt bike anchored to an alley wall by a chain wrapped around one of its wheel spokes. Watching the reactions of a pair of old men playing backgammon in a cafe across the street, he casually broke the spoke free with a strike from the heel of his shoe. Wheeling the bike into the street, he pulled the clutch to the left handlebar and jumped on the kickstarter. Smiling at her once more, he revved the engine and accelerated away in a cloud of blue two-stroke exhaust, gunning for Luxor along the arrow-straight Al Ismaileya frontage road following the Suez Canal.

He had no more than disappeared from sight when her phone rang again.

"Change of plans, Agent Eaves. Forget Port Said. You'll meet us on the easternmost edge of Lake Bardawil. There's a 12th century fortress there—the only one for miles. We'll be arriving tomorrow morning at eight o'clock. Noah sends his regards. Just a reminder: Try anything clever and I'll butcher him."

FORTY

Luxor, Egypt

The shores of the Nile stirred with life. A string of cormorants passed overhead, flying low between towering palm trees. Shirtless men slipped into the water up to their waists, clearing brush, flotsam, and garbage from irrigation ditches, their soft murmurs echoing across the surface. An outboard motor grumbled from somewhere downriver.

A tourist might have found the star-lit Egyptian sky and the soothing wash of the Nile commandingly beautiful, but Lane took no notice. Flipping through his notes in the back of Pernier's journal, he strained his eyes to see the ink by the dim morning light. Before him stood the statues of Ramesses II and the granite obelisk guarding Luxor Temple's towering pylon. Originally, there had been two obelisks here. He'd seen the shorter one while in Paris years before. It had been taken from

Egypt and reassembled in France in the early 1800s. They'd managed to turn a once-impressive piece of historical architecture into an incongruous eyesore standing awkwardly at the center of *Place de la Concorde*.

After hours spent scouring the temple complex, he still hadn't found a royal seal that matched what he was hunting for. Early-rising tourists watched him as though he were a zoo animal on display. They pointed at him, whispering about the crazed man talking to himself as he crawled on hands and knees in the temple's dark recesses, searching frantically for the faintest sigil or inscription indicating a connection to the Phaistos Disc or the Minoans. Doubts about his research began to creep in. Maybe this wasn't the correct spot after all. The translation was vague to begin with, and they'd been in a hurry to decipher the inscription. Any minor error they may have introduced had the potential to steer them completely off course, potentially hundreds or thousands of miles from where the second temple actually stood.

Lane slammed the journal shut and shoved it in his pocket. He just couldn't believe this wasn't the place. The temple complex fit the timeframe, the geography, and was even referred to by the Egyptians as *ipet resyt*—the southern sanctuary. Sanctuary. *This disc will guide the deserving to salvation*. Everything about it was correct, and yet there wasn't the faintest indication of Minoan script or symbols anywhere.

Nearby, a museum guard waved off a *gali-gali* street magician who had been pestering a few of the temple's early visitors with his routine—manipulating an armful of Chinese linking rings. Lane's eyes followed the rows of human-headed stone sphinxes fringing the avenue leading away from the temple toward Karnak. He cursed himself for not investing more time deciphering the disc and determining other potential temple sites.

If the second temple wasn't here, where was it? The Egyptians during the Middle Kingdom had constructed major cities hundreds of miles to the north and south of Thebes, many of them prominent sites with great political and religious significance. Heliopolis? Memphis? Edfu? A man could spend a dozen lifetimes searching up and down the Nile and getting nowhere.

Sighing, he removed his glasses and shoved them in a pocket. His ass still hurt from the 10-hour ride to Luxor, ears ringing from the persistent whine of the motorcycle's motor.

He'd wanted to avoid what came next, but it was looking like he would need to rely on some local help to find the second temple. He returned to his bike, handlebars pinching a palm tree's trunk against the motorcycle's gas tank. Firing it up, he accelerated along the riverfront, turning into the dusty, crumbling stone thoroughfares of Luxor. He rolled through narrow streets overshadowed by derelict apartment complexes and gold-domed mosques. Men with features obscured by shadow watched him distrustfully from alleyways and balconies.

He was unwelcome here. But if anyone knew the ruins in the area, it was Chigaru—southern Egypt's premier antiquities dealer. Finding him would be easy. Surviving contact with him might prove more difficult. The man had developed a reputation, even among thieves, as untrustworthy. Dealing with him was a risk: He was knowledgeable, and had eked out a considerable fiefdom of antiquities dealing in the country, but he never played fair, never negotiated, and had a history of killing those he felt hadn't paid him adequate respect—

which happened more often than not given the man's fragile ego and temper. Rumor had it Chigaru had once ruptured an exporter's testicle for pointing out a scratch on his Mercedes— the same car Chigaru rolled into an irrigation ditch a week later while high on heroin.

Pulling in the clutch, Lane downshifted, letting the bike coast to a stop at the end of a meandering alleyway. A haze of smoke from a poorly ventilated fire blended with that from the mouths of a half-dozen men encircling a *hookah* pipe nearby. One of the men sat in a dry concrete fountain, leg dangling carelessly over an edge. A woman watched him from a rooftop as she flogged the dust from a rug with a crude wooden carpet beater.

His phone buzzed in his pocket, and he eagerly looked to see if it was Susara. He could use her expertise about now—or even some friendly reassurance—and he was concerned with her sudden change in demeanor and her request to stay behind. Something wasn't right. Either she was in trouble, or she had reconsidered working with him and was working an angle to bring him in. He didn't want to think it was the latter.

"So there I am, just enjoying my morning cup of coffee at this adorable little cafe on the east side of Lichtenberg, when what do I see on the television?"

He smiled at his lawyer's comforting Southern drawl.

Dorothy continued, "Some museum in Crete was broken into last night, and an ancient Greek disc was stolen. But more importantly, they found a dead body where that disc should have been. Now, because you picked up the phone, I'll assume it wasn't you, which comes as no small relief to me, you should know."

"I'm fine. I met that guy briefly, though."

The men seated before Lane spoke softly as they smoked, watching him curiously.

She sighed. "First, you need to call me more often so I don't learn about these things over the television. Second, honey, when are you going to give this up? You're smart enough to get a job working at any museum or teaching at any university you'd like. Why keep risking your life?"

"You know why." A stray cat rubbed against his ankle, purring softly, a cloud of fleas radiating from its body. He shooed it away and wiped at his pant leg.

"That NERO agency still giving you trouble?"

"Not much." He paused, then said, "I'm actually working with the agent who arrested me on a private case."

He could picture Dorothy rolling her eyes on the other end of the line.

"What am I going to do with you? It's as though you're trying to find every possible way to get yourself into trouble. I've never had so many bizarre, challenging court cases as I have when you're the defendant."

"She's trustworthy."

"Ah, so it's a she." He could hear the smile forming as she said it. "That's telling."

"It's nothing like that. This is strictly business."

She cooed. "Oh, sweet thing, it's never just business. You're wiser than to think that. Just don't be blinded by a pair of pretty blue eyes."

"Green, but point taken."

"You must have spent some time staring into her eyes to know that," she teased. "I'm just saying, if she arrested you once, she'll set you up to do it again. As charming as you are, people don't change that dramatically. Don't trust her."

"I'll keep that in mind."

"Where are you now?"

Tapping a finger on the cracked glass face of the motorcycle's gas gauge, he watched the needle hop around E. "You sure you want to know?"

"Just give me a little hint so I know which region of the international news to follow," she said.

"Think camels, mummies, and bad sanitation."

A telephone rang in the background, and she spoke quickly. "If, hypothetically, you took that Greek disc they're looking for, what possible reason would you have for traveling to your current location—which shall remain undisclosed over an unsecured phone line?"

He opened his mouth to speak, but paused. Her question had struck a chord. They'd assumed from the beginning that the Phaistos Disc was pointing them to Egypt given the hieroglyphs on the cipher stones. But what if the hieroglyphs were meant only as a way to safeguard the Minoan language, and had nothing to do with the inscription on the disc? Then the second temple would likely have been located somewhere within the Minoan kingdom. He was in the wrong goddamn country.

"I've gotta go. I'll call you as soon as I get back."

"Just stay alive," she pleaded. "I can always get you out of prison, but I don't make morgue visits."

"I'm doing my best. You take care, too." Tapping the screen to end the call, he shuffled the phone into his pocket just as a mighty force wrenched him from his bike and pitched him violently into the side of an overflowing dumpster.

FORTY-ONE

A towering behemoth, draped in a billowing, cream-colored *gellabiya* and without one intact tooth in his mouth, grinned at Lane.

"Your boss around?" Lane asked in Arabic, making no attempt to stand.

The man kicked over the motorcycle, then raised his fists and banged them against his colossal chest like a gorilla.

"I see," Lane said, returning to English. "You must be Chigaru's receptionist."

The man smiled again, wide enough to reveal his bare gums, as he dropped into a fighter's stance.

Shuffling off his backpack and clambering to his feet, Lane sized up his opponent. The man would probably rely on his superior size to take him to the ground, and once he got him there, the fight would be over. No amount of hand-to-hand combatives training could offset a one 100-pound weight advantage. Speed and elusiveness would be his only edge.

Waiting until Lane had assumed a stance mirroring his own, the Egyptian attacked, leading with a front kick that would have snapped the smaller man's leg in two if he'd waited for it to connect. Dodging the strike, Lane wrapped an arm around his attacker's leg and pulled it tight to his side. Slamming his palm against the outside of the giant's kneecap, he then attempted a leg sweep. He might as well have kicked a tree trunk. The big man recovered his balance using the alley's wall, then drove an elbow into Lane's cheek.

Darkness blotted his vision. The metallic taste of blood filled his mouth. Stumbling, he tried to right himself before his attacker could reach him again.

The pounding of the earth signaled the big man's approach for another strike. Slipping to his left, Lane felt the wind from a fist passing near his face. Planting a foot on the Egyptian's thigh, he heaved himself upward, swinging onto the man's back. In one fluid motion, he slipped a leg over his opponent's left shoulder, wrapped his arms around the Egyptian's right armpit, and pitched his body forward—rolling as his weight pulled the big man to the ground. They crashed to the brick street together, but Lane now had the man in a secure arm-bar—the limb trapped between Lane's arms and chest, his legs wrapped around his adversary's trunk for leverage.

In a civilized match, the fight would have been over. But this wasn't civilized, and although he had tried not to end up on the ground, there he was. Surrounded by enemy combatants. Vulnerable. He'd have to dislodge his opponent's arm from its socket in hopes of disabling him, and then regain his feet before the others got close enough to engage. The smokers nearby had already stood and were beginning to make their way over to him. He couldn't stay here. Just as he began to thrust his hips upward, the big man crying out as muscle separated from bone, Lane heard a shrill, high-pitched voice.

"I see you still know your way around a street barrier, Mr. Lane."

Standing barely five feet tall and wearing a cartoonish eye patch, Chigaru stroked the wrapped leather of the bullwhip at his belt. His dark skin blistered with acne, further adding to the image of an ungainly teenager playing dress-up.

"Brawl," Lane grunted, not relinquishing control of the big man's arm.

"What?"

"You meant brawl, not barrier. Although your version is pretty fitting for this guy. Where'd you find him, anyway? A livestock auction?"

Chigaru nodded slowly, mouth open in a confused half smile. "Care to come inside?" he asked, gesturing toward a nearby bicycle-repair shop. "We just got satellite television." His tone was deceivingly anodyne. Lane knew better.

"You going to tell your boys to stay civil?"

The small man tittered. "You're funny, Mr. Lane. Let him go and I'll get you a drink."

Freeing his assailant's arm, Lane stood and collected his bag. Following Chigaru inside, he exchanged hostile looks with his wounded opponent as the giant rose slowly from the dirt, cradling his injured arm. Clenching his injured hand, Lane tried to calm his heart rate. The wound from the museum assassin's garrote had reopened during the scuffle. Blood trickled to his fingertips, dripping onto the dusty street.

At this point, he didn't even want to go through with the meeting, particularly after his conversation with Dorothy. The more he thought about it, the more he believed he'd been wrong about the second temple's location from the beginning. But he'd rung the doorbell, so to speak, and now he had to come up with a valid reason why. And quickly.

They entered a cramped room illuminated by only a single bare bulb swaying on a frayed wire, and a small flat-screen television in the corner playing a rerun of *Tom and Jerry*. Bicycle tires, chains, and frames lined the walls, all of them caked in a thick layer of dust. The shop hadn't been used legitimately for years.

Chigaru gestured for Lane to sit across from him at the table. The stale air reeked of tobacco smoke and onions. Steam jetted from the mouth of a teapot as Chigaru filled two glasses with *Saïidi* tea, moving one across the table to Lane before sitting down. The tea, in keeping with Chigaru's demeanor, was a deceptively accommodating gesture. "Why are you here, Mr. Lane? We haven't spoken in some time. I thought you'd been arrested or killed. When people go quiet in our business, it usually means they've met an unpunctual end."

"Unpleasant," Lane corrected under his breath.

"Yes, very," Chigaru agreed, nudging his cup of tea with his thumbnail.

"I just came by to see if you could move a few antiquities for me," Lane lied. "Nothing huge, but they're hot, and with the scrutiny I've been under lately, I need a little help getting them to a buyer." Touching the glass before him, he drew his hand back and rubbed the pads of his fingers together where they'd been burned. The Egyptians, shop owners especially, always poured their tea boiling hot. That way, you were forced to stay put until the tea became cool enough to drink, giving them more time for their sales pitch.

"That seems unlikely, Mr. Lane. I've never known you to depend on someone else to move your products. Too much risk."

Lane contemplated accepting the burned fingers and tongue and downing the tea anyway. "Times have changed."

"But people don't." Leaning back in his seat, Chigaru crossed a leg, angling his foot toward him.

To those less worldly, such a gesture would seem perfectly meaningless. And in another region, it might have been. But in the Arab world, showing the sole of one's shoe was a significant insult. The bottom of the foot—being the lowest part of the body and considered unclean—when pointed at someone, implied they were beneath the shoe. Dirt. Chigaru was doing it partially for his own amusement, and partially to test Lane's patience and perception.

Before Lane could rebuke him, one of Chigaru's men entered, eyes submissively adhered to the floor as he slipped behind his boss and discreetly placed a slip of paper in his lap. The man whispered in his ear, and then retreated to the shadows.

Chigaru waited for his man to leave the room, then lifted his eyepatch to reveal a perfectly intact, functioning eye. He began reading the note in his lap. His expression darkened. Pushing away his tea, he drummed his fingers atop the table. "So, the Phaistos Disc has been taken from Heraklion. There are only a few thieves in the world veracious enough to try a heist like that, and fewer still able to pull it off."

Lane swallowed hard. "Audacious."

"What?"

"You said veracious. Means truthful. I think you meant audacious—you know, fearless. Intrepid."

Raising his voice, Chigaru stabbed a finger in Lane's direction. "You have that disc, don't you?" Leaping to his feet, chair crashing to the floor, he drew the bullwhip from his side. "Give it to me, and I'll let you live."

"I don't know what you're talking about. I don't have the disc." Lane used his foot to scoot his backpack closer to him beneath the table.

With a flourish, Chigaru cracked his whip loudly, the leather carving a shallow gouge in the worn wooden floorboards.

"So I take it we're done here?" Lane slapped his glass of tea with an open hand, sending a shower of the steaming drink toward Chigaru. Scooping up his bag, he scrambled for the door. A sharp rush of air blew by his right ear, the tip of the bullwhip snapping near his head.

Dashing outside, he shrugged into his backpack, leaving the motorcycle behind. No time. Chigaru's men leapt up, shouting as he ran by. A rifle barked, the round thudding into the doorframe above him, showering him in wood splinters.

He dodged through the shadows, ducking through low archways and beneath waves of air-drying laundry spanning the narrow alleyway. Chigaru's men followed. His path opened into a street covered in a patchwork of brightly colored awnings, lined with roll-down security gates and open shops. The *souq*, an open-air market, was just beginning to stir with the morning's first patrons. He sprinted by stalls selling shisha pipes, pottery, T-shirts, and vegetables. The air was filled with the smell of seared meat and garbage, exhaust and dust. Somewhere, a welder crackled and spat.

Diving behind a display piled high with mounds of fresh spices, Lane held his breath as he pushed himself tight to the wall. A *muezzin*'s voice moaned over a distant loudspeaker, announcing the call to the *Fajr* prayer—the first of five spread throughout the day.

"*Sabah el kheer*," someone whispered.

A street peddler stepped beside him. Barefoot, bearded, and reeking of tobacco and days-old sweat, the man looked down at Lane, over at his pursuers—now milling in the street, scanning the area for him—and back. He cast a yellow-toothed smile and held out a scarab pendant.

Lane waved him off.

The peddler shrugged, moving in the direction of Chigaru's men.

"Fine. How much?" Lane whispered, urging him back.

The man gestured with one hand, all five fingers outstretched. Fifty Egyptian pounds.

Lane glanced at the trinket, and then shook his head. "No way, man. That's not even real jade."

The man shrugged and pocketed the jewelry, turning back toward Chigaru. The little man had just arrived on the scene, his face covered in bright red spots where the coffee had scalded him. His miniature frame heaved with rage, a frustrated whine squeezing between his lips with each exhale. He kicked dirt at a pair of stray dogs resting in the shade.

"OK, OK," Lane said, pulling the peddler back. "Here." He shoved a handful of bills into the man's hand before bringing a finger to his lips in the universal sign for quiet.

The peddler beamed, handing him the trinket before pocketing the money. The old man whistled at Chigaru and gestured wildly toward the next street.

"Thanks," Lane said after his attackers had disappeared from sight. He patted the old man's shoulder, slipping the trinket into the peddler's pocket with his other hand. He might be able to sell it again. Lane turned to go back the way he'd come. If he could make it back to the motorcycle—

"Lane Bradley, I will martyr you, you...apostrophe!" Chigaru screamed from the end of the street, his voice quivering as he aimed a finger at Lane.

"Chigaru, come on. Even you've got to know that doesn't mean—" A shot rang out and a bullet ruptured a bowl of turmeric beside him. A woman screamed.

Diving out of the street, Lane plunged into an empty laundromat. Scrambling into a darkened stairway, he batted away a veil of cobwebs. Legs churning, he took two stairs at a time to the top floor. Apartments, all locked. He kicked open a door and found himself surrounded by reclining and mostly unconscious forms scattered amidst piles of faded pillows and sweat-yellowed bed sheets. Waving away the dense cloud of opium smoke on the air, Lane paused, searching for an exit. He listened closely for the sounds of pursuing footsteps. Chigaru and his men stood below, a torrent of frustrated Arabic echoing up the stairwell.

A woman approaching him drowsily. Petting his back, she offered him a pipe. He gently pushed her away, moving a step closer to the door. The stairs creaked as the group of men ascended.

"Sorry guys, but I'm gonna have to open a window." Grimacing, knowing this next part would hurt, he rushed toward a smoke-stained glass pane on a far wall. The window buckled and burst from the impact of his body, a cascade of glass shards falling around him. His momentum carried him over the adjacent alleyway, directly into the arcuated stained-glass window of the mosque next door.

A second impact. More glass crumbled. A breath-robbing collision with the floor. Uncurling himself, Lane looked up at the path he'd taken. Brightly colored glass fragments glittered on the rug around him like confetti burst from a broken piñata. A focused beam of sunlight shined through the aperture he'd made. The mosque worshippers paused in their ceremony, raising their heads from their prayer mats and staring at Lane, bewildered.

"Sorry to drop in like this," he said, achingly rising and dusting bits of debris from his shirt and pants, "but could someone point me in the direction of the train station?"

FORTY-TWO

Without NERO's assent or support, Susara had neither local law enforcement nor so much as a sidearm to help her rescue Noah. She could do nothing about the former, but the latter was attainable if one knew where to look. Security contractors stationed aboard merchant vessels, upon their arrival in port, were required to lock up their firearms according to Egyptian law. If she could infiltrate the armory where those guns were housed, she'd have her pick of a broad assortment of the best firepower those contractors could afford.

Of course, they weren't going to just let her walk in. She didn't have the money to bribe her way in. Her NERO credentials wouldn't mean anything to the port authority. It was a classic example of a catch-22: She needed a gun to get at the guns.

Though she loathed the thought, she knew she had only one remaining tool at her disposal to access the armory—her looks. Tying her shirt in a knot at the waist and tugging her jeans down to reveal her toned abdomen and the tops of her hips, she moved from the shadows of the sidewalk into the port authority office in long, seductive strides. Running her fingers along the steel mesh outside the night guard's position, she asked timidly, "Excuse me, could you help me? I've lost my passport, and I don't know where the American consulate is." The guard, a man with a porcine build and a protuberant lower lip, turned his chair slowly to face her, but didn't unlock the gate between them.

"I can't help you," he said flatly. "You'll have to go somewhere else. You shouldn't be here."

She leaned forward until she was certain he had a good view of her body, then said, "I'd *really* appreciate your help."

"And I'd really appreciate you turning around and leaving," he said, reaching for a folded newspaper on his desk and kicking his feet up.

She hadn't expected that. Turning toward the door, she paused, her mind racing. "Hey, this is weird, but I saw this guy when I was walking in who was stuffing a rifle into his bag. He looked like he was in a hurry to leave here. That's not something I should be worried about, is it?"

"What?" The guard sat upright. "No one has been here in hours."

She shrugged. "He looked real to me. I just assumed he was in the army or something."

"Did you see where he went?" the guard stood and began unlocking the gate. The second the latch opened, she had a handful of the guard's hair in her grip, driving his skull down to meet her knee.

With a groan, the man slumped unconscious, collapsing on the concrete floor. She slipped his keychain from his belt and raced inside, looking for the armory.

It didn't take her long to locate what she'd been looking for: a room lined wall to wall with guns of every size, make, and model. Unlocking the steel cable woven through each rifle's trigger guard, she scanned the assortment of heavier armament, settling on a belt-fed Belgian Minimi machine gun. She wasn't going to take down Agapito halfheartedly. The man had tried repeatedly to kill Lane and her, but like any skilled predator, when he'd failed, he'd adjusted his strategy. Now, he was aiming for their weak points—in her case, Noah. But like any predator, he could be stopped with one well-placed bullet. Or one hundred.

Searching the room, she found a black duffel bag large enough to cover her find and two spare box magazines. Hefting the bag over her shoulder, she stepped over the fallen guard, only just beginning to stir, dropped his keys, and left the building.

Upon hitting the street, she woke a dozing taxi driver parked in a nearby alleyway, waved the few dollars she had beneath his nose, tossed her bag in the trunk, and told him to drive eastward.

Climbing into the back seat—ignoring the crumbs, fingernail clippings, and cigarette burns on the upholstery—she felt for the phone in her pocket. She desperately wanted to tell Lane what was happening, if only because Agapito's new strategy could mean danger for Jordan and her mother, too. A cancer-stricken child would make an easy target, and nothing, not even torturing or killing a sick kid, was beneath Agapito. She patted her pocket, but stayed the course. She would eliminate the threat. Then, she could tell Lane all about it.

An hour later, the vehicle slowed at the rise of a hill overlooking an oasis. The fortress Agapito had indicated in his phone call stood alongside the water like a forgotten sandcastle eroded by the tide. The crenellated battlements had worn to rounded knobs. The ramparts, like untended fences, had crumbled, leaving long breaches between towers. Only the gatehouse and bartizan remained standing, the overhanging turret barely clinging to the high stone walls after centuries of exposure to unrelenting sandpaper winds.

"Are you sure you want me to leave you here?" the driver asked, a sudden gust of wind tugging at the windshield wipers. He glanced uncomfortably at the fortress, fingers tapping a nervous rhythm on the steering wheel. A silver crescent moon and star dangled from the rearview mirror, rocking gently with the car each time a gust kicked up.

She only nodded and disembarked, then slapped the trunk with her palm. Hefting the FN Minimi machine gun from inside, she racked the bolt, opened the feed tray, and pulled the first link in the ammo belt into the receiver. Slapping the feed tray closed, she rested the skeletonized stock on her shoulder and said, "I'll be fine on my own, thanks."

The taxi driver didn't wait around to see if she would change her mind, pulling a K-turn and gunning back toward the city.

She set out, shoes sinking in the loose sand. Approaching the fortress, she considered her strategy. Agapito held the advantage of superior manpower, and consequently, firepower. But his advantage could be exploited: He would be so confident he was the one in control, he would never expect Susara's ambush.

The wind was picking up, lifting sand into a swirling, fog-like miasma that burned her eyes. Though painful, she considered it another advantage. When Agapito and his men arrived, the low visibility would help conceal her position. Finding a small depression in the soil with a good field of view of the fortress, she unslung the rifle and unfolded the bipod, anchoring it in the dirt. She took up a position lying prone behind the weapon, concealed by the scattered detritus of the fallen fortress walls.

An hour passed. The wind calmed, the desert sun rising. Sweat formed on her neck, tickling as it slipped down her back. They were late. Had Agapito changed his plan? She checked the time on her phone. Looked for missed calls. Debated calling Lane. Doubt took hold again. This was desperate, and she knew it.

The distant groan of struggling truck engines echoed across the barren terrain. She sank lower into the sand, burying the machine gun's stock against her shoulder and sighting down the barrel.

Desperate or not, she was committed to seeing it through, now.

Blinking to clear her eyes, she aligned the machine gun's front sight with the first vehicle as it came into view.

The SUVs stopped in a semi-circle. Men disembarked. She identified Noah, head down and hands bound, pushed forward by one of Agapito's men. There had to be a dozen or more of them, each carrying a rifle or submachine gun. Still no sign of Agapito. That had her second-guessing her plan for a moment. But she reminded herself who she was dealing with. Agapito wouldn't phone this one in. He was obviously the type to micromanage everything, especially something as crucial as getting the Phaistos Disc from them. He'd be there.

Sure enough, less than a moment later, one final vehicle rolled into formation and came to a stop. Agapito jumped from the passenger door, the tails of his tweed jacket tossed by the breeze. Snapping his fingers at his men, he grabbed Noah by the back of the neck and shoved him into the open terrain in front of the fortress.

This was her shot. Letting the breath slowly escape from her chest, she focused on the sights, lining them up with Agapito's chest, and squeezed the trigger. The rifle roared, a zip of gunfire flinging sand at Agapito's feet.

She'd misjudged the distance.

His men dropped to their bellies. Agapito did not. Twisting Noah around, the young man frozen in his confusion, the assassin drew his pistol and buried the muzzle in Noah's hair before Susara could readjust and cut him down.

"Agent Eaves," Agapito called out, "I thought we had an understanding."

"Oh, I understand you perfectly," she shouted back, pulling back the trigger and raking two of the SUVs with gunfire. Glass shattered. A tire heaved and went flat.

Agapito didn't flinch.

Sliding the muzzle of his pistol down from Noah's ear to where his jaw met his neck, Agapito said, "Ms. Eaves, I will shoot your lover in the throat and let him bleed out in your arms unless you put down your weapon and approach with your hands above your head."

She bit her lip, her ears ringing. This had been a gamble, and she'd lost. Agapito was stone—totally composed and unshaken. It all came down to who was willing to lose more: Agapito would give his life, but Susara would have to give Noah's in the exchange. And he knew she wouldn't do it.

Letting the rifle's stock drop, she stood, muscles stiff from hours spent lying in the sand. Agapito's men approached, guns trained on her.

"Wise choice, Ms. Eaves," Agapito said, shoving Noah toward the stronghold's entrance. "Wise choice."

FORTY-THREE

A gapito's men circled her like ravenous coyotes surrounding a wounded fawn, shoving Noah into a chair in the corner to watch the spectacle.

"*Bagascia*," one of them said, slapping her face with the back of his hand. *Whore.* "What do you think, Noah, would your lady give me a *bocchino* if I asked nicely?" Grabbing her hair in one hand and thrusting his pelvis toward her face, he and the others laughed raucously. "*Fammi un bocchino! Fammi un bocchino!*" he chanted, unzipping his fly.

The door swung open, and Agapito's lanky form ducked through the frame. His men went silent, looked to the floor, cleared their throats, and gripped the backs of their necks nervously.

"Are you tormenting our guests?" Agapito asked, approaching the man whose fly remained open.

"No, Mr. Vicente. No. We were just teasing."

Agapito looked unamused. Pointing at the man's fly, he shook his head, and then slammed his fist into the mercenary's groin. With a gasp, Susara's tormenter dropped to a knee, cradling his manhood.

"The next time you find yourself thinking with your *pisello*, you *fessacchione*, remember the sensation of my knuckles against your genitals."

The man whispered something unintelligible, still drawing air in ragged gasps.

"What did you say to me?" Agapito asked, leaning over and turning his head expectantly.

The injured man looked up at his boss maliciously and spat, "*Bastardo. Frocio.*"

Agapito sighed, stood up, and drove a knee into the man's chin. Before his back struck the dirt, Agapito had drawn his gun and planted two 10mm slugs center mass, followed by one that smashed the man's nose through the back of his skull.

Thumbing the safety back on, he returned his pistol to its holster—the thunderous reports dying away and leaving only a shrill ringing in everyone's ears. Agapito turned to his captives as if he'd only just entered the room.

"Noah, is it? I believe that's Hebrew for 'rest' or 'comfort'. Are you comfortable?" He ran a finger along the young man's forearm and up his shoulder before slapping his cheek. Noah recoiled more from surprise than pain, his cheek turning rose-colored from the impact.

"He's handsome, Agent Eaves. A little young for you, though, isn't he?" Agapito strolled deliberately around the dead man still twitching on the packed-dirt floor, a growing pool of glistening crimson surrounding his form. "But not too

young to die today. In my line of work, I've learned a great
deal about inflicting pain. For the sake of transparency, allow
me to explain what I had in mind." He shifted his path and
began orbiting around Noah. "I'll begin by cutting from the
corners of young, handsome Noah's mouth," he hooked a
finger between Noah's lips, pulling tight against his cheek,
"here, all the way until we hit the hinge of his jaw." Agapito
snaked his finger up the younger man's cheek to his ear.
Resuming his ambling path, the assassin slipped a stiletto knife
from his jacket's inside pocket and flicked it open—the abalone
pearl handle and sharp blade glinting in the low light. "This
isn't particularly painful, at least not as painful as what's to
come, but it's meant more to emphasize how serious I am. I'll
let him sit here for an hour or so, perhaps park a mirror before
him so he can admire how wide his jaw can open when the
muscle and skin holding it together are no longer attached."

Agapito looked from Noah to Susara, gauging their
reactions. Noah wept softly, head against his chest.

"Then, if you still haven't complied, and I still haven't gotten
what I want, I'll try something…historical. Perhaps you've
heard of the blood eagle? The Norse torture? I've always
wanted to try it—for curiosity's sake. Cutting down to the ribs
near the spine, breaking the bone to clear a path, I'll pull your
lover's lungs out through his back. The question I have is, does
he die from shock? Blood loss? Or asphyxiation?" Leaning in
toward Susara until she could feel his breath against the skin of
her cheek, he whispered, "Agent Eaves, find a way to get me
the Phaistos Disc, or this will be only the beginning of a long,
arduous, excruciating end to your boyfriend's existence. And
rest assured, you will bear witness to every cut, every smashed
bone, every violent shock he endures. And he will curse you

for it." Tossing Susara's phone into her lap, he motioned for her to pick it up as one of his men freed her from her restraints. "Call Lane and tell him to meet you here. Tell him to bring the disc, or I'll take a walk outside and leave you to the mercy of these men. We'll consider that just another step in the suffering young Noah will endure as he watches them desecrate your body. No doubt that will resonate with Lane, too." Leaning over as if to whisper to Noah, Agapito said, "With how much time those two have spent together in the past week, you may have reason to be concerned."

Susara forced herself to speak calmly. Though she didn't know Agapito's background, and couldn't tell if he was bluffing, she refused to reveal how shaken she was and that his intimidation was working. "He kept me in the dark. Do you really think a criminal like Lane Bradley would ever trust me?"

"What surprises me is that you trust him," Agapito mused, folding his knife and returning it to his pocket. The lanky man sauntered toward Noah, planting his palms on the young man's shoulders and squeezing. "A man willing to leave his dying daughter in another country while he selfishly goes about stealing artifacts is hardly the kind of person I would want to associate with." Giving Noah's shoulders a final painful squeeze, Agapito moved a hand to Noah's hair and, grabbing a fistful, yanked his head back. Sliding his pistol from its holster, he scraped the weapon's front sight across Noah's throat, leaving a rose-red scrape in its wake.

"I didn't say I wouldn't call him. Please, just leave Noah alone," she pleaded.

Agapito licked his lips, his face inches from his captive's scalp, as if savoring the man's fear. "Then hurry."

FORTY-FOUR

Bats. Susara couldn't see them in the darkness, but she could hear their scratching—like mice behind drywall—as they burrowed in the fortress walls, their wings fluttering as they jostled amongst one another.

Left alone with Noah inside the stronghold's atrium, bound to the chair upon which she sat, she could do nothing but think about the phone call she'd made to Lane hours before and listen to the rodents go about their business.

She'd given in to Agapito's demands, telling Lane what had happened and where they could be found. He'd listened silently, only concluding the phone call with, "OK." She felt guilty for not telling him about Agapito's demands sooner, and even guiltier now that their rescue was entirely in his hands. She'd failed everyone in her desperate attempt to save Noah by herself, and now Lane would be forced to do exactly what she'd been trying to prevent all along.

Battling a powerful wave of anxiety that threatened to make her vomit, she pinched her eyes shut. It didn't help that she could sense Noah's anger as he stared at the wall. There was no point in trying to speak with him. It was like sitting beside him in the car during one of their fights; he'd just stare out the windshield, eyes burning a hole in the road ahead, silently ignoring her attempts at reconciliation.

The scuffling of the bats grew louder. Something scraped loudly against the fortress wall. A body squeezed through one of the room's clerestory windows.

"Sorry to intrude, but it looks as though my taxi dropped me off at the wrong stop. Which way to the Bellagio?" the shadowy figure asked as he slid to the floor, dusting off his shirt and jeans as he approached and tugged her restraints loose.

"Lane, tell me you worked up some kind of distraction to keep Agapito away. He knew you were coming," she said, urgently untying Noah, who continued to look at the wall dejectedly—as though he'd given up and was awaiting death.

"Don't worry about it," he said, extending his hand to Noah for a handshake. "You must be Noah. Nice to meet you."

The door swung open and smashed against the wall as Agapito and his men stormed into the room. Agapito clapped his hands slowly. "This is it? Lane, I expected so much more from you. You've really slipped in your old age."

"Better to have slipped than to have never had it to begin with," he countered. "I suppose you want the disc. Fair trade for these two? I'll throw in a Cal Ripken Jr. rookie card to sweeten the pot."

Agapito tilted his head and snorted. "My friend, you have nothing to barter with. I'll take the disc, certainly." He waved his men forward to take Lane's bag. He gave it willingly.

Withdrawing the protective case from within, Agapito opened it to find the disc half buried in thick foam. A small light bulb blinked on as the case opened, switching from green to red.

"Nothing's free, Agapito. You just activated the pressure-sensitive switch," Lane said casually. "You lift the disc, the three ounces of Semtex I stuffed in there will send it and most of your upper body through the ceiling." Stepping back, he withdrew his phone from his pocket, finger hovering over the screen. "Oh, and just in case you're feeling froggy and try to kill me, I've added a remote trigger too. I just send this little text message—which reads, 'Bye bye, Agapito. Heart. Winkey face. Smoochey kiss'—and you and the disc go molecular. Welcome to the 21st century. Technology's really something, isn't it?"

Undaunted, Agapito smirked.

"We can play the back-and-forth game as to whether or not I'm serious," Lane continued, "but you remember that armored car in Lebanon as well as I do. Would you have bet your life against me back then?"

The briefest flicker of doubt passed over Agapito's countenance. Slowly closing the case in his hands, he said, "So you think I'll let you and your friends go based on your threat to destroy the disc? You've clearly forgotten who I am." He stood up straighter, a defiant glint in his eyes. "But I haven't forgotten who you are. You've spent your entire life trying to save artifacts like this one from destruction. You'd never be the one to ruin it. Not even if it cost you your life."

"Then go ahead and try to take the disc out of the case," Lane challenged, not backing down. "Find out how well you know me."

Agapito raised the lid of the case slowly until the indicator light came on again. He abruptly closed it. "How do I know you won't just blow the charge when you leave?"

"One, it'd be irreplaceable history wasted on someone like you. Second, unlike you, I'm a man of my word. You let us go, I'll disarm the case and you can have the disc. I just came to get my friends back."

Taking his silence as implicit consent, Lane, Susara, and Noah moved through the crowd of men to the door. Susara paused, returning to Agapito. Reaching a hand inside his suit jacket, she ripped out her phone.

"This is mine."

After Noah and Susara had passed through the door, Agapito shouted, "Lane, you should know who your true enemies are. You know me, you know my motivations, but your friend there? She's deceived you."

Lane hesitated at the door. "I know what your angle is, Agapito. It won't work."

"Don't be so quick to discount my warning, old friend. Ms. Eaves possesses a cutthroat sense of self-preservation. Or didn't you notice that she called for you to save her, knowing your life would be at risk? She doesn't care whether you live or die. After all, you're a criminal, like me, and she's the law. The classic cop and robber paradigm. Even children understand the two can't work together. Trust me, she will betray you."

"Trust you? Agapito, putting aside our past, ignoring the fact that *you* betrayed me by leaving me in that hole in Lebanon, you kill people for a living. You kidnapped a guy who had nothing to do with this and threatened to murder him just to get to me. You'll understand if I don't exactly look at you as a shining beacon of morality."

"I could have kidnapped your daughter instead," he said solemnly. "But even I have my limits."

"You want a pat on the head for that? You're still a murderer, Agapito. Makes it hard to take your advice seriously."

"Do murder and honesty exclude one another?" He stepped forward and leaned in, his voice a whisper. "You know, the Greeks often considered the act of killing to be a reflection of the gods' will. The ancients possessed this inexorable sense of fatalism when it came to death. As though it was all preordained. Accidents didn't happen. If you were slain on the battlefield, you must have angered Athena or Ares. Killed by a wild animal? You must not have sacrificed enough cattle to Artemis. Plague decimated your village? Apollo, that naughty boy. Only the gods possessed free will. They toyed with mortals like playthings. Selfishly and without care." He tapped Lane's chest with his pointer finger. "That man you killed in Heraklion: It eats at you, doesn't it? You were always one to languish in your remorse, self-flagellate for those you've destroyed. You bear the guilt like a heavy stone on your chest, obvious and crippling. But why? We should feel honored to have survived this long. The gods favor us. We may be pieces in their chess game, but you and I are knights. Those we've killed? Pawns. Disposable and meaningless. When we battle, so do the gods. Someday soon, we'll finally learn whose god is strongest."

Susara shouted to Lane to hurry up. Lingering a moment longer as he stared at his adversary, Lane slowly closed the door behind him.

She met him outside, tugging his arm. "Did you actually wire the case to explode?"

Moving into a dense fringe of low palms and grass surrounding the oasis—the only greenery visible in the miles of open sand—he began pulling brush away from a steel frame. A military fast-attack vehicle took form. "Do you know how hard it is to find ordnance like Semtex on such short notice? I was lucky the Egyptian Army had a surplus of these bad boys lying around or I would have shown up on a camel." Leaping into the driver's seat and pumping the gas pedal a few times, he slid a key from his pocket into the ignition. The vehicle rumbled as it awoke. Susara and Noah piled in behind him. "I bought a radio from a street vendor, harvested the parts, and wired the case to turn red when the lid opened. It's not hooked up to anything. I just hope it takes them a while to figure that part out."

A door swung open and a submachine gun spat rounds into the sand a few feet from the buggy's oversized rubber tires.

"I guess it didn't."

He hit the gas. The sudden acceleration nearly toppled Noah backward into the gravel. Cutting through the trees, the buggy leapt into the sand, building speed as it motored down a large hill heading toward Lake Bardawil.

"It kills me that we had to give up the disc," Susara shouted, her mouth an inch from Lane's ear so she could be heard above the rushing air. "Are we writing it off like the stones?"

"That wasn't the real disc."

"What do you mean, that wasn't the real disc?"

"Let's just say I owe the gift shop at the Heraklion Museum 30 euros," he said, reaching under the driver's seat and withdrawing a case holding the authentic disc.

Headlights, bouncing wildly in the distance, shot over the rise. Agapito's men had boarded their SUVs and given chase.

Noah slapped Lane's back and pointed fearfully at their pursuers, the blinking of their distant muzzle flashes like popping firecrackers in the dying sunlight, the sound lost amidst the roaring of engines battling loose sand.

Nodding without looking back, Lane guided their vehicle down the slope toward a thin spit of land fringing the lake. "Herodotus' Serbonian Bog is going to get us out of our own Serbonian Bog."

"What?" Susara yelled, her hair flailing in the wind.

Slowing down so he could be heard above the fast-moving air, steering with his knees to free his hands for gesturing, Lane explained, "Herodotus called this area the Serbonian Bog. It looks like solid land, but isn't. It was fabled to have swallowed entire armies. A Serbonian Bog is also a simile for a quagmire. Like the one we're in. So this Serbonian Bog is going to save us from our own Serbonian Bog."

"Why are you slowing down?" Noah cried out, resuming his backslapping with more urgency.

The vehicle continued to slow, the SUVs nearing. A bullet twanged off the dune buggy's roll cage.

"Lane, get us out of here!" Susara screamed.

Turning to face her, his expression went dark—as cold as if he wore a mask forged of iron. "You should have told me."

She held his stare, feeling the intensity of his disappointment searing a hole straight through her.

Glancing over his shoulder to ensure Agapito's men were following closely—too closely to stop in time—Lane jammed his foot down upon the accelerator, shooting the lightweight dune buggy across the quicksand of the bog. The vehicle slowed only slightly, wide tires slinging arcing rooster-tails of muck into the air as they slogged forward.

The SUVs, three times as heavy as the dune buggy and further weighed down with men and guns, hit the bog and nosed to an immediate, jarring stop, the sludge pulling the vehicles in.

FORTY-FIVE

Outskirts of Port Said, Egypt

The fast-attack vehicle thundered over the earth, following a string of power lines looping toward Port Said. Lane squinted against the fine, fast-moving sand stinging his eyes. Obscured behind the tears, distant houses crowded the shoreline of the Mediterranean. Sporadic patches of thin, sun-bleached trees dotted the landscape, clinging thirstily to the edges of dry *wadis* as they struggled to survive in the hostile sands. After an hour, the dune buggy choked and sputtered, its small fuel tank empty. They stopped, leaving the vehicle behind as they set out on foot toward a cluster of distant buildings in the nearest town. Lane led the way. He could feel Noah staring at his back as they walked.

"That was a close call back in that swamp."

Susara's voice sounded false in its cheerfulness. She was trying to break the silence, cut the tension by getting them talking, but it was a weak attempt, and everyone knew it.

"Hey, did either of you get shot today?" Lane asked, scanning the streets.

Under his breath, Noah mumbled, "No. But the day's not over yet, either."

Lane stopped walking, and without turning to look at them, said, "None of us have any extra holes, and you're free and unharmed. You're welcome."

He didn't need to look behind him to envision Susara's surprise. She'd never seen him this bitter. But he had good reason to be upset. She'd lied to him, and in so doing left him no choice but to risk his life to come save them. This was just another delay keeping him from the second temple and yet another opportunity for Agapito to gain the upper hand. She'd quickly gone from being an asset to a handicap, and he began considering whether it wouldn't be prudent to abandon her and her boyfriend at the first sign of civilization and finish this himself.

"This guy was the reason you were gone all the time?" Noah asked, doing his best to wipe the thin layer of fine sand from his suit jacket, bits of white padding poking through ragged tears in the shoulders. He tripped on a deep crack in the asphalt, got up quickly, and looked around to see if the others had seen him fall.

"What are you implying?" She stopped near the entrance to a church, a strange sight in contrast with the dozens of mosque minarets dotting the skyline. The areas above the glass-shattered windows had been scorched black—the lasting scar of a conflagration that had once burned within. "We've been working together on a case. That's it. And that's the first thing you can think to say after we both risked our lives to save you?"

"It's your fault I'm even here!" Noah shouted. "One minute I'm leaving my office on my way to my car, and the next minute I'm on a plane flying over the Middle East with some French guy waving a knife under my nose whispering that he's going to castrate me. All this time I thought you were into archaeology. Harmless stuff. But you've obviously gotten yourself into something completely different, and I want nothing to do with it."

"I'll work on getting us a ride out of here." Lane fished his phone from his pocket as he attempted to withdraw. "Give you two some alone time. Sounds like you've got plenty to talk about." He wanted nothing to do with their drama. God knows he had enough of his own to deal with.

"No way, man. You're not going anywhere."

Footsteps approached behind him and fingers hesitantly grabbed his shoulder and pulled. He allowed himself to be turned around. Noah stepped closer, the toes of his Ferragamo loafers nearly touching Lane's worn-out high-tops.

"I'm sure all this has been pretty shocking for you. Maybe you should take a few minutes to decompress," Lane suggested.

"I had a ring," Noah said through clenched teeth.

"I don't understand."

"I had a ring in my pocket the night Susara got the text message telling her she had to leave. And now I finally get to meet the guy she left me for, and this is it? You?" Noah's voice cracked, his eyes filled with resentment. "Not a doctor or fitness model, but some roughneck criminal?"

Lane took a deep breath. His voice was even and calm when he spoke. "Like Susara said, we're not together." He glanced at her over Noah's shoulder, making sure she met his eyes. "I'm sorry you got dragged into all this. I'm going to go make a call and get you a flight out of here."

As he left, he could hear Noah redirect his anger toward Susara. "You know, you always called the shots in our relationship. I always supported you, even when you disregarded me. Well, it's my turn to disregard you. I don't want to ever see you again, Susara. I don't want my name associated with you. Forget you ever knew me. Just get me to an airport and leave me the hell alone."

Chin up, she looked disdainfully upon her ex. "You're such a child." Brushing past his shoulder, she followed Lane down the street.

Someone had hastily parked a tangerine-colored Lada Kalina hatchback with two wheels on the curb. Lane tried the door, and it gave. Legs draped on the pavement, his upper body resting on the floorboards, he dug under the dashboard in an attempt to hotwire the car.

"Looks like I can add grand theft auto to your list of offenses," Susara joked as she approached.

He didn't reply.

"Hey, I owe you one for getting us out of there," she continued. "That was quick thinking with the Serbonian Bog and the fake disc." She climbed into the car's passenger seat and smoothed the curled-up floor mat with the toes of her shoes.

Twisting free a bundle of wires from under the dash and flicking aside a dusty mouse nest that followed, he continued to ignore her.

"Lane? Look, I'm sorry I didn't tell you where I was going, but—"

"A few days ago, back at your apartment, you thought I'd taken the photos of the cipher stones and left without you," he interrupted. "The truth is, I'd walked out that door after you'd fallen asleep with that exact intention. I felt really bad about it—bad enough to go back for you. I'm wondering now if that wasn't a mistake."

"Why would you say that? We've come so far, accomplished so much already."

Dropping the wires and using his elbow to pull himself up into the seat, he turned toward her and said, "You were nearly killed tonight. And your boyfriend, too. This isn't your world. You belong back in D.C. with your steady job and your steady guy and your very nice apartment in the city." He paused. "And at this point, you're not helping me anymore."

His words struck a nerve, he could tell. She looked confused, betrayed, and hurt. Those emotions seemed to meld together like chemicals that, when mixed, bubbled and smoked, ready to ignite.

Her hand shot out. Fingertips snapped against his cheek. The sound of her hand impacting his face echoed in the narrow street. Waiting for the sting to subside, he locked his eyes on the dashboard clock. It insistently flashed 12 o'clock.

"You have no idea what I've given up for this, for you. You dare to tell me that this isn't my world?" Her hands shook. "Did it ever occur to you that I've felt that way about every day I've spent at my desk, behind a computer, then going to the same restaurant to eat the same meal with the same perfectly content man because it's what society says I'm supposed to do?" Opening the car door, she went to leave, but stopped. "I've risked and lost almost everything for your ridiculous fixation on a fairy tale. And now, after all that, you tell me I should just go home?" She moved to the sidewalk. "You want to find that second temple, Lane? You know where you should go next? Straight to Hell." The car door slammed and she stormed down the darkened street. "*Jou bliksem*," she cursed under her breath, ducking a piece of construction lumber nailed across the church doorway and disappearing inside.

Well, that was it. This was his opportunity to shed his baggage, to go solo again. After all, he had a mission that surpassed any affection he might have developed for Susara, any sense of loyalty for her he might possess. His first priority had been, and continued to be, his daughter. Plain and simple. Hotwire the damn car and leave these two behind to bicker amongst themselves. They were safe now, and he had somewhere important to be.

But there he sat, ass planted on the stained cloth of the driver's seat, staring at a prominent cigarette burn on the steering wheel. He wanted her to come with him. It wasn't just about how useful she was to his mission. He wanted her to believe the legend, to see that he'd been right about it all along. To share as much in his triumph as she had in his trials.

He followed her into the church. The fire had gutted the building, its timber framework exposed like ribs on a decaying carcass. The soles of his shoes scuffed through a thick layer of ash, the nave empty and open except for the charred remains of the pews. Black, rotted tree stumps in an empty forest. In the dim light, he could make out the silhouette of Susara's slim body as she sat atop the church altar, her arms wrapped around her legs, knees pulled tight to her chest. At first, he thought maybe she hadn't heard him come in. But then she spoke—her voice hauntingly soft, like a whispered prayer spoken inside a confessional.

"This wasn't your fault. You just showed up at a time when my life was falling apart. If anything, I'm mad at you because you always seem to possess this...I don't know...resolute purpose. You never doubt yourself; you just work off of pure instinct and roll the dice. And I guess, in a way, I hate how easy you make it all seem. With all my carefully laid plans and discipline and training, everything just fell apart anyway. And I made you my whipping boy because of it. I don't resent you, Lane, I envy you."

Shoving his hands in his pockets, he stepped beside her and leaned against the altar. He bumped her shoulder with his and said quietly, "We haven't found that temple yet. If you can put up with me for a while longer, I think I know where it is."

FORTY-SIX

Sunlight poured through the Lada's dust-covered windshield, the vehicle idling feebly as they waited in a long line of traffic on an already packed highway. Ninety-nine percent of Egypt's 80 million people lived packed into only five percent of the country's land, and it showed. An accident or government checkpoint had forced them to a standstill. Or perhaps it was just an ordinary day on the road. Drivers exited the vehicles ahead of them, shouting and gesticulating at one another.

Susara picked at the peeling synthetic leather on the dashboard, glancing at Lane occasionally. The car was a furnace; the fans of the air conditioner whirred, but only hot air came out. He seemed not to notice. Instead, he fidgeted like a man who had just given up smoking, twisting in his seat as if fighting the urge to rummage through the trash in search of his last pack of cigarettes.

Noah had insisted on taking a taxi to the airport the night before. He'd left without fanfare, eager to conclude this nightmare and return to a normal life back home. Susara still wasn't sure she'd made the right decision by not going with him. Some part of her knew that Lane meant what he'd said about her not being helpful to him anymore.

Reluctantly breaking the silence, she whispered, "I know I told you this already, but I'm sorry. I should have told you about Noah's kidnapping right when I found out. I just thought I was protecting you from Agapito, and figured I could handle him myself."

He shrugged. "Yeah, Agapito's not a guy to trifle with. He's homicidal and intelligent, which makes for the kind of scary combination that usually ends up showcased on true crime documentaries." He tapped an impatient beat on the floorboards with his foot, fingers kneading the gear shifter, resisting the urge to move it away from neutral.

"What is it?" she asked.

"Nothing, really."

"You can tell me."

He glanced at her doubtfully. "Just Agapito getting inside my head."

"How? What did he say?"

"Nothing. It's stupid."

She gestured at a tour bus parked in front of them. "Not like we're going anywhere. Come on. What did he say?"

He coughed up a forced laugh. "He said you would betray me. That you had a cutthroat sense of self-preservation." He waved a hand dismissively. "It's just Agapito playing mind games—his own little brand of psychological warfare."

The car went silent.

"What if he was right?" She didn't know what possessed her to say it—maybe her exhaustion or maybe Lane's insistent but undeserved trust in her—but it slipped from her lips before she could stop herself.

He turned to look at her, jaw set. It wasn't his anger that bothered her, but his lack of surprise.

"I only agreed to come with you because I thought I could arrest you after you stole the Phaistos Disc." Her words came faster. "When we first set out, my life was coming apart at the seams. Noah had left, and I had just been put on unpaid leave, which is the first step in being terminated from the job I promised my father I would someday get—one I've worked damn hard to be the best at." Drawing a deep breath, she looked out the window at the pedestrians walking by, wishing she were one of them. "I thought that if I were the one to capture you after you stole the disc, I could get back into Ruben's good graces and salvage my career. But the more time I spent with you, the more I realized how good a man you are. You're honest and compassionate, and I couldn't bring myself to—"

"Don't." He shook his head. "Spare me the emotional storytelling. I've had enough."

"I'm not lying, Lane. I only kept all this to myself because you would have sent me away if I'd told you." Her fingers pinched the fabric of her pants at the knees.

"Why would it matter if I sent you away? You don't believe in any of this. The legend is meaningless to you."

She paused and looked at him, blinking away tears. "I may not believe in the disc's legend, but I believe in you."

The muted honking of horns and shouts filled the cab. They looked away from one another. Finally, she said, "I'm just...I'm gonna go." Swinging the door open, she planted a foot on the pavement.

A tender hand came to rest on her wrist, softly pulling her back inside.

"Long walk home from here," he said.

"I'll figure it out."

"Get back in the car, already."

She slowly sat back down.

He stared out the windshield. "You remember when I told you I felt like I've known you a long time? That's part of the problem, isn't it? You spent years trying to track me down. Then, overnight, you had to turn that instinct off and work with me. No one could authentically do that, especially if they had the commitment to their work that you do. I guess I should be flattered you changed your mind." He turned to look at her. "You still want to come with me?"

"I'm not a quitter."

"You never got to hear about my little misadventure in Luxor, did you?" He tenderly massaged the large bruise on his shoulder that had formed following his fall through the mosque window.

She shook her head. "No, what happened?"

He reached below the dashboard and untwisted a wire, turning the car off—giving up on the possibility of them moving anytime soon. "Nothing good. Long story short, I don't think the second temple is here. I think we misunderstood the disc's translation. I got caught up in the hieroglyphs on the cipher stones and instantly thought of Egypt, but even as trade partners and allies, it's unlikely the Minoans would have built a second temple in Egypt. You and I are friends, but that doesn't mean you'd let me build a summer home on your front lawn, you know?"

A man led a donkey through the halted traffic, then stopped at the hood of the Lada, waiting expectantly for them to back up enough to allow him and his mount passage. Lane looked behind them at the car parked on their bumper, back at the man, and shrugged apologetically.

"Anyway, the interpretation read, *two palaces a sea apart*. We took the word 'sea' literally, which made sense if the second temple had been directly across the Mediterranean in Egypt. But to the Minoans, even the hundred miles between Crete and, say, Santorini might have been considered a sea apart."

"Why Santorini, though? she asked. "Doesn't that interpretation open up almost every island in the Dodecanese and Cyclades chains? Homer wrote that the Minoans had 90 cities at the height of their civilization. That's a lot of ground to cover."

"Most of those were on Crete itself. The interpretation rules out all but those settlements located off the island."

"That still leaves Karpathos, Saria…"—she counted off with her fingers—"…Kasos, Kythira—"

"Call it a strong hunch, it's Santorini," he interrupted.

"Don't tell me you're one of those lost city of Atlantis theorists. A magical island that might have been the site of your magical temple?" She gave his shoulder a playful shove.

A man tapped on the window, offering a resin model of the Great Sphinx of Giza for sale. Lane waved him off. "I'm not. Besides, Plato ripped off the story of Atlantis from the

Anatolians. The capital city of ancient Lydia was Tantalis, and it fits his exact description and timeline better than Santorini or anywhere else. And, of course, the name is too similar to ignore—Tantalis, Atlantis?" He waved his hands as if wiping down a chalkboard. "Forget all that. The legend of Atlantis has nothing to do with this. What's important is that we know the Minoans had expanded beyond Crete. The architecture, tools, and writing uncovered on Santorini leave no doubt that it was, at the very least, part of the Minoan empire. Plus, it has what those other islands don't: It fits perfectly with the disc's translation. *Built beside a mighty river* may not have meant the Nile, but instead the waterways into Santorini's caldera."

"Wasn't the caldera a result of a volcano erupting? You know, the one that killed everyone on the island and initiated the decline of the Minoan civilization in its entirety? There's no way the terrain matched the description on the Phaistos Disc before the eruption."

He shook his head. "Pumice deposits from the eruption have been found in the caldera wall. That could only be if the walls were there before the eruption."

"So you're thinking, what, Akrotiri?"

"A confirmed Minoan Bronze Age settlement that fits the disc's description pretty closely, yeah. If nothing else, it's a much smaller place to search than all of the Nile River basin."

"*Under the crest of the king.*" She leaned back in her seat, staring up at the flaps of torn upholstery hanging from the roof of the car. "King Minos's symbol was the same as we found on the clay tablet in Chávez's collection: the double-bladed *labrys*. We find that, we've found the second temple."

"Exactly." He grew somber. "But none of that matters, since you don't believe in any of this."

Their eyes met.

She whispered, "I'm learning to take some things on faith." A repetitive, deep-bass palpitation rattled the car's windows. Distracted, she looked away. "Do you hear that?"

The throngs of people stepped away from the street. They looked up, shielding their faces with their arms as the *thrump thrump thrump* of a helicopter's rotors grew in volume. A tornadic swirl of orange dust cloaked the street. Lane tapped his phone's screen, pointing at a glowing dot hovering over a map of the city. He shouted into her ear to be heard above the noise. "There's our ride. You're not afraid of heights, are you?"

"That depends on how high we're going." She followed his lead and exited the car, hair swirling in the helicopter's downdraft.

He shouldered the bag holding the Phaistos Disc. A pair of STABO harnesses dropped from overhead, followed by two canvas bags filled with rope—causing the crowd to scatter to the sidewalks.

She shook her head as she stared at the bags. "I know what those are, but why? Why can't we ride *inside* the damn helicopter?"

He pointed up at the hovering craft, then down at the crowded roadway. "We can either spend the rest of the day in this heat on our way back to Yuri's ship, or we can leave now. Your call."

Glancing back at the Lada, she let out a deep breath and reached to unpack one of the bags. He guided her into one of the rigs, securing the straps over her shoulders and tugging the steel clips around her thighs. Hooking himself into a rig, he tethered their risers to the ropes and raised his arms to signal the crew above. The straps tightened, their feet leaving the ground. Obscured by dust and sunlight, the helicopter lifted over the buildings, Lane and Susara suspended below.

FORTY-SEVEN

Letting the towel slip from his waist to the intricate tile mosaic underfoot, Agapito breathed deep the steam hanging on the air of the Turkish bathhouse. Stepping inside the domed building's hot room, he reclined atop a centuries-old stone platform carved to fit the contours of the human body.

He was proud of himself for showing restraint. His pistol had remained holstered following their hapless pursuit of Bradley and Eaves across the Serbonian Bog. Instead of gunning down the imbeciles he'd hired for security and leaving their bodies to mummify in the bog—though tempting—he'd taken the one vehicle that hadn't become inextricably entrenched in the quicksand to the nearest town, found a quiet Turkish bath, and waited.

Dragging a thumb across his phone's screen, cutting a path of transparency through the fogged glass, he followed a red dot as it tracked across the Mediterranean toward the Cyclades Islands.

He hadn't anticipated Lane's last move with the replica disc and rigged case, but conversely, Lane hadn't anticipated Agapito's safeguard, either. It had only taken a few seconds to download off-the-shelf parent monitoring software to Susara's phone. Now the device's built-in GPS would transmit her location directly to him as long as it was powered on. He only had to wait until the tracker stopped moving to learn where the second temple was located.

His adversary had many shortcomings, but his skill as an archaeologist and procurer of the unobtainable was unmatched. Why not let Lane do the work for him, and then simply take it from him? Such a scenario played to both men's strengths.

His phone buzzed, interrupting his contemplation. Clearing his throat, Agapito took a final deep breath before answering. He'd been expecting the call, but hadn't been looking forward to this moment.

"Father."

"Tell me you have the disc," Musarde said. A fork clattered atop an empty plate. He sounded as though he hadn't yet finished chewing his last bite.

"In a manner of speaking, yes, I do." Agapito nodded to a young man who approached with a sponge in hand and rolled to his side. "I'm letting someone hold it for me while they track down the second temple described in the translation." He could hear his father take a deep breath in preparation to berate him, but cut the elderly man off. "You should send word to your pilot that you'll need a flight scheduled immediately."

Musarde resisted the temptation to yell despite being given an opening. "Where am I going?"

Removing the phone from his ear and following the red dot as it hovered over Santorini National Airport, Agapito smiled. "Santorini. Looks as though we're heading back to Greece."

FORTY-EIGHT

Akrotiri dig site
Santorini, Greece

Jagged streaks of sunlight crept over partially unearthed stone buildings and rows of cracked clay amphorae vessels, a lattice of steel rafters and purlins overhead covering the site in a patchwork of shadow. Lane sidestepped stanchions rising from the dirt and hopped over pine boards braced against unstable walls, Susara following close behind. Her fingers brushed the handle of a pistol stuffed in her belt, concealed beneath the waist of her T-shirt. The gun had been part of a resupply Lane had requested his helicopter pilot friend bring along when he came to get them in Egypt. Lane had declined when she offered him the gun's twin.

"We probably won't even need the one. Besides, I shoot like a Star Wars Stormtrooper. Safest place to be is standing in front of the target." He'd given the pistol in his hand one final glance—a shadow of doubt or regret passing over his features—before tossing it back inside its case.

"Well, where do we find this second temple?" Scanning the area, she batted away a persistent fly as it circled her head.

"The Minoans were very advanced for their time—indoor plumbing, ventilation, the works. This palace, if you can envision it, probably featured colonnades, sweeping courtyards, theaters, and crypts. The question becomes, if you were trying to hide your most sacred temple, where would you put it?" Reaching into his pack, he withdrew a water bottle and took a long drink. Sweat beaded on his brow. The afternoon sun, even diffused by the canopy overhead, had raised the temperature to Hell-like levels. In Greece, everything seemed to come to a standstill in the heat of the afternoon. Everyone made an effort to avoid being outdoors, closing up shops and pausing in their work until the evening, when the temperature became bearable again. It gave Lane and Susara full run of the dig site without fear of interruption by other visitors or staff.

"I keep coming back to the legend of Theseus." Dusting off a stone seat, she eased herself down and reclined.

"Ah, the labyrinth."

She shrugged. "Well, consider this: If you had a sacred temple containing your culture's most precious possession— the curative nostrum or whatever that Pernier was talking about—wouldn't you want to stop people from just dropping in to use it? And of course you'd want to keep enemies from taking it. So why not build the temple inside a convoluted maze and invent a legend of a violent, carnivorous man-bull that wanders the halls, waiting for the undeserving to step inside?"

He knelt down and offered her the water bottle. "I could see it. But the labyrinth was built at Knossos, beneath the king's palace. Doubtful they'd go through that trouble a second time, let alone for a distant island colony."

"Or maybe that was the architectural norm for Minoan palaces," she said, taking a quick drink and reaching to return the water bottle to his pack. "Either way, look around. There's not one structure that hasn't been reduced to a chalk outline of its former glory. If the temple were to survive for millennia intact, it would have to be hidden underground."

"Then we look for a *labrys* marking the entrance to an underground passageway." Dropping his pack in the dirt, he climbed halfway up a steel buttress and surveilled the grounds.

After five minutes spent hanging like a monkey from the beam, he descended, grabbed his pack, and marched down the line to the next vantage point. He repeated the process for an hour, covering every angle of the dig site. Finally, he shook his head and slid down from the last buttress.

"Maybe I was wrong about this place, too." Ducking beneath the framework of an ancient doorway, he strolled along a rickety wooden bridge, each footstep causing the deck to creak. Upon reaching a large, flat stone in a dark corner of the dig site, he took a seat, elbows on his knees, hands rubbing his eyes.

"You're not giving up, are you?" she asked.

He folded his hands and held them before his mouth. Looking straight ahead, eyes red and dry, he whispered, "Have you ever watched orange juice being made?"

She knelt to face him.

"The really fresh stuff. You know, slicing the orange in half and impaling it on that little plastic thing—"

"A juicer?" she asked.

"Yeah. And you have to kind of grind it on that sharpened point, mashing it until the insides turn to liquid and pulp and there's nothing left but the used-up, hollow shell."

"OK, yeah, that's how it's done."

"That's how I feel right now. Like I'm the orange."

"I don't understand. We're almost there."

He adjusted his stare to her eyes. "Susara, be honest: Is she right about me?"

"Who? Nicole?"

"When we first separated, she told me that I was only lying to myself about trying to save Jordan. That this was my addiction, and I was a selfish man…"—he choked, tears forming—"…What kind of father would use his daughter's sickness as an excuse for his own sickness?"

Tenderly, she placed a hand on his shoulder, but she didn't speak. No one could know his true motivations but him, and nothing she could say would alleviate his misgivings.

"My soul's worn thin, you know? I don't want her to only remember my absence during her struggle." He stared at his hands, his anguish turning to anger as tears struck the dusty soil. "But I couldn't just sit there and watch her die."

"Then finish this." She rocked his shoulder, then gently punched his arm. "Let's talk it out. Where could this symbol be?"

He wiped his eyes and cleared his throat. "Well, pillars were sometimes used as symbols of the threshold to an otherworldly passage or an entrance to a sacred place. So that would be a start, assuming the Minoans had used something permanent like stone for their pillars instead of upside-down cypress trees."

"OK, so that's off the table." Urging him on, she asked, "What else?"

He continued, but he sounded dejected. His fire and passion for the hunt had vanished. Now he was just going through the motions. "We know we're looking for the palace's megaron— the principal hall. It'd be oblong, with sloping sides and a flat top. That's where the Minoans typically built passageways leading to their underground burial chambers."

"OK, that's good. That's more than we had to work from before. Can you think of anything else? Something in Pernier's journal, maybe?"

He buried his face in his hands again. "Susara, I've read that journal front to back every night for years. There's nothing in there beyond what we already know. Trust me."

"Humor me." Reaching into his bag and withdrawing the journal, she began flipping through the brittle pages. Beneath Pernier's notes, covering the margins, Lane had added notes of his own, the ink fresh and dark. Scrolling past the original stone rubbing of the Phaistos Disc and Pernier's crudely sketched image of the clay tablet, she stopped on Lane's carefully penned translation of the Phaistos Disc's symbols.

Two palaces a sea apart. One, ruled by royal blood, the other, built beside the mighty river. Within their temples, beneath the royal crest, hides the source of the kingdom's eternal beauty. This disc will guide the deserving to salvation.

Scraping the heels of his PF Flyers into the dirt, he sighed. "Told you. Nothing new."

She shook her head. There was something about the translation that had struck a chord. "*Beneath the royal crest*. We assume that's the *labrys*, right? King Minos's royal crest? But let's roll with my idea for a second. What symbol would represent a labyrinth? A bull's head, maybe? Like the Minotaur?"

"Yeah, maybe. I guess if we're diving down the rabbit hole of Greek mythology, the Minotaur was actually known as Asterion, the bastard son of Pasiphaë, wife of King Minos. The oracles convinced Minos to banish him to the labyrinth."

"But he was still a son of the king. Royalty. And Asterion was symbolized on Minoan coins as a star, right? Wouldn't that be considered a royal crest?"

He recoiled as though he'd been kicked in the shin. His back straightened, and he groaned. "Not a word about this to anyone." He shuffled two steps to his left to reveal the faint outline of a star—washed by coarse volcanic sands—on the face of the stone he'd been sitting on.

She crossed her arms and stared at the gateway.

This was it. What they'd been searching for. The find they'd flown around the planet to reach. Shed blood for.

And she felt...nothing.

"You aren't excited. Why?" he asked, his voice instantly brightening. "I mean, this is it, right? We found it!"

"Is it weird that I feel like this is all a bit anti-climactic?" she asked. "I mean, when we first decoded the disc, I envisioned some derelict pharaoh's tomb in the middle of the desert, lined with gold and relics that had survived grave robbers, storms, thousands of years under the sand. Here, it feels, I don't know, like the discovery's already been made." She held out a hand as if to point to the excavation site's many modern fixtures.

"Like we're just tearing down the caution tape and taking credit for someone else's success."

Moving with a newfound energy and resolve, Lane stepped on the stone. He looked at her with a puzzled expression. "I don't see how this is anti-climactic. What do you need? Fireworks?" I can do fireworks if you think it'll help you feel more accomplished." Withdrawing a brick of plastic explosive from his backpack, he wedged it beneath a corner of the stone.

"Tell me that isn't C4." She stared at him with the disapproval of a parochial school nun.

"OK, it's not. It's C3. Older stuff. I may or may not have taken it from a Greek military base during the government protests a few years back."

"How the hell did you manage that?"

"I flashed a contractor's ID badge and they let me walk right in. I was kinda surprised how easy it was to pull off, especially considering the guy I stole the ID from was a six-foot-tall, bald, Japanese guy."

As he poked an electronic detonator into the soft, clay-like explosive, she turned away.

"I'm not seeing this."

"It might turn out to be a dud," he said as if to reassure her. "This stuff is probably 50 years old. And it's just a teensy charge, anyway. Won't even wake the neighbors."

Unwinding the wire connecting the detonator to the switch until they reached a safe position behind a monolithic statue of a bull, Lane knelt beside Susara. She had covered her ears and pinched her eyes shut in preparation for the blast.

He tapped her shoulder. "Keep your mouth open during the blast, and take shallow breaths—don't hold air in. The shockwave might burst your lungs, otherwise."

She had no trouble complying; her mouth hung agape at the advice.

"What happened to it being a teensy charge?"

"I sometimes confuse my adjectives." He triggered the switch. Nothing happened. He tried again, then waited a few seconds before standing and following the wire leading to the explosive.

"Must be a faulty switch. You know, this is the problem with using military surplus—"

The delayed detonation blew him backward, depositing him on the ground as a pulse of intense heat blew by.

*****

Castelnaudary
Lauragais, France
2003

Castelnaudary possessed all the features of a sleepy French town one might expect to see in a World War II film. At first glance, it would be easy to think such a place was populated only by friendly old men who wore tweed caps and rode bicycles with baskets mounted on the handlebars. Despite its peaceful facade—old-world church spires soaring over the surrounding stone buildings, brightly painted launches and skiffs rolling leisurely on the water of the *Canal du Midi*—the town was also the home of the French Foreign Legion's 4th Foreign Regiment. And today, the town was at war.

Lane re-adjusted for the fourth time that morning the sling attached to his FAMAS rifle. The buckle was worn and had bent when he'd fallen on it during the unit's last exercise. He feared it would let go of the canvas strap completely at an inopportune time. He had some expensive hardware mounted on his rifle, too, and couldn't risk it being damaged by a fall. The bulbous laser module attached to his weapon's barrel would send a pulse each time the rifle fired a blank round. Every soldier in the exercise wore a vest and helmet cover bedecked in sensors to indicate if they'd been hit by enemy fire.

Lined up in the shade of the town's bakery, he and his squad mates awaited orders. The building was closed today, but the smell of fresh bread still filled the street. From where Lane stood, the town appeared abandoned. Even the local dogs, always eager to see new faces, had cleared out.

His unit had taken over the village, flooding the cobblestone streets as they hunted down the opposing forces hiding out in alleyways and on rooftops. His platoon had been tasked with raiding one of the town's decrepit hotels, clearing it of enemy combatants. The building showed signs that it had been used for this exercise before: Black scorch marks painted the doorway Lane was expected to breach, and the door itself was new—likely just installed the day before. His role in the raid was to plant a breaching charge and create an entryway into the building for his men. He had to get it right. Too little explosive, the door wouldn't be blown off its hinges, and he and his platoon would look like buffoons in front of the adjutant—a hawk-nosed man observing the exercise from a balcony across the street. Plus, the sound would alert the enemy inside of the impending assault, eliminating their element of surprise. Too much explosive, on the other hand, and the overpressure could kill those inside, or cause enough structural instability to collapse part of the old brick building and bring it down on their own heads.

"*Premiere Classe Bradley, êtes vous prêt à faire tomber la porte?*" his sergeant called to him from across the street, waving him toward the door.

Lane nodded. Gripping the handle of his heavy canvas gear bag, he sprinted across the street and knelt beside the hotel's foundation. He'd spent the past 10 minutes staring at the door, scanning it from top to bottom, taking in every detail. It looked to be made of solid wood, of frame-and-panel design. A glance at the jamb revealed no exposed hinge pins, meaning the door swung inward. The charge he'd prepared—three lengths of detonating cord—would be just about right.

As his men swept the adjacent rooftops with their rifles, Lane peeled back the cover from his charge, exposing the sticky tape that would hold it in place. He adhered the detcord to the door. Satisfied with his work, he hustled into cover around the side of the building, dragging a shock cord lead line behind him.

"*Etre prêt. J'avoir le contrôle,*" Lane said, his hand cradling the rig's pull-pin ignitor.

Slipping into his mouth a chrome whistle hanging from his neck by a lanyard, the sergeant gave three shrill whistles.

"*Etre prêt.*" The sergeant gave him a nod.

Lane drew the pin on the ignitor, expecting to hear a thunderous boom, followed by the shouts of his comrades as they poured into the building, rifles shouldered. Instead, he heard only a hollow *click*. Before he could check to see what had gone wrong, the report of a single rifle shot echoed through the narrow cobblestone street. An enemy sniper had targeted his platoon.

Men began shouting orders and obscenities. Small-arms fire crackled in the street like a fireworks display building up to an inevitable, thunderous finale. Before Lane could sweep his FAMAS to his shoulder and join in the fracas, the sergeant tapped him on the back and pointed to Lane's helmet. The sensor mounted on it blinked red.

"*Tu es mort. Vous avez échoué vos hommes.*"

You've died.

You've failed your men.

FORTY-NINE

Coughing and wiping the dust from her arms and face, Susara crawled to where Lane had fallen. His body lay still, obscured by a veil of dust hanging on the still air. Planting a hand on his shoulder, she shook him.

"Lane? Lane! You OK?"

He sat upright, blinking and stretching his jaw, ears throbbing. "Teensy was definitely the wrong word." Turning, he looked back at the smoldering hole he'd created in the earth. The explosion had flipped the heavy stone to its opposite face, revealing a subterranean passage diving downward into the bowels of the ruins.

"You've got a little cockroach in you, don't you?" She wiped the dust from his shoulders. Dirt clung to his hair and eyelashes. "A normal week for you would kill most people."

As if to reinforce her statement, a bullet tore through the air an inch above Lane's head, whining loudly as it ricocheted against a rock. They both dropped down, diving in opposite directions for cover behind an excavated stone wall. Peeking out, they watched a crowd of armed men approach.

Behind them, shouting orders, stood a short man with a bullwhip and an eyepatch.

"Friends of yours?" she asked.

He cursed. How could Chigaru have followed him? He'd ditched them in Luxor. He was sure of it.

"Lane, you've got a better angle. Take the gun." She lobbed the pistol toward him.

Staring at the weapon at his feet, he shook his head. "No thanks." He dug himself deeper into the sandy ground as another round snapped overhead and shattered the bulb of a halogen work light left behind by the site's archaeologists. "You go right ahead, though." He tossed the gun back toward her.

"Are you serious right now?" she shouted as she picked it up and began firing at the approaching men. "You picked a hell of a time to become a pacifist."

Bullets thunked into the stones of the temple wall above their heads.

"I just don't want to shoot anyone today. That's not what I came here for."

"Yeah? Why don't you try telling them that?" she said, firing the last of her rounds at a fast-approaching gunman. She slid back into cover, staring at the empty pistol in her hand for a moment before letting it drop to the dirt.

"That sounds like you're out of bullets, Mr. Lane," Chigaru taunted from behind cover.

"Wasn't expecting to go to war today, Chigaru," he shouted back. "And I was really hoping not to see your ugly face again so soon."

"Step into the open, and I'll show you my ugly face up close. Maybe you won't think it's so ugly, then. Especially with my fist inside your ribcage."

"How'd you find us here?"

The little man laughed mockingly. "You think you can hire a helicopter pilot in my neighborhood without me hearing about it? I knew exactly where you were going before you even got off the ground. Oh, and don't bother calling your pilot to come take you home, either. I had him depopulated with the blades of his own helicopter."

"The word's decapitated, you evil little amoeba." Lane stared at his hands as they tightened into fists.

Another rifle round impacted above their heads.

"I won't tell you again, Mr. Lane. Get up and give me that disc."

"What are you going to do with it, Chigaru? Nobody's going to buy this thing while it's all over the news, and you don't have the patience to sit on it for a decade to let it cool down. We both know that."

"You let me worry about—" Chigaru didn't get the rest of his sentence out before all sound was replaced by thunderous gunfire.

Daring a glance over the wall, Lane spotted another group of men enter the ruins, exchanging rounds with Chigaru's crew as they approached. He caught sight of a tweed jacket. Agapito.

"You mention an open bar and everyone in town shows up." Lane motioned for Susara to follow him as he moved along the dug-out trench, crouched down and head low, moving toward the still-smoldering entrance to the underground passageway.

"Wait, Lane, we could just leave," she shouted, tugging the tail of his shirt to get his attention. "We have the disc. Now we know where the temple is. We can come back later, when they've left."

He shook his head. "Agapito will post guards all over this place, and they'll be expecting us. No telling how long they'll be here. I'm not waiting another day. Jordan needs this. We can get down there and test the disc's powers, then wait until they're done killing each other to leave. But we need to get down there now, before they see us."

"But if they find us down there, we'll be trapped."

He looked at her with pleading eyes. She moved her hands as if to give him a gentle shove toward the temple entrance. "Fine, let's go."

The cries of wounded men filled the dig site, bullets snapping overhead and caroming off stone and steel. Then, suddenly, silence. Lane and Susara stopped. They'd closed the distance to the temple entrance, but to reach it, they'd have to cross over exposed ground.

"Lane, does this...creature...belong to you?" Agapito called out.

Lane closed his eyes and let his chin drop to his chest. Agapito knew he was here, which meant what little chance they had of slipping into the temple unnoticed, or escaping, had vanished. He raised his head over the lip of the trench. Agapito's men held Chigaru upright by his arms. The man was barely conscious, bleeding from his mouth and a weeping bullet wound in his abdomen.

"Nope, afraid that's not mine. Better return it to the lost and found."

"Joking aside, come out here and give me the disc. I'll let this man live if you do it quickly."

One glance at Susara told him her thoughts on what they should do. *Forget these guys. Let's run for it.*

"I promise, you won't be harmed. Come on out," Agapito coaxed.

Undecided on what course of action to take, Lane stayed silent.

Susara called out, "Call me skeptical, but you've tried to kill both of us a whole lot in the past few days. We're not too eager to make ourselves a target, least of all when all we have is your word that you won't kill us."

"I'm graciously accepting your surrender. If you choose not to comply, I'll first shoot this man, then I'll have my men come for you. They'll not be as polite as I've been. You're both smart people. You know when you've been beaten, and today, you have. There's nowhere to run, and you have no way of fighting back."

Resting against a stone wash basin, elbows on his knees, Lane clasped his hands before his face as if praying. Motioning for her to stay down, he stood.

"No more killing today, Agapito." He approached his adversary, drawing the backpack from his shoulder and holding it out.

Agapito accepted the bag. Drawing the Phaistos Disc from inside, the assassin looked relieved. Without looking where he was aiming, Agapito used his free hand to draw his pistol. Planting the muzzle against Chigaru's eyepatch, he pulled the trigger. The bullet punched the man's brain matter through the back of his skull, showering the dirt in pink mist.

Lane jumped back, hands on his head. "Oh come on. Why, Agapito? He was wounded. Harmless. You didn't have to kill him."

"You truly are a gentleman thief, aren't you? That vile little man just tried to murder you. Would have, I think, had I not arrived when I did, and yet you wanted me to save his life. Now *that's* nobility." He swept aside the flap of his tweed coat and returned the pistol to its holster. "However, had I been as honorable as you and let this man go, he would have healed eventually. He would have come back. He would have hunted me down, like the ignorant little savage he was, incapable of realizing that he's only a lowly street thug—a minnow that slipped from its little pond into the ocean. Men like that, they're mosquitos, buzzing about and taking stinging little bites until—" He slapped his hands together loudly. "So why delay the inevitable? I'd have had to kill him eventually. You'd do well to learn such things, my friend."

He waved his men forward, and they began patting down Lane and Susara, taking their phones. One took apparent delight in searching Susara, his hands boldly sliding up her thighs toward her crotch. Planting her thumb into the man's eye, she then delivered a sharp palm strike to his nose.

Guns were raised as the man dropped to his knees, crying out as blood poured between his fingers.

"Tell your dogs to behave themselves," she said, staring at Agapito.

"Of course." He eyed the wounded man as he rolled in the dirt. "My apologies. Men in this line of work tend to lack our...civility."

Lane straightened his shirt following his pat-down. "Agapito, we've known each other for years, and if there's one thing I've learned about you, it's that you'd struggle to find your own ass with both hands and a spotlight. How'd you know we were here?"

A devious grin crossed Agapito's face as he grabbed Susara's phone from one of his men. He held up his phone beside it, the screen showing the blinking dot over Santorini. "We all have our little tricks." Letting her phone drop to the dirt, he smashed it with his heel. "Take you, for instance. I smell...what is that? Tar? Coal? It does have a unique, bituminous scent about it. Judging by the dust in the air and the guilt written on your face, I believe you've been toying with plastic explosives. You found something, didn't you? Oh you naughty boy."

Lane looked at Agapito dispassionately without saying a word, but Susara glanced away, just for an instant, in the direction of the passageway. Agapito noticed.

"I just knew I could count on you, old friend."

The air temperature suddenly dropped, the sun disappearing behind the clouds as a breeze whistled through the ruins. A hoary form approached, shuffling through the rubble, emitting a rasping cough every few yards like an antique farm tractor belching exhaust.

Musarde.

"You." The old man stabbed a crooked finger at Lane as he neared. "You're the one who stole my journal."

"Does it count as stealing if you stole it from someone else?" Lane asked. "Your sense of ownership is a bit misguided considering the circumstances." Eying the gold ring on Musarde's finger, he whispered, "But then, this wouldn't be the first time you've taken something that didn't belong to you, would it?"

The old man stepped close. Near enough that Lane could smell the decay of the old man's teeth and see in great detail the buff-colored tobacco stains fringing his mouth, blending with the deep shadows between sagging skin. Though bent slightly at the waist, Musarde still towered over him.

"You recognize my ring. Of course you do, you disgusting wretch. You've been hunting all the same relics I have to get here. But I've beaten you, haven't I?"

"Well you've had plenty of experience beating people, and judging by your face, plenty of experience being beaten, too." Nodding at the old man's hand, Lane said, "That's the Ring of Mavro Spelio, isn't it? A fascinating bit of Minoan craftsmanship, that. You're a pretty clever guy, so I'm sure you've learned by now that it's not much help in this little pursuit of ours. I took the liberty of jotting down its symbols when I took the journal—you're adorable when you're sleeping, by the way—and what a disappointment that ring turned out to be." Lane reached into his pocket, withdrew Pernier's notebook, and shoved it against Musarde's chest. Before releasing his grip, Lane leaned toward him and whispered, "How much blood did you shed for that ring, only to have it tell you where the disc was located a century ago?"

The elderly man, with no small amount of effort, swung a fist at Lane, knuckles connecting with his cheek.

Rubbing his jaw, Lane chuckled as he righted himself. "Did your wrist just break? Felt brittle."

Musarde rocked back to deliver another blow, but Lane dove into him, the two men falling to the dirt. Agapito's men quickly pulled him off the older man and proceeded to beat him into compliance.

Standing slowly, Musarde spat at Lane. "The man's not worth the bullet it would take to end him. An uncouth stealer of antiquities, that's all you are." He took the Phaistos Disc from Agapito and held it against his chest like a child selfishly gripping a toy.

Lane smirked, his teeth covered in blood. "Old man, you *are* an antique."

"Enough," Agapito ordered, pointing toward the smoldering hole in the earth. "Down you go."

Musarde stepped forward eagerly. "Come, bear witness to my rejuvenation, Lane Bradley. Bask in my greatness as you contemplate your failure."

FIFTY

Blinding white light floodlit the narrow cavern walls, Agapito's men sweeping the path with flashlights as they traveled deeper into the Minoan temple, pushing Susara and Lane along. The dust on the air settled on sweat-beaded skin, the atmosphere oppressive and still. One of the men sneezed as he inhaled a cloud of dust. Another complained of the spider web he couldn't seem to wipe from his face.

Musarde followed close behind Agapito, his timeworn hands clenching the disc. The soles of his loafers scraped along the stone stairway as he shuffled along, careful with each footstep as he blindly sought the next step down. His countenance was blank—his mind elsewhere. The elderly man muttered to himself, beseeching the gods to let the legend of the disc prove true.

"What I find most bewildering about all this is your insistence on trying to best me, Lane," Agapito taunted as he shoved over a crude statue partially blocking their path. His voice echoed dully against the stone walls. "For as many years as we've known each other, there has never been an instance of you coming out on top, and yet you persist."

"Agapito, you're running at the mouth. Nervous about something?" Lane replied, his countenance relaxed.

Susara smirked. Lane could sense Agapito's anxiety in his father's presence and was rubbing salt in the wound.

One of Agapito's mercenaries—a dwarfish, bug-eyed man, slapped the slide of his pistol against the back of Lane's skull. Catching himself before stumbling, he tenderly touched his fingers to the fresh wound.

"Hands too soft to do the bloodletting yourself, Agapito?"

Stopping in his downward path, Agapito turned and gently placed a hand on Lane's arm. Leaning in until his mouth was an inch from Lane's ear, he whispered, "You'll see my capacity for bloodletting in a few minutes. I wouldn't waste any more of your precious breath castigating me. Perhaps you should pray, instead." With an insincere smile, he patted his shoulder.

Plunging downward, the narrow passageway began to widen. Upon reaching the end of the stairway, they found themselves inside a vast grotto blanketed in skeletal remains. The space had been festooned in brightly painted murals—perfectly preserved in the darkness for thousands of years—portraying religious ceremonies and dark-haired men leaping over the heads of charging bulls. Unadorned bronze braziers nestled inside the many shallow alcoves carved in the walls, cloaked in a thick crust of verdigris that camouflaged them when flashlight beams flicked by.

Ignoring the scene, Musarde marched urgently toward the room's central altar—a crude stone edifice upon which rested several ornate clay vessels. Cradling the disc in his hands as he genuflected—a slow, labored movement to the foot of the altar—Musarde muttered, "Grant me beauty."

Minutes passed in silence. Everyone, even Susara, watched attentively to see if the legend of the disc's healing power would prove true. Musarde's head hung down against his chest, his eyes closed, while his men clutched their guns closer and shuffled uncomfortably in the darkness. Soon, it became clear the old man's supplications had gone unanswered. He shifted the disc about the altar's surface. Cradled it in his hands. Flipped it to the opposite face. Placed the cipher stones in a semicircle around it. Still, nothing happened.

Lane chewed his lip, scanning the cavern with the same attention he gave to the Heraklion Museum before attempting the disc's robbery. She heard him take a sharp breath. He wore the look of someone who had just realized a profound mistake they'd made.

"What is it?" she asked, leaning toward him.

"*Beneath the royal crest hides the source of the kingdom's eternal beauty. This disc will guide the deserving to salvation,*" he whispered in her ear, his breath cool against her skin. "Look at the frescoes on the walls. The figures in red rushing toward the boats, the ones in white retreating into the mountain. In Cretan art, white skin was meant to symbolize a woman or royalty. Those with red skin were men."

"I don't understand."

He gestured toward where Musarde knelt before the altar at the cavern's center. "Look at the skeletons in here. The Minoans preferred to bury their dead in terra cotta *larnakes* or *sarcophagi*, but these bodies are out in the open and in natural poses, as if they were sleeping. And look at them: They're small and without weapons. These were women and children. The frescoes, the bodies, the disc's inscription, they all say the same thing. *The kingdom's eternal beauty* was referring to the empire's children, their legacy—the future of their civilization. The Phaistos Disc wasn't some key to lifelong beauty and health, it was an emergency plan. *This disc will guide the deserving to salvation.* The two temples were the kingdom's fallout shelters, meant to protect the women and children from danger. They came down here to escape the volcano, seeking salvation, but they must have become trapped inside. God, how could I have been so stupid?"

"What's he saying?" Musarde turned around. "You, what are you going on about?"

Clearing his throat and forcing a laugh, Lane asked, "You enjoying the weather here?"

"What? Why?"

"I really hope you are, because it's the only thing that'll come from your journey. Pernier's legend is a lie. You're praying to the same deaf gods these skeletons entreated when they were sealed in here 3,000 years ago."

"No, it was in his journal. He was healed, restored. Made beautiful," Musarde protested.

"A fairytale," Lane said coldly. "The disc was meant to reveal the hiding place of the Minoan women and children should the island come under attack. The cipher stones were paired with the disc so even the Egyptians—their allies—could find and rescue the Minoans should enemy forces succeed in overtaking their capital cities. But before the disc and the stones could be delivered to the Egyptians, a seismic shift that completely changed the ancient world brought the Minoan empire to its knees. Thera's women and children were sealed in this vault by an erupting volcano, and no one ever found them. Until today. You can take pride in that, Musarde. It's the one decent thing you've ever had a hand in."

Musarde looked around, finally taking in his macabre surroundings. Realization dawned on his face as he shifted his expectant gaze to Agapito. The younger man looked to the dirt floor, his mouth moving emptily as he sought an explanation.

Musarde swung his cupped hand against his son's ear. "You cretin."

Looking at Lane with contempt, Agapito called after Musarde as the elderly man moved to leave. "Father, wait. The Minoans were said to have practiced human sacrifice in some instances."

Lane scoffed. "Like twice in their entire history."

Agapito glowered at his adversary. "Perhaps the disc requires blood for its curative powers."

Musarde paused as he lifted a foot to the first step leading out of the crypt. A part of him was just desperate enough to try it, and his hesitation proved it. "Let blood if it pleases you, but the journal never spoke of such a thing," he said. "This isn't the second temple. Keep looking. Next time, don't contact me until you're sure of it. Deal with these two and meet me at the car." He slowly ascended the stairway.

Lane shouted after him, "Musarde, you'll spend the rest of your days hunting that temple, but the one in your mind doesn't exist. Pernier lied about the disc's power. It's all imaginary. This is all there is."

From the top of the stairs, Musarde called back, his voice echoing distantly, "Then so be it. Let that be my hell, and let this be yours."

As Agapito and his men filtered into the stairwell, the assassin turned and withdrew his pistol. Without a word, he thumbed the 1911's safety off and fired a single round into Lane's leg. The impact drove him to the floor, his face filled with more surprise than pain. Susara followed him down, kneeling before him protectively as she glared at Agapito.

"Come on, Agapito. That was just mean," Lane said with a groan.

As the ringing of the gunshot died away, Agapito moved forward, shoving Susara aside. Stepping over his fallen adversary, he wrapped a hand around Lane's *fravashi* amulet. With a swift tug, he unsnapped the chain. "I've always admired this little charm of yours. I think I'll take it to remember you by." He placed the necklace in his breast pocket. "Oh, and Ms. Eaves, I'll pass along your regards to your supervisor, Director Luis. He and I have struck up something of an alliance during all this. He's been very amenable to monetary persuasion and the promise that I'd leave you to die in a far-off corner of the globe. Apparently, he felt threatened by you. Peculiar." He shrugged nonchalantly as he looked her over. "Regardless of his motivations, I'm sure he'll prove to be an indispensable resource should your organization choose to pursue me again in the future."

What could he have meant by that? She and Ruben had never seen eye to eye, but there was no way he wanted her dead. He'd never...would he?

Lane grimaced, blood trickling through his fingers as he applied pressure to his wound.

Taking one final look around the space, Agapito sniffed imperiously, then swept his palms over the graying hair at his temples. "Well, for the final time, Lane, goodbye. I'll always hold your memory in high regard. You were a worthy adversary until the last." Grabbing a flashlight from one of his men, he tossed it at Lane's feet. "I'd hate to leave you in the dark."

Agapito and his men climbed toward the surface, their footsteps echoing and fading to silence. The eerie scrape of a heavy stone pushed atop the cavern's entrance resonated like a final death knell.

FIFTY-ONE

Silence hung over the necropolis as Lane probed the wound in his leg. With an accepting grunt, he removed his shirt and wrapped it tightly around his thigh to stanch the flow of blood.

"Well, let's get out of here." He wiped the blood from his hand on his pants before reaching to Susara for help standing.

"We're locked in." She could hear the despondency in her own voice, but did nothing to hide it. They'd been dealt a final, staggering blow. The fight was over, and now there was little left to do but lie broken on the mat and await the ten-count. "You're bleeding—a lot—and we're trapped."

"You underestimate the intelligence of ancient people." His face contorted in pain as he rose to his feet and tested his weight on his wounded leg. "Who would dig a cavern like this one without leaving themselves a way to breathe? There's no way the volcano blocked all of the vents. We find where the air is coming in, we find our way out."

"How can you be so calm at a time like this?"

"What other option do we have?" he chuckled. His jovial demeanor vanished with a groan as his wound pulsed a painful reminder. "I'm a solutions guy. If there's a problem, I attack it until I solve it or it beats me. *Res ad triarios venit.*"

"Go until the triarii. Carry on to the bitter end."

Hobbling along the wall nearest to the caldera's exposed face, he swept a hand over the stone. With effort, he managed to climb atop a *pithos*, an enormous clay vessel once used to store olive oil, and ran a finger along a dark fissure. "That's our fresh air. We just need to get through this wall, and we're home free."

"That's solid stone. I don't care how many push-ups you can do, you're not pushing through that."

"Gotta be smarter than the rock." He climbed down and knelt in a dark corner, stabbing a finger into a brown puddle. Limping back to Susara, he held his finger beneath her nose. "Smell that?"

"This isn't the time for playground antics."

"Smell it."

She cautiously sniffed at the substance on his finger. "Smells like gas."

"Natural gas condensate."

"So your big plan is to what? Ignite it? Blow a hole in the rock?"

"Something like that. My version has a little more romance to it, though. What do you know about Greek fire?"

"Ancient napalm," she said unenthusiastically.

"You sure know how to take the shine off a cool story. Couldn't even muster up a positive inflection in your voice? A little fake enthusiasm for your dying friend? Yeah, it's ancient napalm, or more specifically, naphtha. The Greeks figured out how to launch the stuff on enemy ships, and it became one of the most devastating weapons developments of the ancient world. Given the advantage it served on the battlefield, the Greeks compartmentalized the formula to keep it a secret. Like so many secrets, it died with those who kept it. No one really knows exactly what was used to make the stuff. But I've got a pretty good idea what went into the recipe."

Swinging the flashlight around the cavern, he settled on a skeleton clutching a crude bronze knife. "Mind if I borrow that for a minute?" he asked the corpse. Plucking it from its grasp, he approached a line of *pithoi* lining the cavern wall.

"You may not want to watch this part. It's criminal to have to do this, but dire circumstances…." He moved the flashlight to his mouth to free his hands. Using the heel of the knife, he smashed into the clay shell of the first container. He went from one to the next, pausing briefly to explore the pottery's contents before smashing another hole.

"What are you looking for?" she asked.

He plunged the knife into another vessel and let out a grunt of satisfaction. "Pine resin. The Minoans added it to their wine." He scraped a softball-sized globule of the syrupy substance onto a large clay shard and limped over to the pool of natural gas condensate. He began blending the two ingredients together using the knife blade.

Suddenly feeling lightheaded, Susara realized how much she was sweating inside the dark cavern and how dehydrated she was becoming. The air was still and oxygen-poor. Lane's plan had to work, because even another few hours like this could bring their deaths. She glanced at his bloody pant leg and suddenly felt panic. If they couldn't escape, he would almost certainly die first, leaving her to face her end alone.

Lane clearly didn't share her apprehension. Satisfied with the mixture, he hobbled over to the fissure in the temple wall, stuffing the concoction into the seam.

"This is where things get exciting." He tamped the goop down with the knife blade. Tossing the artifact into the shadows, he knelt gingerly and pulled free one of his shoelaces. "Find me a long stick, will you?" he asked as he unscrewed the lens from the flashlight.

Shaking away her dizziness, she began fumbling in the dim light, eventually finding a crude wooden pole supporting an unlit torch. Returning with the find, she looked hard at Lane. Perhaps it was just the effect of the flashlight's beam on his features, but he looked deathly pale.

"You doing OK?"

"I'm fine," he said dismissively, accepting the pole and lashing the flashlight to its tip with the shoelace. "Take cover behind the altar."

"And where are you going to hide?

He said nothing.

She prompted him again, "Lane——"

"Get behind the altar. It'll be fine."

"If you're going to touch that thing off, it could kill you."

"And if I don't, we'll die anyway." He carefully broke the flashlight's bulb with a stone to expose the leads. Shuffling back as far as he could while remaining within distance to touch the pole to the mixture, he asked, "Ready?"

"What happens when the whole cavern explodes and we die?"

"Well, then we'll know I was wrong." He angled the flashlight toward the naphtha. "And you can hold that over my head for all eternity."

The leads, glowing dimly, hovered in the darkness like fireflies. They disappeared amidst a flash and puff of smoke. The explosion was small, a sudden hiss, neither loud nor dazzling. Then, darkness.

"That was anticlimactic," she said.

The cavern groaned. The floor of the temple trembled and clods of dirt and fine, powdered stone began to drop from the ceiling.

"It's caving in!" He shuffled past her on his way toward the center of the room. "Grab the other side of the altar's top."

"Why?" Her hands fumbled for the large stone in the darkness.

"Not really the time to ask that question." He grunted, struggling to support the weight of the massive slab without transferring it to his injured leg. The walls shook visibly, and a corner of the cavern crumbled and collapsed.

Together, they drove the stone into the spot where the naphtha had exploded, striking the wall like driving a battering ram into a castle door. A small pinhole of sunlight shot inside, a spider web of jagged cracks surrounding it. With each strike, more sunlight entered the cavern. Finally, muscles burning and exhaustion setting in, they managed to create an opening large enough for them to squeeze through.

"Go!"

"You first!" she shouted back.

Grabbing her shirt collar in one hand and her belt in the other, Lane hefted her through the hole. "A gentleman always holds the door for a lady," he said, lunging through the aperture behind her. A mighty rushing noise followed, pouring forth from inside the cavern. A violent cough of dust blasted through the hole behind him.

Toes overhanging a narrow ledge carved into the caldera wall, they looked down to find themselves hundreds of feet from the water.

"Out of the frying pan." Her fingers dug into the friable rock slope with animal-like desperation.

"Well, we either wait here in hopes that someone will notice us before we die of dehydration—or, in my case, blood loss— or we jump." He stared at the pounding surf below.

She balanced unsteadily on the edge of the precipice. "Jump? Are you out of your mind? That's easily a 200-foot fall."

"I know, right?" He chuckled and reached for her hand.

She gave it, wrapping her fingers tightly around his.

"Come on. Live a little," he said, eyes aglow and the makings of a smile on his lips.

Her heart beat wildly in her chest as Lane gave her hand a squeeze. Though terrified, she couldn't suppress a smile. "OK."

Together, they leapt from the cliffside and plummeted into the azure waters below.

FIFTY-TWO

Santorini National Airport

The runway crackled in the midday sun, a heat mirage rising from the distant tarmac. A wall of storm clouds approached. Agapito flung the car door open and disembarked, shuffling his tweed jacket off, revealing his holstered pistol. He ignored the startled stares of the baggage handlers nearby as he hastened toward his father's plane.

Musarde, supported by one of his men, followed. He called after his son, "You behave as though I've slighted you, as though I'm somehow at fault for your negligence. But you have made yourself appear the fool today, and in so doing, made me look a fool."

Already enraged by the day's events, Agapito had no remaining patience to absorb his father's upbraiding. "That's easy to say." The younger man turned and stormed back toward his father, stopping with his face inches from Musarde's. The old man flinched, uncomfortable having anyone so close to his disfigured skin. "You sit behind your desk in the safety of your fortress, but send me out like an errand boy to fetch your trinkets. And I do. I go out and get these things for you. But still you rebuke me as though I've suffered no pain or risk at all. Today, I put the Phaistos Disc in your hands and delivered you to the Minoan temple. Everything you asked for. What does it take to please you?"

Musarde's smoke-yellowed teeth showed in a mocking smirk. "You didn't deliver me the correct temple. I gave you a job—a very specific task—and you failed. How can you not understand my disappointment?"

Agapito turned and stared at the runway's yellow lines trailing off into the distance. There was no other temple. Lane was right. It was a myth. And now, Agapito would spend the rest of his days hunting a mirage, all for a man incapable of showing appreciation for his doing so.

"I've given you everything," Musarde continued, donning a pair of oversized sunglasses. He took careful steps toward the waiting aircraft. "I paid for your education, and the life lessons you couldn't learn in school I taught you myself. I took you off the streets and I gave you work. I gave your once-miserable life purpose. Yet you have the gall to think me unjust?"

Tempted to break off the argument before it reached a crescendo, Agapito instead blurted, "I do. I always have."

Musarde stopped at the base of the rolling stairway affixed to the plane's fuselage, one hand on the chrome railing. "Then you are a weaker man than I thought. I demand success because you lack the impetus to demand it of yourself. When you fail, I make you better by punishing you for it. And look where you are today; you couldn't have become what you are without me."

His lips quivering, Agapito balled his hands into fists, knuckles turning white. "You're right. And I wish every day that I never would have become what you wanted. Perhaps I could have been a decent man, instead."

The first raindrops fell, the temperature plunging.

Chuckling as he ascended the stairway, the plane's engines building in volume, Musarde said, "A decent man is vulnerable. If you'd been decent, you'd be dead by now."

FIFTY-THREE

The sky, only hours before as bright blue and clear as the Aegean below it, had been blotted out by slate-colored clouds rumbling ominously with thunder. A drenching rain fell. Crawling beneath a beached, overturned sailboat long abandoned on a pebble-capped alcove, Lane and Susara huddled against one another for warmth.

"We should give it half an hour to make sure Agapito and his men are gone. It'd be a disappointing surprise to go through all this only to run into him again on our way out," he said, teeth chattering. He reached into his pocket and pulled out a gold ring. "The Ring of Mavro Spelio. You like? A parting gift from Musarde." He slipped it over his middle finger and clenched his fist. "I'm not really a jewelry guy, but this has a certain...*je ne sais quoi* about it. Think he'll miss it?"

"When did you take that?"

"During our scuffle. Popped right off."

A rat poked its head out of a knot in the boat's hull, causing him to jump.

"Tough guy. Letting a little mouse scare you," she teased.

But his stare remained locked on the animal, his expression fearful and the color drained from his face.

"It's just a mouse," she said, patting his arm.

"No, it's a rat. Totally morphologically different."

Rolling the waist of her shirt to ring the water from it, she shook her head. "What's so scary about a rat? He's just trying to stay out of the rain. Calm down."

"Yeah, well this seat's taken. He should go do rat stuff somewhere else."

"What's the big deal?"

Resting his head against her shoulder and sighing as though he'd just climbed into bed after running a marathon, he continued to watch the rat distrustfully as it groomed itself. "The prison in Lebanon. There weren't enough guards on staff, so they could only come around once a day to feed us. And to take away the bodies."

Blood dripped from his leg, slipping through his fingertips and blending with the puddle of rainwater pooling at their feet. Thunder crashed and he jumped—his grip tightening on his wound, skin pallid. She could hear his breathing becoming more rapid and shallow.

"Lane, stay with me. Five more minutes and we'll go for help." She rubbed his cheek with her hand to keep him conscious.

"There was no room in those cells." He pinched his eyes shut as if to hide from his memory. "Suffocating and putrid. Like being trapped inside a dumpster with a dozen other men." He began to slide lower on her shoulder, and she pulled him against her for support. He looked up at her, but his eyes held the same absent, far-off look of an inebriate. "We stacked them in the corner when they died to save space—feet of one over the head of the one beneath, interlocking like a pile of firewood. Then, at night, the rats would come. Some of the prisoners were so hungry, they trapped and ate the rats. Then, when they died, they were eaten by the rats. A miniature, macabre ecosystem. Some were so desperate to escape, they'd lie with the bodies for hours, pretending to be dead. They played the part pretty well. But then, we all did." His voice grew weaker, his eyes barely open.

She shook him. "OK, we're going now. Come on." She pulled him to his feet and rubbed his back until he seemed more responsive. Then she reached for his belt.

"Really? Now? I don't think my performance is gonna be too impressive considering all the blood loss," he joked, his voice weak.

Working quickly, she slipped the leather through his belt loops. Wrapping the belt around his thigh, she cinched it tight and twisted it until she'd stanched the blood flowing from his wounded leg. He groaned, gripping the overturned boat's deck for support.

"Just buying you a little time until we get you to a hospital," she said.

Leaning out from beneath the boat's hull, he blinked away the torrents of rain coursing down his face. "No hospital. Gunshot wounds get you a visit from local law enforcement. It's OK. I've got a guy. But when he finishes patching me up, we go get that disc and those stones back, straightaway."

She joined him outside the boat, wiping the rain from her eyes as she looked for a path they could use to ascend the caldera's sheer face. "At what point do we just cut our losses? We've had so many near-misses since this all began, all for the sake of a legend that turned out to be fiction. The disc won't save Jordan, so why don't we just let Musarde have it? We can put the authorities on his trail and go back home. After all, that was the point of all this, wasn't it? To help Jordan? Well the most help you can offer now is to be there with her."

"We can't go home yet, even for Jordan." He stared out at the open water, the surface battered by the rain. "There's no telling how many more people Musarde will kill in his pursuit of Pernier's mystical catholicon. It's my fault he has the disc. Without it, his fantasies would have stayed in that journal."

FIFTY-FOUR

She'd spent the past hour rehearsing exactly what she'd say. But even after readying herself, Susara found herself stuttering, stumbling over words as she explained her situation to NERO's managing director. During her tenure at NERO, she'd only exchanged a few hallway niceties with Dr. Rutendo Mosi, and despite the elderly Nigerian's soft-spoken and thoughtful demeanor, his diminutive build and shuffling gait, he intimidated her. He had more academic credentials than an Ivy League review board and an encyclopedic knowledge of everything even peripherally related to archaeology. He was the highest-ranking member of NERO save for the founder himself.

And here she was, telling him that his subordinate, Ruben, the man he'd personally selected for the position, had been working with an assassin to have her killed. To Dr. Mosi's credit, he listened to her entire explanation without interruption. Only his soft breathing into the receiver indicated he was still on the line.

When she'd said everything she could think to say, she listened intently for his response.

A moment passed as he considered her explanation. "I'll look into this. I suggest you come back to the office as soon as you can."

Dropping the phone's receiver into its cradle on the store's front desk, she peeked into the next room. Opening the door invited the scent of wet earth and clay. A smoke-blackened kiln loomed in a corner. Rows of decorative vases and bowls in various stages of completion lined the walls. Illuminated by a dying flashlight perched on a shelf, two forms reclined side by side in a pair of steel folding chairs.

Lane had known a guy, just like he'd said. A phone call to a contact in Athens had produced the name of a local doctor, one who wouldn't ask where the bullet hole in Lane's leg had come from and could be counted on to avoid contact with the authorities. Obviously using an unscrupulous medical professional came with drawbacks. She didn't have to look hard to figure out which ones this guy came with.

Translucent tubes ran from both men's arms, snaking their way to an IV pole draped with bags of saline, both fed by a morphine drip machine.

Approaching Lane, she touched his shoulder. He stirred. "How are you feeling?"

He looked at her dreamily. "I should ask you. You're the one with four arms and two heads."

She nodded toward the unconscious doctor beside him. Saliva dripped from the corner of his mouth and puddled on the floor. A guttural snore rumbled past his lips. "How do you find these people? Is there some kind of criminal directory?"

"Shows up on the front steps like the Yellow Pages every six months."

"Let me guess. He's actually a large animal veterinarian," she said.

"No, he's a real doctor. Pediatrician, actually. Great with kids. Excellent bedside manner." He glanced over his shoulder at the morphine drip machine, the screen flashing red. Tapping it a few times, he shrugged and settled back into his seat.

She knelt beside him and examined the dressing on his leg. The drug-addict doctor seemed to do good work—while he was conscious. "What's our next move?" The way she asked it was meant to convey to him that she already knew his answer, but was hoping he'd reconsidered.

"We need to take down Musarde and Agapito."

"How? We have nothing on either one." Neither man had ever been directly linked to a crime given their many layers of scapegoats and fall guys. "No one's going to help us. You suggesting we storm Musarde's mansion ourselves?"

Shifting in his seat and looking around, as if suddenly noticing his surroundings, he said, "Of course not. There has to be some way to get the authorities involved. Tax evasion? Mail fraud?"

"The Al Capone angle."

"Is it such a terrible idea? I mean, Musarde's been a player in the criminal world since public transportation ran on steam. He must have slipped up somewhere along the line."

"We could suggest the French authorities look into his finances, but something tells me he keeps two sets of books.

Besides, you really think they'd be able to put him away on an accounting error? And even if they did, would they be able to link him to the theft of the Phaistos Disc? You might get him behind bars, but he'll still have his stolen relics."

He looked up at the ceiling, trying to dig through the painkiller haze to figure out another way.

"I have an idea, but I doubt you'll like it very much," she whispered.

"Let's have it."

"You worked for Musarde once. Maybe you could make up a story about working for him again when you stole the disc." The thought had come to her hours ago, but she'd resisted telling him for fear he'd think she was still trying to get him behind bars.

He nodded slowly, the pieces falling into place. "I agreed to steal it for him. But when my partner—the guy who attacked me at Heraklion—killed the guards, I couldn't stand to be a part of the operation. When I tried to quit, he assaulted me, I defended myself, and the rest is history. So I turn myself in, testify against Musarde and Agapito, and take them down with me."

"I wish I could think of something different. Something better." If Lane went through with this, it meant a certain, lengthy prison sentence. Men had been murdered that night. If he admitted complicity, there'd be no negotiating, no chance for Dorothy to get him off the hook.

"That may be the only card we have left to play." Tugging the IV needle from his arm, he stood unsteadily, favoring his good leg. "Make the call. I've got a few I need to make, too."

FIFTY-FIVE

Ajaccio, Corsica

Musarde's estate still bore signs of the vineyard it had once been. Grapevines had been left to grow wild, the once neatly trimmed rows now a sweeping, tangled mess blanketing the arid hills. Terra-cotta roof tiles sloping over limestone columns and cedar-beam pergolas evoked a recognizably Mediterranean wine country flare. But instead of Western tourists casually strolling across the grounds cradling wine glasses in hand, solemn-looking security contractors with rifles, like restless underworld shades, roamed the property.

Black SUVs rested in the shade of a grove of clementine trees half a kilometer away. The French National Gendarmerie Intervention Group to whom they belonged prepared for their assault on the estate. Light rain ricocheted through the leaves of the trees overhead as Lane helped Susara tighten the shoulder straps on her plate carrier, glancing at the nearby operators suspiciously.

"You sure about this? Why not let the GIGN take care of Musarde? They may be French—they've got that working against them—but they're some of the best soldiers in the world. They don't need your help."

"Lane, I'll be fine."

"I bet you said that before the raid on Poldi's castle, too. You should let me come with you in case you need rescuing again," he said, half teasing, half pleading.

"You were shot only a few days ago." She reached down and gently patted the thick bandage pushing against his pant leg. He winced. "So you stay on the bench for this one. Watch the car. There's a tire-pressure gauge in the glove box you can play with."

Lane fixed his attention on using the toe of his PF Flyers to break loose clods of dirt from the treads of an SUV's back tire.

Susara raked a fingernail back and forth over a Velcro patch on her vest. "I'm sure you're having some second thoughts about all this—"

"It's fine," he interrupted. "Nicole should have enough money to pay for Jordan's treatments while I'm gone, and you promised you'd look after them."

"I will."

They'd known that raiding Musarde's estate to recover the artifacts would require an army, but they hadn't expected the French to send the GIGN, the country's premier anti-terror group, to conduct the raid. They soon learned that the words "stolen Middle-Eastern antiquities," especially when spoken to certain individuals in the French government, evoked images of black-clad men destroying Syrian and Iraqi historical sites, then selling the pillaged antiquities to help fund their murderous campaigns. The purchasing of said relics, as Musarde was sure to have done given his opportunist nature, his blatant disregard for human life, and the nature of his collection, could be considered bankrolling a terrorist organization. The French had no qualms about sending their very best to deal with someone like that.

"And you'll water my plants for me, too, right?" Lane joked. "And forward me copies of National Geographic? Makes a great makeshift baton if you wrap one up tightly enough."

She laughed. "Sure."

The GIGN operators motioned for Susara to join them, running their final weapons checks.

"Well, looks like it's go-time. Wish me luck." She turned to leave.

He placed a hand on her shoulder. "Hey, do whatever it takes to come back alive, OK? Put these guys away if you can, but just make sure you come back. There's always tomorrow. The planet's not that big, and there's nowhere they can run where we won't find them."

She nodded and offered her hand. He shook it, but pulled her in for a hug. "Hey, try not to get shot again. I won't be in there to save you this time."

"You should try listening to your own advice." After giving him a final squeeze, she approached the GIGN operators. Swinging open the cylinder on the Manurhin .357 revolver they'd given her, she rubbed a thumb over the huddle of brass rounds. Straight out of the '70s and the darkest, dustiest corner of their armory, it wasn't exactly the cutting-edge firepower of the GIGN's P90 submachine guns or FAMAS bullpup rifles, but it was reliable, and a good-faith gesture from their agency to hers. Besides, she wasn't looking to shoot anyone today. Her job was to recover the Phaistos Disc and the cipher stones, and ensure they were properly secured and transported back to Heraklion as soon as they were recovered.

Unless, of course, Agapito gave her the opportunity.

She owed that man a bullet.

As they set out on their approach, sweeping aside the dense tangle of grapevines and crouching low to avoid being seen, she caught a glimpse of a distant figure. It wasn't one of Musarde's security guards. Whoever it was seemed to be moving *toward* the building from the opposite side of the driveway.

"Dammit, Lane."

She should have known better. He would never just give up on those relics, helping the authorities to recover them in exchange for a prison sentence. Instead, he was using the brute force of the GIGN to engage Musarde's private security while he made his entrance. He'd get everything he wanted: Musarde and Agapito would be arrested or killed, he would make his escape with the Phaistos Disc and the cipher stones in tow, and he'd never see a day behind bars. She wasn't even upset. It had been brilliantly orchestrated, and she'd played right into it. There was no malice behind his plan. It was just what he did.

FIFTY-SIX

The thunderous cacophony of flash-bang grenades and gunshots disturbing the picturesque villa grounds provided ideal cover for Lane's ingress into the estate. A second-story window, the same one he'd used to enter Musarde's study years before, had once again proven the ideal point of entry. The old man, no doubt despite persistent warnings from his security team, always left it slightly ajar, likely to diffuse the constant haze of cigar smoke with a little fresh air. Just that slight lapse in caution was all Lane needed to get inside, and with any luck, retake the Phaistos Disc and the cipher stones before the GIGN had cleared the building.

The artifacts may not have possessed any magical beautifying power as he had initially hoped, but they were still enormously valuable. If he could get them before the GIGN did, he could make a small fortune on their sale—enough to build his own cancer research laboratory for Jordan if he so chose. Stealing and selling an artifact that had been kept in the safety of a well-funded, secure museum went against his code, but the thought that the years of physical and mental suffering he'd endured to get those relics had been wasted, and the knowledge that a huge score like this one would free him to spend some much-needed time with his daughter, had made his code much more flexible. He only hoped Susara would forgive him.

He moved quickly through the building's broad corridors. Each time he turned a blind corner into a medieval suit of armor or looming stone statue, his heart heaved violently. Although he'd been here before, lifting a journal from Musarde's desk and extracting a relic from his vigilantly guarded vault were two very different things.

The sound of approaching guards caused him to hang an abrupt right turn into the nearest room. The shades were drawn, the lights off, but he could still make out the looming outline of a grand piano in the room's center. The mercenaries stopped just outside the door. Their breathing was labored. They shuffled their rifles and mumbled into their earpieces.

"The principal has been escorted off-site. We're covering the rear entrance."

Lane pushed himself tight against the wall, holding his breath. He silently prayed they'd be called away or would move somewhere else quickly. He didn't have much time to pull this off.

A grenade detonated, followed by the sound of breaking glass. Urgent shouts erupted in their earpieces, and the men hastened down the hallway. Without waiting to see if the two would return, Lane slipped out of the room.

The corridor swept left and terminated in a spiral staircase leading down to the estate's cellar. The air became cool and dry as he descended. Soft yellow light illuminated rows of oak casks, kept by Musarde only to help further the impression to outside visitors that there was nothing of note to be found here beyond the standard vineyard fare. Lane knew better.

Upon reaching the end of the hall, where he'd expected to find the vault door, he found instead that it terminated in a very solid-looking wall. Musarde was a cautious man—at least as far as protecting his treasures went. He would take every measure to conceal the entrance to his private museum.

"Where'd you hide it, old man?" Lane muttered, running his fingertips over the rough stone as if divining a message from endless lines of Braille.

The estate had been renovated, the centuries-old structure given modern updates and amenities. Any hidden rooms would likely have been part of the original structure and later concealed when Musarde purchased the property.

Hallways always lead somewhere.

Slipping a wireless signal detector the size of a pager from his pocket, he swept it along the wall, listening for the device to indicate a strong signal—one not generated by his phone or an internet router somewhere nearby.

There was no way of knowing if Musarde had hardwired the vault's security panel or if it was wireless, but if it was the latter, he'd find out quickly.

After a moment of frustration edging on despair, he found a hotspot. The device in his hand chirped excitedly when held above a bronze candelabrum, one crafted to look like a dragon gripping a doorknocker in its claws—probably purloined from an old-world European castle or church.

With a firm tug on the knocker, he swung the candelabrum, and the stone upon which it was mounted, out to reveal a modern touchscreen.

Given his time constraints, an electronic hack-box or auto-dialing safecracker had been out of the question. They could take hours, and on a lock this complex, would more likely take weeks. A brute-force attack—using explosives to breach the vault door, or a thermic lance or cutting torch to bore his way to the lock's mechanism—would have been more feasible if it weren't for the door's many vibration sensors, its extreme thickness, the team of mercenaries swarming the building like termites, and the fact that he'd been under close supervision until just 15 minutes ago.

Musarde's vault had, since the day Lane discovered it, been his fixation. Breaking into it surpassed mere personal challenge: He had a personal stake in defeating the old man, proving no amount of money or advanced technology could protect his ill-gotten hoard of treasure. But fate had a sense of humor. With all the hours he'd spent contemplating this moment, deliberating the best strategies for gaining access to the vault, it had all come down to entering the correct code.

Slipping a small ultraviolet flashlight from his pocket, Lane flashed the alphanumeric keypad in hopes of finding fingerprints that might give him an indication of which numbers were used in the passcode. It had been wiped clean.

"So you're more clever than you let on." Lane stared at the screen for a moment, contemplating the most likely password.

"Seven digits, seven letters. *Agapito*."

The panel flashed red. Wrong answer. Lane shook his head. "Not much love for the loyal son, hmm? Should have figured."

He entered his second choice. *Minoans*.

The panel flashed red with more urgency.

"I get the sense you're telling me I have one more shot." He craned his neck as the volume of the shootout increased, the GIGN making forward progress into the estate. He'd have to hurry. If they found him here, they might just think he'd reneged on their deal and really *was* working for Musarde.

"What, or whom, does Musarde love?" Lane remembered the journal he'd stolen from the old man. "Luigi Pernier. P-E-R-N-I-E-R," he whispered, pressing the corresponding numbers on the digital keypad.

The stone wall before him divided with a hydraulic sigh, revealing the colossal vault door. Grinning at his success and rubbing his hands together expectantly, Lane waited for the vault to open. Nothing happened.

"You've got to be kidding me. So now you're telling me I need a key or the old man's eyeball, aren't you?" He looked over the door and found an iris scanner and a circular token slot. The eye was off the table, for obvious reasons. The token could have been stored somewhere in Musarde's study, but he didn't even know what it looked like, nor did he have time for a search. He kicked the chrome-plated door angrily, then slid down with his back to it. Spinning Musarde's ring on his finger, he deliberated what he'd do next. He was out of options.

Then it dawned him.

He tugged the Ring of Mavro Spelio from his finger and shoved it into the token slot. A series of loud clunks thudded from the other side of the door as the hardened steel locking bolts slid out of the way. With a pull, the heavy door swung open smoothly. He cautiously stepped inside.

"You survived," a voice echoed distantly from deeper within the stone labyrinth. "How can I even be surprised?"

In that instant, Lane's joy at overcoming the mighty vault door evaporated, replaced by a sinking feeling in the pit of his stomach. "Agapito? Don't you think it's time we had a sit-down heart-to-heart to talk about everything that's happened lately?"

"We should, certainly. I've been very curious to learn about your imprisonment in Lebanon and your escape all those years ago. Truth be told, I figured you for dead. But then again, you've made a habit of escaping certain death, haven't you? Your lover's apartment in Washington, the museum at Heraklion, the fortress at Lake Bardawil, and most recently, your escape from the crypt in Akrotiri. You're a modern Houdini, aren't you?"

"Three shows a day at Caesar's Palace." Sliding against the wall, Lane glanced around the next corner. The passage opened into a broad showroom illuminated by conical beams of yellow light cast down from between steel joists overhead. Wandering paths, like narrow cobblestone streets, spread out between seemingly endless rows of artifacts on display, the entire room framed by those finds too large to fit inside a showcase. Agapito, bent at the waist, examined a Roman gladius through the glass, hands cradled behind his back.

"Please, come join me. Let's settle this in a manner befitting men of our civility and intelligence." Agapito slipped his shoulder holster off and hung it on a nearby wall sconce. "See? Now we can do this equitably."

"That'd be a first." Stepping into the open, Lane slowly approached his rival.

Agapito waved him toward him. "Do you like my father's collection? The few people who have seen it thought it comparable to most impressive museums in the world."

Distrusting his conversational bearing, Lane kept his eyes locked on Agapito.

"But you know what? I look at these relics I've found for him, and I feel...nothing." Agapito shrugged indifferently. "They're just old things, the desperate, pleading attempts of those who mistakenly believed they could carve or write or construct something that would outlive them."

"Didn't they succeed? Look in front of you," Lane said.

Agapito sneered. "Naivety. That's one of your endearing traits. Fine, let's say these people succeeded. Look at it. What stands before us today is as deteriorated and hideous as their designers' skeletal remains must be now. How's that for a lasting legacy?"

Approaching the opposite side of the display, Lane stared through the glass at his adversary. Shadow from the lights overhead sharpened his features. "You've let nihilism cloud your view. Not surprising for a man who's spent his entire adult life murdering people on behalf of a father who doesn't care if his son lives or dies."

That one was barbed, and it had drawn blood. Agapito glowered, drawn in, curled and hissing.

Lane continued, his tone calm, feet anchored shoulder-length apart, prepared to withstand a blow or launch himself away from danger should Agapito tire of talk and make a move. "These artifacts aren't meaningless. They embody the optimism and ambition that makes our species so unique. We battle against our mortality, as inevitable as it may be."

"Let us build a city and a tower, whose top may reach unto heaven," Agapito said, reciting the King James Bible with a dramatic flourish. "A tale as old as time itself. We ants, scurrying about, obsessed with finding meaning in our existence. But it's narcissistic, isn't it? Animals don't hold such delusions of the value of their lives. In fact, they seem to possess a cold complacency when meeting their ends. But humans, oh how they thrash and cry and beg, as if their preservation is crucial to some larger purpose."

Stepping around the display to better see his rival, Lane said, "For years, I hated you, Agapito. As I sat in the corner of my crowded, dirt-floor prison cell, I blamed you for putting me there. I never would have dreamt that I'd pity you."

Cocking his head as though Lane's words were pleasing music, Agapito smiled. "You know, in spite of this ongoing rivalry we've found ourselves in, I've always considered you something of an estranged brother to me."

"If this is how you treat your brother, I'd hate to see you around your in-laws."

Unbuttoning the sleeves of his dress shirt, Agapito began rolling them in precise folds to his elbows. "We're two men cut from the same cloth. You're the worthiest of adversaries because you're my mirror image. My doppelganger. My perfect opposite. We're Romulus and Remus, Lane. And like Romulus, I must kill you before I can go on to grander things. That makes you no less vital to the undertaking, you understand. You're essential to the story. What is a story without conflict, without a challenge?"

"Who's naive now, Agapito? You've built this up to be some kind of grand climax to a deluded fantasy." Lane turned his head slowly from side to side, stretching his neck in

339

preparation for the impending struggle. "Well, if it's a conclusion to the story you need, let me give it to you."

Arm cocked back, fingers pulled together in a tight fist, Lane leapt toward Agapito. He drove his knuckles into his adversary's jaw while still in the air, his body crashing into him. The two men slammed to the floor. A mad scramble followed, a blur of desperate strikes and grappling as the two men fought for survival. Lane possessed superior fitness and a decade of youth over his adversary, but Agapito had spent his entire life fighting. It showed. Blows that would have felled a larger man glanced away with little effect. Submission moves that would have had most men incapacitated in seconds were expertly countered.

Agapito, hair wild and eyes aglow in a primeval frenzy, broke free from Lane's grasp. Drawing his stiletto from his pocket, he flicked the blade into position and lunged for Lane's chest. Sidestepping the attack, Lane delivered a quick jab to his adversary's hyoid. Gripping his throat and making a pained, gurgling sound, Agapito kicked out, landing a strike squarely above Lane's knee, driving a heel into the bandages covering the still-fresh bullet wound. Crying out and collapsing, Lane clutched his injured leg.

After a few seconds of swallowing deeply, his breath returning, Agapito stepped to his holster and tugged free his pistol. He deliberately checked the action as Lane writhed in pain, blood soaking through the bandage and staining his jeans. "I've always liked your spunk. You're one of those incurable optimists, the kind that just will not give up even when they're clearly defeated. All the same, I would have thought you'd learned your lesson all those years ago in Lebanon."

Lane looked up, fury smoldering in his eyes. "I'm a slow learner."

He slammed his shoulder against the nearest display. The impact jolted the glass sensors. A pneumatic *hiss* filled the room as thick steel doors slammed down, blocking the exits and sealing them inside. The mechanical whir of a vacuum followed.

"What have you done?" Agapito let the gun fall to his side, his hair blowing wildly in the swiftly moving air. "You've killed us both."

Lane flashed Agapito a sly grin, the kind worn by a man who'd just had a one-night stand with his mortal enemy's sister. The air became scarce. "May we meet in another life as friends," he shouted, reciting the same lines his adversary had spoken when he'd left Lane to be captured in Lebanon. "Hell, let's go there together."

FIFTY-SEVEN

The estate, only moments before ringing with the concussion of flash-bang grenades and screamed orders to surrender, had fallen hauntingly silent. Susara stood by as two GIGN operators whispered in French, mumbled communications pouring through their headsets. Suddenly taking notice of her presence, one of them spoke in English, "Musarde is gone. Escaped through..." he sought the word, "um, *souterrain*." He let his rifle hang from its sling and used his hands to illustrate a subterranean passage.

"A tunnel. Probably an old cryptoporticus," she said. "Great."

The operative shrugged apologetically, and then resumed his discussion with his comrade.

Suddenly, the floorboards beneath her feet rumbled with the sound of large motor coming alive somewhere in the building.

Recalling Lane's explanation of Musarde's security system, and specifically the auto-lockdown function designed to evacuate the air inside the vault, she panicked. Someone had activated the security system. Who was she kidding? She knew it was Lane. And if he'd activated it, he must be trapped inside the vault. She needed to find him before he suffocated.

Sprinting toward the sound, she entered the cellars. Picking up her pace, she tripped on the uneven stone floor. Striking the ground hard, she cursed and forced herself back to her feet, ignoring the new pain from the ragged gash in her knee. Rounding the corner, she found the vault door open, but the way inside was blocked by a colossal steel barricade spanning from wall to wall. She could hear Lane's voice in her head: "...seven-digit security code...10 million possible number combinations." She looked around until she found the system's keypad. Squeezing her eyes shut, she silently prayed that the seven-digit code wasn't a random jumble of numbers, but an alphanumeric code that spelled something recognizable. The word 'Phaistos' had eight letters, so that couldn't be it. 'Minoans'? No, too obvious.

"Please, Lane. What was it?" She chewed her lip and rested her forehead against the wall as she considered the possible combinations. The rumble of the vacuum distracted her. She pushed against the door and tried to focus.

Seven letters.

Pernier.

Musarde had proven his obsession with the archaeologist's account of the Phaistos Disc. It was her best shot.

Tapping the corresponding numbers on the keypad, she grabbed her hair in both hands and stepped back. A light flashed red. She slammed an open hand against the barricade.

What now? She tried to think of another password, but her mind couldn't focus. She could only think of Lane, face turning red as he desperately sought another breath, one that wouldn't come. Like drowning on dry land. She saw Jordan, bedridden, as she received the news of her father's death. It would kill her.

Susara stared at the keypad. The red light had stopped blinking. An agonizing second trickled by. Then, the light turned green. The rumbling motor stopped, the steel barricade retracted into the floor, and the rushing air of the ruptured vacuum pulled her inside.

She scanned Musarde's underground museum, ignoring the mountain of relics, in search of Lane. Her eyes settled on two forms on the floor in unconscious heaps. Rushing to Lane's side, she pressed her ear to his chest, waiting to hear a heartbeat or feel his chest rise.

Nothing.

Her revolver clattered to the floor as she placed the heels of her palms against his sternum and thrust against him in pulses.

"Dammit, Lane, you reckless jackass. I told you to stay behind. Why can't you ever listen?"

She checked for a pulse, and then held a hand over his mouth, hoping for the lightest kiss of breath against her skin.

Nothing.

Impossible. She felt the heat from his chest on the palm of her hand. He couldn't be dead. A personality as big as his couldn't just expire on a cold concrete floor. If such a man could die, his death should have brought the world to a grinding halt, shaken it to its core. He wouldn't just drift away quietly. But as the seconds ticked by without him stirring, she began to doubt.

Cradling his head in her arms, her anger gave way to tears. She stroked his cheek gently. "You selfish bastard. We came all this way, and you're going to leave me now? After all we've been through together, you're just going to take the easy way out? What about Jordan? What will she do without you?" Pulling his limp form tight to her chest, head resting against his cheek, she said, "I hate you for this."

Spine arching upward as if he'd just been electrocuted, Lane pulled desperately at the air. As he struggled to get his breathing under control, he whispered, "You're a bad liar."

She abruptly dropped his head to the concrete and punched him in the chest. "You ass. I thought you were dead."

Agapito coughed loudly from behind them.

Grabbing her sidearm from the floor, Susara trained the .357 on him and said, "You stay right there." Stepping forward and kicking away Agapito's pistol, she noticed Lane's *fravashi* charm poking out from the man's pocket. "This doesn't belong to you." She took it.

Shoving it against Lane's chest, she said, "You don't get to die again, understood?"

"I'll try harder not to. Promise."

Rubbing the back of his head where it had struck the concrete, Lane slowly approached Agapito. "Remember what you said to me back at NERO headquarters? Well maybe this time, *you* should have just stayed dead."

FIFTY-EIGHT

The rain stopped, skies clearing as the sun warmed the vineyard's damp soil. Lane watched as Susara packed the Phaistos Disc and the accompanying Minoan stones into a watertight protective case.

"I bet you think less of me for having believed Pernier's story," he said, kneeling beside her and running a finger along the disc's face. "It all seems so ridiculous, now."

"Desperation will always win out against skepticism." She plucked foam squares from the case's gridded padding to perfectly fit the relics. "I'll bet that millennia from now, no matter how advanced technology and education become, people will still suspend their disbelief if there's even the slimmest chance that something like this will improve their lives. No one could blame you for believing it." She turned to him, her knee touching his. "The truth is, I wanted you to be right. As much as I didn't believe the legend, I really hoped I was wrong." His expression was one of exhaustion and loath acceptance. She wished she could think of something optimistic to say, some way to comfort and reassure him. But there was nothing. This disc hadn't just represented an ancient mystery, it had been a reservoir for his hope, the focal point of a man's desperate yearning to save his dying daughter. And that elixir had proven to be little more than snake oil.

Handcuffed wrists lifted behind his back by a burly GIGN operator, Agapito struggled against his restraints, shoes slipping in the mud as he sought purchase. "This isn't over," he shouted to Lane as he was forced into the back seat of a waiting SUV. "My father will have me out the moment they lock me up, and I'll be back to find you, old friend. The gods aren't through with us. We'll finish this someday."

Lane only smiled and shook his head. Musarde had fled, leaving Agapito to defend his treasures. Agapito was merely a tool in his father's arsenal to be leveraged for the old man's personal gain, even if it meant Agapito's death or incarceration.

"*Qui totum vult totum perdit.*"

"He who wants everything loses everything," Susara said.

A pair of GIGN officers approached slowly, allowing the two of them to finish their conversation before cuffing Lane.

"My chariot awaits." He nodded at the two men and stood, then offered Susara his hand. She shook it. "Partner." Reaching around his neck, he unclasped his *fravashi* charm and ran a thumb over the figurine. Slowly, he reached for her wrist. Placing the necklace in her palm, he folded her fingers closed atop it. "Hold on to that for me until I see you again."

FIFTY-NINE

Washington, D.C.

The metro hissed and decelerated, passengers leaning with the transfer of momentum. Light from the approaching station throbbed in the car's windows, pulse slowing as the train eased to a stop, finally giving steady illumination. Ruben jostled uncomfortably as waves of passengers brushed and bumped his knees, disembarking. A baby cried. An old man sneezed into his hand. A woman sat down across from him.

"How much did Musarde pay you to make it worth throwing away your career?" Susara's stare was cold—filled with disgust.

"I don't even know what you're talking about. But I do have to wonder what would compel you to show your face after going rogue. The agency knows all about your latest illicit activities." He clicked his tongue and shook his head. "How the golden child hath fallen."

"The only way the agency would know what I've been doing on my leave would be if you told them. And the only way you would know what I've been doing is if Agapito Vicente told you."

He sneered and lowered his voice. "You have nothing on me. Only hearsay from a disgraced agent with an axe to grind."

"You're absolutely right, I have almost no evidence," she admitted.

Smug, Ruben leaned back in his plastic bucket seat.

"Except for the fact that you handed over stolen property to a man identified on NERO security footage as a Corsican antiquities thief. Now, that alone isn't adequate to convict. It could have been an accident. You were misled. He had his paperwork in order. All the same, it was enough for internal affairs to hear my appeal and look into your recent financial transactions. Care to guess what they'll find?"

His face blanched, the confident lines vanishing as self-doubt and anxiety took hold.

She leaned in. "So, like I asked, was it worth the money?"

Sucking in his cheeks and looking away, he whispered, "You're such a simpleton, Eaves. It wasn't just about the money. You were always showing me up. You don't think I heard the talk? Even Mosi was beginning to think it had been a mistake to promote me instead of you. If Agapito had done what he was supposed to, you would have been out of the picture for good. My career was on the line. You would have done the same thing if you'd been in my position. The same thing."

"You tell yourself whatever lies you have to, but know this: You and I are nothing alike," she said. "Do you understand me? Nothing alike." A fresh influx of passengers boarded the train, stepping between them. She held his stare.

He stood. "You've ruined me, Eaves. You can be smug about that for now, but we're not done. Not by a long shot."

An automated voice chimed above the din, warning of the train's imminent departure.

It was like a starting gun. Ruben turned and scrambled toward the exit. Gripping a chrome stanchion, Susara propelled herself forward. Her fingers brushed the shoulder of his jacket, but he ducked out of her grasp. The doors began closing.

Squirming through the narrow aperture, he broke free to the platform. He turned and watched as the doors clicked shut, locking her inside. She could only follow the fleeing man with her eyes as he vanished into the dense crowd, the train crawling forward, entering the darkness of the tunnel ahead.

SIXTY

NERO headquarters
Washington, D.C.

The last straggler, dragging a briefcase and rubbing his eyes as the cleaning crew made their rounds, had long since departed. A few hours later, the custodians followed. Midnight came and went, and now, only the night guard remained to let Susara in. She began to explain why she had come, only to have him raise a hand as he held the door open for her.

Say no more.

The late hour and emptiness of the building made it feel like a sort of corporate cenotaph—an homage to workers past. The receptionist had left her desk fan on. The sandwich guy had forgotten to turn off the coffee brewer. It percolated quietly like a softly snoring night watchman.

A sensation that she was doing something wrong followed her, lurking in the shadows, just out of sight, as she traversed the main hall and entered an elevator. Her phone rang a meeting reminder. Before, she'd thought it was a mistake; someone had accidentally scheduled it thinking they'd selected the afternoon. But upon being repeatedly prompted to accept the meeting, she began to doubt. All her messages to the sender—listed only as *corporate*—were ignored. She contemplated not coming at all. But there must have been some reason they'd be so persistent.

With the overhead lights in the main atrium shut off for the night, the room floated in pitch darkness. Strips of softly glowing bulbs traced the curve of the circular walkways, giving the space the feeling of a miniature galaxy of spiraling stars.

She paused at the door of the conference bay. A short, slight figure stood at the end of the room, bathed in dim light. Her hair was gray, but neatly kept. Her hands were aged, but her suit without a wrinkle.

"I'm glad you could make our meeting, Ms. Eaves," the woman said, her back turned toward the door. She'd left all but one light off in the room, and was staring at what appeared to be a jumbled spreadsheet projected on the wall. "Take a seat."

Susara complied, easing a chair out from beneath the conference table and sitting on the cushion's edge.

The woman continued, "We took a calculated risk in promoting Ruben Luis to director of NERO's field agents. You were a top contender for the position, as I'm sure you've figured out by now, but we needed your skills to be applied in the field. We never could have anticipated this."

"Pardon me, ma'am, but who are you referring to when you say 'we'?"

"The council."

She'd never heard of a council. There was NERO's billionaire founder, the managing director, and the director of field agents above her in the corporate structure, but she'd never heard of a council of any kind.

"I'm sorry, but what role does the council have in NERO?"

The councilwoman turned toward her, a look of mild surprise on her face. "We run it, Ms. Eaves."

"But the founder—"

"Is a persistent rumor that works well for public relations. It keeps people guessing who the puppet master behind our operation is. There is no one founder. NERO is the brainchild of our council, made up of the most prominent cultural heritage institution curators in the world. You keep doing the work you've been doing, and someday you'll join us. In the meantime, I invited you here so I could personally congratulate you on your promotion."

"Am I to assume that means—"

"Yes, Director. Starting immediately, you'll report directly to Dr. Mosi. Assuming, of course, you accept the position."

"Not to sound ungrateful for the opportunity, but I thought you said you needed me in the field," Susura said.

"And you will be. Leading from the front. Dr. Mosi has already agreed to take a more active role in managing the other agents from headquarters. I'll only say this: There had better be no further indiscretions." She withdrew a small remote from a pocket and aimed it at the room's projector. Stills from surveillance footage covered the wall. The Heraklion Museum's front gates as Lane and Susura strolled in. Their conversation with the museum guard. The two of them arm in arm in front of the Phaistos Disc's display. "The council is well aware of your activities this past week."

Heat escaped Susara's collar. She scrambled for an explanation.

"We recognize that there were extenuating circumstances surrounding your actions. All's well that ends well." The councilwoman smiled curtly as she approached and offered her hand. "We're confident you'll excel at this position, Ms. Eaves. I know your father would be proud."

Susara fought for breath as she reached for the woman's hand. A sudden pressure had seized her chest, and she felt lightheaded. Images of her father's face flashed through her mind. "You knew him?"

Still holding Susara's hand, the councilwoman leaned in and whispered, "He was one of us. One of the originals. And he had big plans for you, Miss Eaves."

SIXTY-ONE

Sibley Memorial Hospital

Knocking softly above the cardboard cutout of the sparrow taped to Jordan's door, Susara peeked inside the hospital room. A gray-haired black woman sat at the foot of the bed, the book in her hands angled toward the bright sunlight flooding through the windows.

"I'm sorry, I thought this was Jordan Bradley's room," Susara mumbled, beginning to back out, feeling both confused and embarrassed.

"It's a joy to me that she still has his last name. If Nicole had it her way, she'd have Jordan take her maiden name." The woman closed her book gently and turned to look at Susara over the rims of her glasses.

Susara stepped inside and closed the door behind her. She gave her name and extended a hand.

The woman shook it tenderly. "Dorothy King. Lane's personal attorney and probably someone whose existence you've been cursing for years." She leaned in and examined Susara's features as if admiring a painting at an art exhibit. "I can see exactly why he was so taken with you. Aren't you just lovely?"

Susara felt her cheeks flush. "That's very kind." She cleared her throat and plunged her hands into her pockets. "I just thought I'd come by and see Jordan. Check on how she's doing." That was only partially true. After several days of putting it off, she'd come to the hospital to tell Jordan and Nicole about Lane's arrest, to soften the blow as much as she could. She wanted them both to know that he'd done an honorable thing, sacrificing his freedom to help bring down Agapito. Nicole, especially, needed to hear it. "Where is she?"

"Nicole took her for ice cream in the cafeteria. The little lady was feeling especially strong today. She's in high spirits."

"I'm glad. I just hope she does OK with Lane gone," Susara said. "He loves her so much. I know it would just crush him if anything happened to her while he was away."

"She'll be fine, darlin'. Just fine."

There was a subtle confidence in the way Dorothy spoke those words that put her at ease. Susara nodded toward the door. "I'm going to take off. Will you tell Jordan I stopped by? Maybe I'll come back another time."

"I'll do that. You take care of yourself, Susara."

As Susara turned to leave, she stopped abruptly. Her skin tingled. On a chair in the room's corner perched a threadbare stuffed animal, the painted metal eyes scratched, staring back at her blindly. A sparrow.

A lucky charm.

EPILOGUE

Crete, Greece

Pieter Doukas was no amateur pilot. He'd flown commercially for 20 years, delivering mail and supplies throughout the Greek archipelago. The short, sometimes poorly maintained airstrips on those islands posed no challenge to him now, and there was little in the way of violent storms or unfavorable weather he hadn't surmounted at some point during his career. Flying wasn't so different from ancient seafaring, he thought. After years, the experienced captain could take one look at the seas and skies and know whether to venture onward or to seek a safe harbor. The same was true of being a pilot. When they'd taken off from the Corsican airfield that morning, the skies had been clear, the weather mild and pleasant. They'd weighed anchor, so to speak, and departed with their precious cargo.

"Where did this weather come from, anyway?" Pieter turned to his copilot, the man's features dimpled by the light passing through the raindrops on the windscreen.

The other man, fresh out of flight school, only shrugged, though his eyes—wide and anxiously scanning the sky—and his vise-like grip on the yoke revealed his trepidation. Pieter didn't hold it against him. It was one hell of a storm. Definitely among the worst he'd flown in.

"We'll get around it." The pilot reached for the digital weather station mounted to the dashboard. "We'll just keep heading southeast until it clears and circle back to Heraklion. We have plenty of fuel."

Daring a glance behind him, Pieter checked to make sure the padded waterproof case was still secure. The woman who had loaded it on the plane had explicitly pointed out that his career was on the line with this delivery, and that whatever was in that case was worth more than his life. She'd punctuated that second point with a finger poke to his chest. It was a milk run, he assured her. He'd made the flight to Heraklion a thousand times.

She'd checked the case's contents—a clay disc and a handful of stones—and adjusted the protective foam inside twice more before disembarking.

"Pieter, ahead." The copilot's face blanched, his arms visibly shaking.

Through the haze of blinding rain, the pilot caught a glimpse of a looming wall cloud rolling forth like black exhaust. It seemed to erupt from the crashing surf of the ocean below, reaching thousands of feet into the sky. The weather station had missed this cell, and now they were heading directly into the heart of it.

"Hold on!" Pieter cried, banking the aircraft in a tight circle, attempting to turn back. But the storm approached too quickly for the small plane to outrun. Like a ship caught in a tempest, the small aircraft rolled and jerked, battered by the winds. A fierce blast of air forced the craft downward, nosing toward earth. The two men cursed and leaned back in their seats, muscles straining to right the plane before it was too late. The turboprop engine roared over the clamor of the storm. The altimeter wound corkscrews as they lost altitude. The instrument panel flickered and went dark.

The next day, the atmosphere held no evidence of the storm. Below clear blue skies, men in matching black windbreakers combed over the crash site. Bits of scattered detritus, flakes of aluminum skin and twisted chunks of the aircraft's framework, speckled the earth. Foam from seat cushions danced over the grass, tossed playfully by the sea breeze.

Overlooking it all sat a battered protective case, plunged deep into the earth like a stray arrow just a few hundred feet from the ruins of the Palace of Phaistos.

An outdoorsman, novelist, and editor, Nate Granzow likes the smell of gunpowder, the taste of gin, the sound of freedom, and the feel of leather-bound books. He worked for years as a magazine editor for a Fortune 500 publishing company before launching Venator Media Solutions, a marketing communications company focused on the outdoor and tactical industries.

His debut novel, THE SCORPION'S NEST, was selected as one of 1,000 finalists in Amazon's Breakthrough Novel Awards, 2012, and was ranked first in the Mystery/Suspense/Thriller category at the IndieReader Discovery Awards, 2012. His sophomore work, COGAR'S DESPAIR, reached top 100 best-seller status in Amazon's 'Men's Adventure' category, followed by COGAR'S REVOLT—a top-three finalist in the Clive Cussler Collector's Society 2014 Adventure Writer's Competition.

www.nategranzow.com

A pharmaceutical research facility in the heart of Venezuela's Amazon Basin goes silent without warning. Primordial beasts never before seen by human eyes annihilate the team sent to investigate. Human eyes. The creatures have human eyes. When a newly discovered, but exceedingly rare plant specie shows promise as a possible cure for cancer, pilot Austin Stewart is ordered to accompany the alluring biologist Olivia Dover and her team of researchers to retrieve another specimen. But as the expedition journeys into the rainforest's shadowy depths, they quickly find themselves hunted by the same creatures that slaughtered the rescue team years before—beasts the local Yanomami tribesmen call *hekura*. Evil spirits. But these are no mere apparitions. The research team, forsaken by those that sent them and racing against a Colombian drug lord to recover the precious catholicon, must fight for survival against ravenous mutants too strong to overpower, too intelligent to outsmart. The jungle guards its secrets fiercely.

Find it at nategranzow.com

April 20th, 2005.
Three days have passed since Ben Williams survived the
harrowing attack on Tucson's Saguaro Towers Hotel.
However, the danger has far from subsided. Unknown to the
public, the Saguaro Towers was a covert CIA station; the
attack, an Iranian false-flag operation aimed at breaching the
American intelligence apparatus. The Iranian operative
responsible for the attack is in possession of sensitive
information and has gone off the grid. Short on options, the
CIA turns to a small start-up private military company to hunt
the Iranian. In turn, that PMC turns to Williams and members
of his old Special Activities Division team. Through bloody
mercenary combat with multiple factions hunting the data in
drug-torn Mexico, Ronin Defense Institute will be born, but
there is no guarantee their company—or the shooters
themselves—will survive.

Find it at stevenhildreth.com

54170169R00221

Made in the USA
Columbia, SC
27 March 2019